Mystery Dis
Disher, Garry.
Kittyhawk down

KITTYHAWK DOWN

KITTYHAWK DOWN

GARRY DISHER

I wish to thank the CIB and uniformed officers of the Victoria Police who gave freely of their time when I sought background information for this book. Any deviations from standard police procedure are mine (the notion of a regional homicide inspector, for example).

First published in Australia by Allen & Unwin

First published in the United States in 2005 by
Soho Press, Inc.
853 Broadway
New York, NY 10003

Library of Congress Cataloging in Publication Data

Disher, Garry.
Kittyhawk down / Garry Disher.
p. cm.
ISBN-10: 1-56947-394-3
ISBN-13: 978-1-56947-394-8
1. Police–Australia–Melbourne Region (Vic.)–Fiction. 2. Melbourne Region (Vic.)–Fiction. 3. Drowning victims–Fiction. 4. Missing Children–Fiction. 5. Australia–Fiction. I. Title.

PR9619.3.D56K58 2005
823'.914–dc22   2004059123

10   9   8   7   6   5   4   3   2   1

To Nora and Henry Hernandez

runners. His hair was straight, dark and lifted a little in the wind. It was cut once a month by a young woman who worked beside her father in a Waterloo barbershop. She was skilful and attentive, and for the sum of $10 returned him to the world with a neatly shaped head. And so Challis was outwardly unremarkable that day, nodding with grave courtesy to the people coming toward him along the track. This late on an Easter Saturday, five-thirty pm, couples and families were streaming back to the carpark. Only Challis headed the other way, happy to leave them to the roads of the Peninsula, which would be choked with holidaymakers right now. Very few noticed that he was wound tightly, as if insulating a knot of powerful feelings, and the sunglasses hid the habitually weary, unimpressed and disbelieving cast of his face.

There were better things that Challis could have been doing. He could have been halfway through an Easter walk of the Peninsula beaches with Tessa Kane, but yesterday he'd had to pull out, and that had been the start of his falling spirits. He could have been at home reading or mulching leaves, but early in the afternoon he'd found himself listening for the phone to ring with more bad news from the women's prison, where his wife was serving eight years, and so he'd left the house. He could have been spending time with friends, but they all had children and Easter was a time for family connectedness and strife, and no one wanted a forty-year-old single man hanging around them.

And so he'd started thinking about murder. As the Homicide Squad inspector for the Peninsula, thinking about murder was his job. In fact, there were two murders to think about, both relatively old and both unsolved. The first involved no body, only a strong suspicion. Ten months ago— June last year—a two-year-old toddler named Jasmine Tully had gone missing. She lived with her mother, Lisa, and Lisa's defacto in a rundown fisherman's shack on the outskirts of Waterloo. CIB detectives at Waterloo suspected the defacto,

Bradley Pike. When they had failed to shake Pike's story or turn up evidence of any kind, they'd called in Challis. Challis was inclined to suspect Brad Pike too, and had spent hours trying to break his story. Cases involving children were the worst. He hated them. They left him feeling scoured and futile.

But it was the second murder that had brought Challis to Bushrangers Bay.

That, and love. If Tessa Kane was sticking to the timetable they'd mapped out with each other, she'd be walking in from Cape Schank about now. Maybe he'd encounter her. Maybe she'd want to talk.

Maybe not.

As for the second murder, this time there was a body, and Tessa Kane had called it the Flinders Floater on the front page of her newspaper. Unfortunately the name had stuck, and now even Challis was calling it the Flinders Floater.

It had been found by a commercial fisherman from Flinders about six months ago. He was pulling in his anchor and noticed how heavy it was. He kept hauling, and that's when he saw the second anchor, caught in the tines of his own. But that alone hadn't accounted for the extra weight. Attached to the second anchor—belted on, in fact, so you could be sure it wasn't accidental—was a body.

The fisherman used his mobile phone to call the police, and bobbed in the sea off Bushrangers Bay for an hour until a police launch arrived to take charge.

No one knew who the dead man was. Challis saw the body before the pathologist had started sawing at it. The flesh was soupy, bloated, chewed about, apt to fall away from the bones like a cooked chicken's. Only the finger-pads of the right thumb and forefinger remained intact, the tips badly softened and wrinkled, but by injecting fluid under the skin the lab had distended them sufficiently to make serviceable fingerprints. No matches with the national computer. Then, when it was suggested that the dental work was foreign, Challis had tried Interpol, the Home Office National Computer in the UK, and the FBI.

Still nothing.

The clothing—jeans, T-shirt, underwear and Nike running shoes—had been made in Asian sweatshops for sale in Australian stores. They were a dime a dozen.

All that Challis knew was, the guy was in his thirties and his skull had been smashed in before he'd been thrown into the water. There were also stab wounds to the stomach, but the cause of death was drowning, the pathologist said, noting the presence of a large volume of seawater in the lungs. The blow to the head? Possibly to stun the victim. The stab wounds? Probably to release gases and so ensure that the body remained under the surface of the water.

The blow to the head was possibly administered by the anchor that had taken him to the bottom, the pathologist reported, after comparing the shape of the indentation in the skull with the shaft of the anchor. The anchor had been intended to hold the body down until the fishes had picked the bones clean. Fortunately the fisherman had happened along about two or three days later. Or unfortunately, because identifying victim and culprit had become a headache for Challis.

At least the anchor told Challis a couple of things: the body had been dumped at sea, not pushed over a cliff, and he'd be saved the tedium of mapping body drift as determined by the tides and the shape of the coastline.

One other thing: the victim had been wearing a Rolex Oyster watch. Silver, with an expanding metal band. It wasn't the costliest Rolex available, but it was a genuine Rolex, not a ten-dollar Singapore or Bangkok fake. If the Rolex spelt a certain level of class or income, nothing else about the murdered man did. The clothes and Nike trainers didn't.

Challis walked on, allowing the Flinders Floater to rest there in his head like a shimmering wraith that would one day clarify, take on a corporeal being and tell him the story of his final days and minutes before he was thrown into the water to die.

He could see kangaroos grazing in the early evening light on the grassy slope above the walking track. He nodded at a young family, stepping off to let them through, and wondered what he was going to do when he got to the fork on the cliff-top above the little bay. Walk down to the beach and commune with the elements in the hope that he'd solve the case? Continue toward Cape Schank and hope to encounter Tessa?

Dusk was settling. He could see lights on the water and the lights of Phillip Island beyond the water. A cool autumn wind blew in from the sea. He zipped up his windproof jacket. He was hungry, sleepy, cold, depressed—and owed it all to one phone call.

An ordinary everyday sort of man might not have answered the phone at seven o'clock on Good Friday morning. But Challis was a homicide inspector and always answered the phone. And had heard his wife, using her phone card at the prison, announce that she intended to kill herself.

Her spirits always deteriorated at holiday time. Her spirits always *fell*.

He'd hung on to the phone for twenty minutes, letting her talk herself out of her depression. But the damage was done. He'd been making love with Tessa when the call came, and an hour later—the mood for love gone and just as he'd been about to set out for the two-day walk of the Peninsula beaches with her—Challis's parents-in-law had rung to say that their daughter had snapped her phone card in two and tried to saw through her wrists with it, and was in the prison infirmary. She wasn't in any danger, but Challis's presence would help stabilise her mood, and if he wasn't busy would he mind . . .

Challis had said yes.

Tessa had said, 'It's time you let go of her, Hal,' then had driven off, announcing that she intended to undertake the walk alone.

Challis had almost set out to find her when he returned from seeing his wife in the afternoon.

Perhaps he should have. He was no good at gauging these things, but suspected that it would have been better then than now, a day later, when she'd had time to stew and set her mind and heart against him.

Self-conscious suddenly, he turned around and walked back to his car.

Almost six pm . . . On the way home he tuned in to the news. Two asylum seekers had escaped from the new detention centre near Waterloo. Challis shook his head, imagining the fallout, the divisions, the extra work for Ellen Destry and her CIB detectives.

CHAPTER **TWO**

Ellen Destry would rather have been home tonight, Easter Saturday, but she was a detective sergeant at the Waterloo station and she could sense the hunger in Dwayne Venn.

What Venn liked to do was drive to three or four of the Peninsula's lovers' lanes and park deep in the maw of the roadside trees and attack couples in their cars. In the watery green light of the night-vision fieldglasses he resembled exactly a creeping psycho in a Hollywood slasher film, but on the two occasions that CIB had shadowed him in the past six weeks he'd never done more than watch. Not even taken his old boy out and tugged on it.

Ellen was almost beginning to doubt the veracity of Pam Murphy's information. 'Maybe your informant's given us a peeping tom instead of a rapist,' she'd said to the young uniformed constable last week after another three hours spent in the dark.

But Dwayne Venn was a nasty piece of work and there had been two rapes late that summer, both involving a knife and a hint of unhinged violence. Now Tessa Kane, Challis's editor girlfriend, was asking questions in her newspaper, and so Ellen would continue to watch Venn for as long as the budget could stand it. Senior Sergeant Kellock had taken a brief hard look at the figures that afternoon and told her, 'Two constables, Murphy and Tankard, that's all I can spare, what with those fanatics escaping from the detention centre.'

Fanatics? Next he'd be calling them 'ragheads' or 'sand niggers', like some redneck in a film. According to the detention centre management, the escapees were Iraqis, one an engineer and the other a taxi driver. They weren't her concern—or not yet anyway. Her concern was catching Venn.

And so now she was in the bushes where she could not be seen but where she could see the station's unmarked blue Falcon as a dense shape against the general blackness. In bushes on the other side was John Tankard, one of the uniformed constables. The other, Pam Murphy, was in the Falcon itself, huddled on the back seat with Detective Constable Scobie Sutton. They were playing lovers. Neither wore shirts. Pam's bra was black, which seemed to indicate passion and willingness for some reason, if you listened to the ads. All four officers were armed, and in radio contact via earpieces and small microphones. To the casual eye, the microphones worn by Sutton and Murphy could have been matching necklaces.

Ellen said softly, 'Destry in position.'

Scobie murmured in her ear, 'Sutton in position.'

'Murphy in position.'

'Tankard ditto.'

Trust John Tankard to be different.

And they settled back to wait. They were a hundred metres away from the tourist road that gave access to the lookout. There was little local traffic—everyone was down on the coastal flatlands, heading herdlike to or from parties, pubs, restaurants and the cinema on this Easter Saturday evening.

Just then a Kombi van drove in. It stopped for thirty minutes, there was soft music, and then it clattered away again, leaving behind a trace of marijuana smoke. There were lights upon Port Phillip Bay, and the distant horizon glow of the

Melbourne suburbs beyond the black water. Cloud wisps obscured the stars and the moon.

Ellen's mind drifted. Back at home in Penzance Beach her daughter was having a party. Ellen fretted a little. It was Larrayne's seventeenth birthday and Ellen wanted to celebrate the fact that her daughter was better now. Just over a year ago Larrayne had been abducted by a man who'd already abducted and murdered three other women. She'd been full of adolescent moody rattiness before the abduction, but since then had become quieter, more studious, inclined to stay at home. The party was also meant to mark her jettisoning of the ratbags she'd once hung around with at school and cementing new friendships. They were decent kids, these new friends, but— along with all the other shit that happened at night on the Peninsula lately—there had been instances of gatecrashing that had ended in violence.

'We could register the party with the police,' Ellen had suggested.

'Sweetheart,' her husband said, 'we *are* the police.'

Alan Destry was a uniformed senior constable in Traffic. He was sour about his prospects. He'd failed the sergeants' exam and was married to a detective sergeant on the fast track. Beating her at something, however trivial, made him feel a little better about himself.

And he was earning brownie points tonight, staying home, watching over a bunch of partying teenagers. Ellen imagined his scowling presence at the door as they arrived, his visual scrutiny, his quick search of jacket pockets, handbags and daypacks for booze and dope.

There was *some* booze allowed. Not enough to cause Larrayne's friends to waste themselves and turn nasty, though.

Drugs were another matter. There was evidence that a major network had taken over on the Peninsula: increased arrests for possession and pushing, more overdoses, reports of ecstasy and amphetamines being sold at rave parties. The rave party scene scared Ellen. Admission was cheap, about $15 to cover the hire of a DJ and portaloos, and the parties were often held in out-of-the way factories that lacked basic safety measures like fire sprinklers. Kids heard about them by word of mouth and liked the sense of community encouraged by the music, the drugs, the secrecy, the air of being outside the mainstream. The drugs were also cheap and readily available, with ecstasy selling for $50 a pop and the effect lasting for hours. The kids believed that ecstasy was harmless and loved the boost it gave them, the ability to dance all night and feel invincible. They had a touching faith in the purity of the ecstasy, unaware that it had probably been made by a bikie gang in some backyard garage and contained heroin, speed and the horse-drug ketamine, bound together with glucose or caffeine. They risked poisoning themselves or fusing their brains in the long term, and at the parties they forgot to drink lots of water, got dehydrated, risked death.

Larrayne had been to one rave party. It had been well managed and publicly advertised, but the pushers were there, she said.

Ellen looked at her watch. Ten forty-five. Where was Venn? Assuming their rapist *was* Venn, he liked to take a knife from his boot and burst in upon a pair of lovers, demanding money. Then he'd threaten to start slicing pieces of flesh from the woman unless she undressed fully and handcuffed her boyfriend's hands behind his back and performed oral sex on him. Finally he'd insert the handle of the knife inside the woman's vagina and leave after cutting clumps of pubic hair from her and pocketing any cash the couple had on them.

Ellen badly wanted to catch him.

Then she saw him. 'He's here,' she murmured.

She had heard the engine and at first thought it was a passing motorist, but then a lowered black Longreach ute with a roll bar appeared in her glasses, slowing for the entrance, then U-turning to make another pass, and giving her a clear view of both its numberplates. She saw the ute enter finally, then coast past the police Falcon and stop some distance away, pointed toward the exit. The Longreach looked fast and hard, like the driver.

They were going to make an arrest no matter what. If Venn simply spied on Sutton and Murphy, then they'd have him on a public nuisance charge and would work on him to confess to the rapes. But what Ellen wanted was to arrest him as far along the stages of assault, unlawful imprisonment and rape as possible, so that she could make a firm arrest yet not imperil her officers.

Venn opened his door. Ellen took the fieldglasses from her eyes and saw nothing: he'd removed the interior light bulb. She put the glasses to her eyes again and saw that he wore dark jeans, a dark T-shirt and lightweight army surplus boots. The balaclava sat like a pelt of short black hair on his scalp. He was big, but light on his feet. The fear he inspired, one person going up against couples, made sense to her finally.

She murmured into her mike, 'Approaching you now, Scobie, coming in on your rear passenger side.'

'Roger.'

The reply was a whisper. She watched Venn reach the Falcon and apparently meld with it as he put his face to the glass and looked in at Sutton and Murphy in their partial nakedness. Then she saw him break away from the car and bend swiftly to his right boot before straightening with a knife and unzipping and tugging out his penis.

'Get ready.'

Venn didn't shout. Witnesses to his previous assaults said he always kept his voice low and even, but crackling with menace. Ellen Destry watched him open Pam Murphy's door and heard him say, 'Surprise! See the blade, lover boy? It slices open your girlfriend's windpipe, you give me any aggro. And feast your eyes on this, sweetheart. I'm gunna slip it up your cunt and your arse and in your mouth and your boyfriend's gunna fucking watch.'

'Don't hurt her,' Sutton said, sounding scared.

Venn's got the knife to Pam's throat, Ellen thought. And he's exhibiting himself to them. She could see the back of him in the open door. Then she saw the hand that must have been holding his penis suddenly slide around to the rear pocket of his jeans.

Handcuffs.

'See these, sweetheart? Cuff lover boy's hands behind his back. Come on! Move it or I'll stick you with this.'

'Don't hurt her.'

'Shut up. Okay, sweetheart, let's see what you got to offer.'

And as he backed away from the door, slicing open Pam Murphy's skirt as he went, Ellen said, '*Go, go, go.*'

John Tankard got there first. He slammed his baton on Venn's arm. The knife fell into the dirt. Venn groaned, hugged his arm to his chest and whimpered.

That's when Pam Murphy's foot caught him between the legs.

Not a happy boy.

CHAPTER **THREE**

After Dwayne Venn had been booked and remanded, Pam Murphy stretched out on the bench inside the locker room, poleaxed with tiredness. She was alone and liked it like that but knew it wouldn't last. There was always someone going on or off a shift or fetching or stowing something. There were separate showers and change rooms but a unisex locker room at Waterloo. It was a meeting ground, a staging ground, a breeding ground for oversexed young men and women and normally she avoided it like the plague, but right now she was too tired to care.

The door hissed on its pneumatic arm and John Tankard came in. His tongue had been hanging out earlier. It was the black bra. Her bareness from the waist up as she'd climbed into the rear of the Falcon to trap Dwayne Venn two hours ago.

'Good result tonight,' he remarked.

She watched him through eyes heavy-lidded with exhaustion. He was unbelting his uniform jacket, releasing the revolver, cuffs and other junk that weighed you down and ruined your lower back.

'Yes,' she muttered.

And it *was* a good result. No doubt some smart-arse lawyer would get bail for Venn, but Venn would go down for rape, attempted rape, false imprisonment and assault with a deadly weapon and whatever else the DPP could throw at him. Plus he'd go on a sex-offenders' register and earn himself a lifetime of official harassment whenever there was even the hint of a sex crime on the Peninsula.

She took a moment to profile Venn in her mind: twenty-two years old, fit despite a diet of beer, hamburgers and amphetamines, poor, poorly educated, face like a child's drawing. He would die before the median age for men—of alcoholism, bad health, work accident, car smash. There were thousands like him living in shabby estates. His parents hadn't known any better, just as he didn't, his children wouldn't. Young men and women like Dwayne Venn spent their lives in and out of courtrooms, lockups, rental houses, welfare offices. They never moved away from the area. Their friends had been their friends at school—friendships based on proximity, familiarity and disadvantages in common. They became parents at sixteen or seventeen. They were mute and vicious and a police officer's nightmare.

It was the interconnections that had surprised Pam when she first came to the Peninsula. Although Waterloo was the main town for the eastern region of the Peninsula it was like a big village compared to her old stamping grounds, the restless inner suburbs of Melbourne. For example, Venn lived with Donna Tully. Donna was the sister of Lisa Tully. Lisa had lived with Bradley Pike before Pike killed her toddler daughter and hid the body—*if* that's what had happened, and Brad Pike was the only person in creation saying that he hadn't done it. Now Lisa was living with Donna and Venn. She didn't want to have anything more to do with Brad Pike, she'd said, and had even taken out an intervention order on him, but recently Pam had seen Brad Pike in the company of Venn and the Tully sisters.

At the pub, in fact. Go figure. They'd all gone to school together. Maybe that was enough to bind them. *She* would never understand it.

Yet it was Pike who'd informed on Venn. He'd stopped her in the street one day with a weird story about being stalked and what was she going to do about it, then suddenly told her that Venn was the lovers' lane rapist. No, he didn't want to go onto the official informants' register. Wanted her to keep his name secret from her bosses too. She'd honoured that, but really, he was weird, they were all weird.

Uh-oh. Now John Tankard was seating himself on the end of the bench beside her stretched-out feet. An unmistakable tremor ran through the wooden legs and padded vinyl seat as the bench surrendered to Tankard's bulk. She'd removed her shoes earlier and now the soles of her feet were touched briefly by his massive thighs, by polyester heated from within by meaty flesh. She drew up her legs hastily.

God. She was too tired for this.

'Want me to massage your feet?'

'No thank you, Tank.'

'Or I could sit on the other end and feed you peeled grapes.'

'What do you want, Tank?'

'Just making conversation.'

'Well don't.'

After a while he said, 'It was good tonight. On any other Saturday night we'd've been cleaning puke out of the divvie van.'

'Yes.'

He fell silent. His body made minute adjustments that were transmitted through the bench to her like shifts deep in the earth. She was almost asleep when she heard an oiled click and a faint, lubricated, whirring sound.

He'd taken out his service revolver.

'Put it away, Tank,' she said, then regretted it. He was the king of the double entendre, after all.

But he didn't ask what was out that should be put away or where he should put it. Instead, he said, 'Pow, pow,' and the revolver dry clicked on an empty chamber.

Shocked, she sat bolt upright. He was pointing the revolver directly at her midsection with the dazed, swollen look of a man aroused by naked flesh.

'Don't point that thing at me!' she shouted, scrambling away from him.

Click.

'*Never* point a gun at someone in fun, you know that.'
Click.

'Stop it,' she said.
Click.

Badly rattled now, she leapt from the bench and shouted, 'Loser!'

He seemed to wake from whatever possessed him—sexual arousal? Power? The gun itself? Or a combination. Whatever it was, he snapped out of it and said irritably, 'Settle down, it's not even loaded.'

'One day it will be,' she said and couldn't keep the shakes out of her voice.

John Tankard lived in a rear unit of a block of four similar units on Salmon Street. He overlooked someone's back yard, a dull reddish Nubrik wall and mouldy PVC downpipes. The front units overlooked weedy grass, a bicycle path and drydocked yachts behind a steelmesh lockup yard, but the rent was higher. Besides, his rear unit was a blind corner in the world, like a burrow away from all of the shit.

He flicked on the TV and sank into the sofa, his usual spot, against the right arm, next to a little op-shop cupboard on which his phone sat in a scattering of beer-can rings. The sofa was op-shop too, a job lot he bought when he first moved into the flat. He'd repaired the vinyl with duct tape that more or less matched, but the tape was lifting here and there, showing the cracks.

Cracks are a metaphor of my life.

Now where the fuck had that come from? He wasn't even drunk yet, hadn't had a beer since lunchtime.

But a crack had shown back there in the locker room, right? When he'd aimed and dry-fired his gun at Pam Murphy.

Wished he'd seen her other crack, nudge nudge, wink wink. He'd stopped thinking she was a lesbian some time ago. Stuck in the divisional van with her day after day, he'd begun to appreciate her close proximity. When she wasn't looking, he'd take in her shape under the shapeless uniform. Her bare arms through the summer and into early autumn. Once or twice out of the corner of his eye he'd seen her wet her lips. Now that was either unconscious and unrelated to him or unconscious but stimulated by his proximity to her, their thighs less than a metre apart there in the divvie van. Or a deliberate turn-on.

Tankard flicked through a week's unopened mail. A couple of bills and credit card statements and the latest *Sidearm News* from the States. He'd found it advertised on-line when surfing the Web for information about the Glock 17 pistol, subscribed to it, half wondering if it was a rip-off and he'd find his card account stripped bare, but it was legit and now the magazine came regularly and was an antidote to the shit he had to face in his job.

Through its pages he'd bought stuff by mail-order. Deerhide holster. Night-vision goggles. Ankle-strap scabbard. Tins of mace. Pistol replicas: a Uzi, a Sig Sauer, a Heckler and Koch.

Plus a Confederate flag—and fuck me if he hadn't seen six Confederate flags in the past six months, usually in some dopehead's scungy flat. Tonight, in fact, he'd gone with Pam to the rundown weatherboard house that Dwayne Venn shared with the Tully sisters and there, in the sitting room, was a Confederate flag on one wall, photos of Sitting Bull and Cochise on the other walls, and sundry Native American beads and blankets and other crap scattered around the place.

The world was full of fuckups whose lives were so shithouse they escaped into dreams of a time and a life where you'd find courage and absolutes and something clean and noble.

Me? I get that from a gun in the hand, Tankard thought. Like earlier tonight.

There was a hot dark corner of his mind—and it made his groin tremble—where he imagined shooting Pam Murphy. Imagined the spurt of it, like an ejaculation. Not destructive, necessarily—though that was part of it. Sort of a pumped-up feeling. Tankard was no longer a porcine, sweaty, unappetising tired copper with a crook back, but as tall and hard and sinewy and unreadable as the Indian chief who wiped out General Custer at Little Bighorn.

But I've never fired a shot on active duty, he thought, and most cops haven't and most cops never do.

God, his back hurt. He stretched out on the floor and visualised his spine as a sequence of knots along a rope and tried to unpick them one by one.

He fell asleep and woke up cold at three o'clock in the morning.

CHAPTER **FOUR**

It was eleven pm and Challis was slumped in front of the television set, thinking about bed, when Tessa Kane knocked on his door, still dressed in her outdoor gear: hiking boots, jeans, padded jacket. She didn't look angry, exactly, but didn't smile either, her face a little sad under the vivid intelligence that was always there, as if the disappointments she'd been bottling up since yesterday morning had worked their way to the surface.

He fetched her a scotch, walking on eggshells, trying to read her. But she said nothing about his letting her down, running to his mad wife instead of taking a camping walk with her.

He'd lit the fire, for the wind had turned sleety by the time he'd returned from Bushranger Bay, and now the house was warm and safe against the squally night. He didn't know what to say to her. Now and then she sipped at her scotch, very still and silent, but finally a grin chased away the blues and she fished around in her daypack. 'I called in at work on the way here,' she said. 'Lots of letters and messages to catch up on.'

This was better. This was something she did from time to time when she visited him. She liked to read stuff to him.

Soon her lap was full of envelopes, e-mail printouts and slips of paper. She flipped through them abstractedly as he watched.

He said lightly, 'Any mail from the Meddler?'

She'd often told him about the man who bombarded her with anonymous letters and phone calls. The Meddler was an appropriate name: he had an obsessive and insane regard for good manners, law and order, and commonsense. He liked to report bad drivers, rubbish dumpers, lazy shire workers, mulish bureaucrats, vandals, property owners who failed to slash their grass in late spring. Unfortunately, you had to agree with him most of the time. Last summer, for example, he wanted to know what bright spark—'pun intended'—had ordered a controlled burn of the nature reserve on Penzance Beach Road when hot northerlies had been forecast for the next day. The resulting bushfire had burnt out half of the reserve, grassland and fences, and come within a few hundred metres of a weatherboard house.

'Roadside rubbish this time,' Tessa said, not glancing at Challis.

'Uh-huh,' he said.

She waved a letter in her fist. 'Garbage bags dumped on Five Furlong Road, to be precise. He actually hunted around in the garbage bags and found a letter, which he's kindly enclosed.' She wrinkled her nose. 'Smells of rotting fish. It's from the Department of Social Security and addressed to a Donna Tully, inquiring as to the status of her cohabitation with one Dwayne Andrew Venn. The Meddler wants me to denounce Venn and Ms Tully in the pages of the *Progress* as dumpers of rubbish. Says he's also sent a copy to the shire, hoping they'll prosecute.'

Challis nodded. At least she was talking to him now. He wondered if she'd noticed the significance of the Tully name. Surely she had. She'd reported extensively on the disappearance of Lisa Tully's child, and left no doubt in her readers' minds that she thought Bradley Pike was behind it.

As for Dwayne Venn, he wondered if he should tell her about Ellen Destry's stakeout.

No.

'The Meddler's offended by everything,' Tessa said. 'The genius who approved give-way rather than stop signs at the corner of Coolart and Myers roads. The woman at Peninsula FM who says "yee-uh" instead of "year", "haitch" instead of "aitch". The residents of Upper Penzance for not wanting paved roads or mains water and thinking themselves better than anyone else. He seems to live in a state of permanent apoplexy.'

Not that she minded. The Meddler's weekly letter had become an institution in the *Progress*, attracting other letters. Tessa's view was, if you're on a good thing, stick to it.

He watched as she continued to sort through the papers in her lap, and as he watched from the other side of the fire, her dark, clever, mobile face relaxed into a shy, pleased smile. 'What?' he demanded.

She might stay the night. She might not.

She waved a flimsy piece of paper at him. 'This is the proof-sheet of next Tuesday's column.'

He crossed in front of the fire, let his fingers brush against hers as he took the proof-sheet, retreated to his armchair again. She wrote a weekly column for the *Progress*. This time she'd tackled wankers.

> Appreciating the wanker and his art, and distinguishing the wanker proper from the wanker accidental, is best undertaken with a close, like-minded friend. Just the other day one such friend and I were shopping in Rosebud and encountered a man walking a ferret on a lead. Our reaction was immediate and simultaneous. We turned to each other and murmured, 'Wanker.'

> But wanking is a fluid notion, so to speak.
> Once upon a time a man with a big bunch of
> keys hanging from his belt was a wanker. Now
> only certain tradesmen and misguided old
> queers clip keys to their belts.

Challis grinned. He'd been the 'like-minded friend' that day. 'Nice one,' he said, attempting to be like-minded again.

Tessa scowled at once, her face sharpening. She straightened her back, folded her arms and looked fully at him. 'How was the little wife?'

'Don't be like that,' Challis said, immediately feeling sulky and small.

'Like what?'

He turned his face to the flames in the grate.

Tessa continued: 'Big emergency, was it? Is she in intensive care by any faint chance?'

Challis flushed angrily. 'If you must know, she had cut herself.'

'Yes, but to what extent, and with what?'

He hesitated fatally.

She pressed her advantage. 'Barely a scratch?'

He shrugged.

'Not a full-blooded attempt, so to speak. Not a proper deep slice down the length of the wrist.'

He sighed. 'No.'

'A cry for help, maybe?'

Challis snarled, 'Something like that.'

Tessa's voice softened. 'It's time you gave her up, Hal.'

Challis crossed the room to the whisky bottle. 'It's not as easy as that.'

'Of course it is. Your wife pulls the strings and you jerk into action. She says "jump" and you say "how high?".'

'*She* didn't call me the second time, her parents did. So why don't you just shut the fuck up?'

The 'fuck' didn't sound quite right. It struck a false note, sounded forced rather than genuine. But he saw the hurt it caused, and then Tessa was turning away from him, staring at the dark shadows in the corners of the room, solitary and chafing. Her voice when it came was low and hollow. 'I was so looking forward to our walk. Mostly perfect weather, perfect company. Well, we all know about that, don't we?'

Challis said nothing. He sipped his scotch miserably and stared down the years to a time and a place that wouldn't let him go. He'd been one of four CIB detectives in a town in the old goldfields country north of Melbourne. His wife, restless and easily bored, had taken up with one of his colleagues. The colleague had become infatuated with her and lured Challis to a deserted place and tried to kill him. Now the colleague was shuffling around a prison yard with a bullet-shattered femur and Challis's wife was serving eight years for being an accessory to attempted murder.

She would phone him from time to time and say she was sorry, then say she *wasn't* sorry and would gladly do it again. She needed him, she hated him. He was too good for her, he was a shit. Most of the time she was full of longing for him and what he'd represented and the times they'd had before it all went wrong. Challis didn't want her back and no longer loved her, but he did feel responsible, as though he should have been a better man or at least the kind of man she wouldn't want her lover to kill. As Tessa Kane kept saying, it was time he shook her off. Time he *divorced* her, in fact.

'I suppose her parents were there?'

'Yes.'

In fact, Challis liked his wife's parents. They were bewildered, apologetic, as tortured with notions of responsibility as he was, and sorry to think that their daughter could do such a thing to so nice a man.

Tessa snorted. Challis read it not as contempt but obscure pain and envy, as though she felt she had no claim on him at all. He put down his scotch. 'Tess—'

'Something unusual happened on my hike. Do you want to hear about it?' She looked at him, brightly blinking her moist eyes.

Relief flooded through him. 'Of course.'

'I was walking along an empty stretch of beach near Flinders this afternoon. There was a lot of seaweed and kelp on the beach, strong winds, waves, you know how windy it was today.'

Challis nodded. Had she seen him? No.

'Anyway, I'm trudging along when a four-wheel-drive appears, roaring straight at me across the sand.'

Challis's nerve endings tingled. 'Go on.'

'White Toyota traytop ute, to be exact. Two men inside. The driver starts shouting at me. What am I doing there? Who else is with me? Have I found some boxes on the beach? Maybe I've hidden them? He was quite aggressive. Then he just sped off further down the beach. I was too surprised to take down the number.'

'Shipment of drugs,' Challis said flatly.

'I'd say so.'

Challis worked homicide, not drugs, but the trade in drugs often leads to homicide, so naturally he was interested. 'There was a gale last night,' he said.

She nodded. 'Either the stuff was tied to a buoy and got dislodged, or it was thrown or washed overboard from some ship or yacht.'

'Or the shipment was ripped off.'

'That too. Or it's entirely innocent. But it didn't *feel* right, you know?'

Things not feeling right is a common instinct in the police and the press, Challis thought. 'What did they look like?'

Tessa shrugged. 'I only saw the driver clearly. Generic Peninsula male, late thirties, beanie, shades, footie jumper, needed a shave. I can't be more specific than that.'

'Even so, it's worth reporting. Our collators can feed it into the system.'

She saluted. 'Yes, sir.'

A silence opened between them. It was clear to Challis now that they were not going to make love and he'd been deluded to think that a reunion after what he'd done to her—as she saw it—could have been passionate. If he reached out and touched her now she'd flinch and say, it's not as easy as that, Hal.

She seemed to read his confusion and unhappiness and got to her feet. 'I'd better go.'

She almost walked out on him coldly but at the last moment stopped and briefly touched his cheek.

She'd left her scotch unfinished.

CHAPTER **FIVE**

At one am, with Dwayne Venn questioned and remanded and most of the paperwork done, Ellen packed up and drove home to Penzance Beach, still dressed in her baggy stakeout cargo pants and cotton windcheater. The Destry family home was a fibro holiday house on stilts in a hollow between the beachfront and hilly farmland. Penzance Beach was a fifteen-minute drive but a world away from Waterloo, with its depressed estates and idle light industry. In summer, Penzance Beach crawled with the four-wheel-drives and German saloon cars of the well-heeled Melbourne families whose fairytale cottages and architect-designed bunkers would one day replace the fibro shacks of families like the Destrys.

Melbourne was just over an hour's drive away so Penzance Beach crawled with outsiders at Easter too. She slowed the car and looked for somewhere to park. The street was full of cars of the holidaying families and the kids attending Larrayne's party. She drove down two adjacent streets before finding a gap large enough to fit her Magna, and walked back. Good: the party was winding up. There were shouts goodbye as kids tumbled out of her front door and away.

She went inside to find a stony-faced husband and teary daughter. 'What's wrong?'

A dirty look from Alan said she'd been out having fun while he'd been stuck at home trying to maintain order with thirty teenagers. She ignored him, placed her hands on Larrayne's face. 'Sweetie?'

Larrayne had lost weight in the past year. She'd been plump and awkwardly shaped before, as though her torso and arms had lengthened but not her legs or neck. Now she was perfectly proportioned: tall, willowy and, when the puffiness and skin blemishes faded from her cheeks in the next year or so, likely to be a stunner. Larrayne raised her damp, blotchy face. 'Someone brought vodka and ecstasy, Mum,' she said, baffled and offended.

Ellen folded her daughter close against her and glanced inquiringly at her husband.

He took offence. 'Lay off. Don't blame me. What was I supposed to do? I'm just one person, not a squad of security guards.'

A straggle of teenagers edged past them in the hallway, eyeing them apprehensively, all of the cheer gone out of their goodbyes. Then the Destrys were alone in the house, the front door sealing them from the night, the last car accelerating through the slumbering streets.

'I'm really sorry,' Ellen said. 'I tried to get home early but we were on a stakeout and made an arrest and it all took a while.'

She lifted a hand from her daughter's shoulderblades and reached for her husband's arm. 'Alan, sweetheart . . .'

Some of the tension left him. He wore jeans and a T-shirt and looked deeply fatigued, rubbing both hands along his bulky jaw. 'One of the kids must have chucked booze and pills over the back fence. It took me a while to realise that half of the kids were stoned and others were coming and going from the back yard all night.' He laughed bitterly. 'I thought they were after fresh air.'

'Do we know who it was?'

Larrayne disengaged herself from Ellen and shook her head miserably. 'I *told* everyone no alcohol or drugs. Everyone *knows* you're both in the police. How could they do this to me?'

'We'd better search the yard,' Ellen said.

If she could find the remains of the stash, maybe she could get some useful prints and track them back to the supplier. It was the supplier she wanted, not the kid. If she arrested the kid, then her daughter's name would be mud. Fetching a torch from the wall hook beside the back door, she stepped out onto the deck that overlooked the yard, and began to poke the torchlight into the shadows beneath her.

Plenty of bottles and cans. Someone's windcheater. Crumpled cigarette packets.

And, half concealed by shrubbery, a pair of slender legs in jeans and trainers.

Beside her Alan said, 'God almighty,' and clattered down the steps then across the blighted lawn.

Ellen followed. Behind her Larrayne wailed, 'That's Skip.'

Skip Lister. Larrayne had brought him home for a meal a couple of times. A slender, edgy but pleasant kid, anxious to please without being fawning, a student at the Frankston campus of Monash University, drove an old Holden fitted with surfboard racks. He lived in an exclusive part of the Peninsula, just off Five Furlong Road in Upper Penzance. Ellen glanced up into the night, past the dark mass that was sloping farmland on the outskirts of Penzance Beach, to Upper Penzance, as if she might see the lights of the Lister house.

Too late, too dark, too far away.

Larrayne pushed past her, knelt beside Alan and reached her hand to Skip's face, then recoiled as vomit spurted over her hand.

'Yuck,' she said. 'Gross.'

'Roll him onto his side,' Ellen said calmly.

Her husband snapped, 'I know, I know, I work Traffic, remember? I know what to do.'

He rolled the boy over, cleared the vomit from the slack mouth, and checked for breathing.

Skip would have choked to death on his own vomit if we hadn't found him, Ellen thought.

Suddenly she was furious. She wouldn't mind betting that Skip Lister's parents had no idea where their son was or what he was up to. The police saw it all the time and were usually the ones to pick up the pieces: brawls, convenience-store hold-ups, cars wrapped around trees resulting in injury and death.

The parents never knew. Most were shocked to find out what their kids had been doing. Some didn't give a damn.

Stewing, Ellen went inside, looked up the number for Carl Lister in Upper Penzance and dialled. It was one-thirty in the morning but the phone was snatched up at the first ring. 'Yo.'

Yo yourself, Ellen thought. 'Mr Lister?'

The tone changed, as though this wasn't the call that Carl Lister had been expecting. 'Yep.'

'Ellen Destry speaking.'

Silence, then, 'Sorry, do I know you?'

A hint of an accent in Lister's voice. South African, that was it. 'Your son attended my daughter's birthday party tonight.'

'Uh-huh.'

'Well, he's lying in our back yard in a pool of vomit.'

A suggestion of matey laughter. 'Little bugger.'

Ellen clenched her jaw. 'Mr Lister? I said, your son's lying here—'

'Look, give him a coffee, put him in his car, send him home. I'll sort him out when he gets here.'

'I can't do that. He's been drinking.'

'Well, obviously, it was a party, wasn't it?'

'Mr Lister, he could crash his car and kill himself. Worse, he could kill or injure someone else.'

Irritation showed in Carl Lister's voice. 'I don't know what *I'm* supposed to do about it.'

'You're his father, aren't you?'

'He's old enough to look after himself. Old enough to clean up after himself.'

'He's barely nineteen.'

'So? When I was eighteen I—'

'Mr Lister, please come and collect your son.'

'Can't he sleep it off there? Drive himself home in the morning?'

'I don't run a hotel.'

'Christ, look, it's not convenient right now.'

Ellen went icy. She disliked playing the cop card, but sometimes it was necessary and it usually got results.

'I know what we can do,' she said. 'I'll ring the Waterloo police station and say to the duty officer, "It's Detective Sergeant Destry speaking. Send a van to my house, I've got a prisoner for the station lockup."'

In the silence that followed, she said, 'How would that do, Mr Lister? You can drive to the station in the morning and fetch your son. That way only a couple of constables—who would be on patrol duty anyway—will be inconvenienced.'

Carl Lister snarled, 'Give us your address. I'll leave right away.'

Ellen smiled and there was no warmth in it.

CHAPTER **SIX**

Mid-afternoon on Easter Sunday. Mostyn Pearce fed Blur, his ferret, then went for a walk. He walked for an hour a day obsessively, counting cars, counting gates and potholes, and his walk always took in Five Furlong Road. You had Ian Munro's paddocks on the left, sloping down to Penzance Beach, and higher up on the right, along a ridge that commanded million-dollar views of the sea, you had Upper Penzance, an enclave of twenty or thirty houses on two- and three-acre blocks, ranging in price from $400 000 to $750 000. Trucked-in palm trees and other exotics, dirt roads, a general sense of shutting out the rat race.

Shutting out Mostyn Pearce in his dingy new housing-estate bungalow at the bottom of the hill, in other words.

What irritated Pearce—and he'd written to the editor of the *Progress* about it—was the air of privilege, like there were rules for the residents of Upper Penzance and different rules for people like him. It was stupid. They resisted mains water, insisting that every householder use tank water. They didn't want made roads, only leafy dirt lanes. They even kept taking down the roadsign to discourage daytrippers.

As Pearce had pointed out in one of his letters to the *Progress*: 'What if there's a house or bushfire in Upper

Penzance? The access roads are choked with trees, the tracks are potholed, there's very little available water, let alone water pressure'.

The editor had printed that one. She didn't take everything he sent her, like his defence of the detention centre and the need to isolate the queue jumpers, but given that he sent her several letters a week and the newspaper came out only once a week, there was always something for her to use. She'd started calling him the Meddler about six months ago. At first he'd been offended—it sounded derisive—but now he liked it. And after every Meddler column there was always plenty of supportive mail for her letters-to-the-editor column.

Not a peep from the residents of Upper Penzance after his bushfire letter, but.

He always had something to write about. Like on Thursday last week he'd been passing one of the houses on Five Furlong Road and seen that they'd fastened an American-style letter box to the front gate, complete with a little red metal flag on the side. He'd been seized with fury. He wanted to sit the guy down and slap him about the face and demand to know *why*, since this *wasn't* America, he'd erected an American letter box? And what, pray tell, is the little red flag supposed to indicate? he wanted to say. Is the postie supposed to put it up whenever he pops mail into your box? If this were America you'd put it up to indicate that you had letters for him to collect—but this *isn't* America, arsehole. Even if the postie could give a shit one way or the other, what makes you think he's got the time or energy or inclination to shift the stupid lever?

The arm was up again today. Pearce clicked it down.

He walked on, coming to Ian Munro's fenceline and the metal sign that read 'Any person caught stealing firewood off this property will be prosecuted', the word 'prosecuted' spraypainted out and substituted by the word 'shot'.

And that's when he saw the sheep. Distressed sheep, a dozen of them, hollow-ribbed, spines bowed in exhaustion, heads drooping. Baked dirt under their feet. No water in the trough, only a greenish sludge at the bottom. A car went by him on the road, a woman driving, and he turned to face her, indicating the sorry spectacle of the sheep with a gesture of his right hand, inviting her to share his outrage.

But the car headed obliviously on up the road toward Upper Penzance, so Mostyn Pearce went home and fired off an anonymous call to the Royal Society for the Prevention of Cruelty to Animals. Then he glanced at his watch. Whoops. Three-thirty in the afternoon, and he started work at four. Time he was gone. He set the VCR to tape tonight's 'International Most Wanted', a true-crime program on one of the pay TV channels, kissed his wife and daughter, and left for work.

As she passed the oddball looking over a fence at some tired sheep, Ellen Destry slowed the car to scrutinise him more closely. Pinched, unhappy face, dainty Michael Jackson nose, scalp shaved within an inch of its life and full of pale, defenceless ridges. But harmless, and so she continued along Five Furlong Road and into Upper Penzance. She was bone-tired after last night, the business with Skip Lister and his father, the cleaning up this morning. And it wasn't finished. There was a leather jacket on the seat beside her. It belonged to Skip Lister and she'd found it stowed behind a sofa cushion just before lunch. It had taken all morning to make the house presentable again. The odour of cigarette smoke lingered in the curtains and upholstery. Puddles of vomit waited for her in unlikely places. The carpet was sodden with spilt beer and spirits—but not red wine, thank God. Cigarette burns on the mantelpiece. Someone's knickers—none too clean either—

under a deckchair on the side verandah. A couple of condoms underneath the ti-trees at the back.

Alan was working from eight until four today, otherwise she might have done her block and shouted, 'Didn't you keep an eye on them *at all* last night?'

She glanced at her watch. Four in the afternoon. He'd be driving home about now. She sighed: she simply felt too fatigued and dispirited to contemplate a row with him later. Besides, in a sense he wouldn't be there but shut inside the dining room to study for another shot at the sergeants' exam. Meanwhile sex had become an infrequent and complicated transaction. Their lives sometimes collided in angry knots but mainly withered in isolation.

She drove on. She could simply have telephoned the Listers and told Skip to call around for his jacket, but she wanted to see where he lived.

Upper Penzance. It was visible from her back yard in Penzance Beach, floating above Five Furlong Road, which marked the top of the ridge above the slope of farmland that separated Upper Penzance from Penzance Beach. Upper Penzance spelt money and a kind of stubborn-yet-stupid exclusivity in the minds of most of the local people. There had been a letter to the *Progress* from one resident, a woman who'd brayed that she and her husband had spent 'a lot of money' establishing their property, and were 'not about to see it spoilt by paved roads, bulldozers gouging out sewage channels or the lopping of more of the Peninsula's magnificent pine tree avenues'.

So that's where Skip Lister lived, in a half-million dollar house with a fantastic view across to Phillip Island, and that's where his father had taken him last night.

There had been another man with Skip's father. No introduction: he'd emerged from Carl Lister's Mercedes, slipped through the cloud-obscured light of the moon into Skip's car, and driven it away. As for Skip's father, he'd slammed the door of his Mercedes in a businesslike way and shaken her hand and gently chastised his son and generally behaved like a responsible, apologetic father. None of the offhandedness that had so angered Ellen when she'd phoned him.

She'd taken one look at Carl Lister and disliked him on the spot. That was why she was delivering his son's leather jacket to his door instead of asking someone to come and collect it.

It wasn't Lister's manner, glossy Mercedes or Upper Penzance address. It wasn't that he was shifty or smelt wrong in any criminal sense, either, for he didn't. And he wasn't like some South Africans she'd met, who'd given off a palpable sense of wanting to firebomb Asians or regretting they no longer had coloured servants to bitch about. No, it was his energy, confidence and general oiliness at that ungodly hour of the morning. She'd watched him stride from his car, throw a stern, bucking-up arm around his son's shoulders and generally take charge, and she'd felt irrelevant and taken for granted. And Skip hadn't liked that arm either. She'd seen the way he cringed beneath the weight and chumminess of it.

Or perhaps she—and Skip—recoiled from the man's impairment. For he'd suffered burns to his face and hands at some stage. They were not particularly disfiguring, but did give a faintly skewed cast to his head, as though he had limited neck movement, and one hand was clenched in a permanent claw-like spasm.

On another man those burns might have elicited sympathy. On Carl Lister they imparted a faint cruelty, encouraged by a grin fit to bruise his face.

Ellen thought that he was probably the kind of man who placed great demands on his son. Not much love there, she concluded as she left Five Furlong Road and made her way along a narrow, potholed track that wound between pottosporums, gumtrees and wattles. There were big houses set well back from the track on either side. Most were two-storey, architectural wet-dreams with tricky bits of modular concrete slabs, corrugated iron or radially sawn weatherboards here and there on the angular walls.

At least the Listers lived in a standard-looking house, even if it did belong more to Toorak or Brighton than the coast. It was Georgian baronial, she supposed, squat and box-like, and reached via a driveway that hooked around a grassy slope set behind an avenue of golden cypresses. The words 'Costa del Sol' had been picked out in mosaic chips on a board fastened to the front gate. Costa Packet, Ellen thought, remembering an old *Punch* cartoon.

The front gate was locked. No answer when she pressed the buzzer next to the intercom.

Ellen crammed Skip's jacket into the letter box then walked along the fenceline until she had a partial view of the rear of the house. Plenty of lawn, mown to within an inch of its life, well-kept shrubs, garden sheds, two vast white concrete rainwater tanks partly buried into an incline, and some other kinds of fancy landscaping, which gave the rear slope a terraced look.

She sniffed. You were always getting the odd unpleasant whiff on rural properties. Weed killer, sheep dip, fuel, creosote.

When Ellen drove back to Waterloo ten minutes later, coming down from the top of Five Furlong Road to where it separated open paddocks from a dismal new housing estate in the middle of nowhere, she thought she saw the man who'd earlier been looking at the sheep. He was standing in the front yard of a new, unfinished-looking brick veneer house, dressed in some kind of uniform and urging a small child to pat a rat-like creature on a lead.

Lunch for Challis on Easter Sunday had been a ham and pickle sandwich washed down by peppermint tea. He let it settle and then took a bucket to gather rotting fruit under the pear trees, but angry bees were feasting inside the shells of the fruit, and the repeated motions of his arms failed to ease his mind, so he wandered down to his front gate in search of a different distraction: his eroded driveway entrance. He lived on an unsealed road. The topsoil had long since washed away, leaving sand and gravel, which in turn was pushed to the verges whenever the shire grader, making its perfunctory sweep, sliced off the tops of the corrugations to create more sand and gravel. The road also sloped uphill from Challis's front gate, and was lined with needle-shedding pines and bark-shedding gums. Whenever there was a downpour the bark and the needles combined with the sand and the water to form dense, clotting mats that blocked the open ditches and stoppered the concrete culvert pipe under Challis's driveway. As a consequence the floods sought new channels of escape, ultimately cutting deep trenches across his driveway and along the road itself.

No one at the shire offices in Waterloo seemed to know who was responsible for his blocked pipe and ditch. Certainly no one was about to admit responsibility for either. He supposed that he'd have to shovel the matted sand out himself. But where should he put it? He was tempted to spread it across the road as a kind of speed trap and invite the shire engineer and the mayor to pay a visit. He was feeling more and more like Tessa Kane's Meddler.

The neighbours were no help. 'You're a police inspector,' one of them said. 'Make use of that. Make the bastards listen.'

The neighbour had pronounced 'bastards' as though wondering, as he said it, whether or not he'd be arrested for swearing.

Challis knew he wouldn't trade on his job to get results. The police were constantly relying on shire officials for information to help their investigations into the citizens of the Peninsula.

CHAPTER **SEVEN**

Challis showered, dressed, then set out in his rattly Triumph, steering among the channels and potholes of the road that went past his house. At the Old Peninsula Highway he turned toward Waterloo, passing through a region of orchards, vineyards and ostrich farms which gave way to a scattering of plant nurseries and riding schools, which in turn gave way to the drab housing estates, car yards, furniture barns, pump suppliers and junkfood palaces that lined the outskirts of Waterloo. Just before the police station he turned right, travelling for five kilometres to the aerodrome, where he drove in, passing a Land Rover that was parked on the track outside the entrance gate.

Kitty's Mercedes was parked behind the main hangar. He pulled in beside it and got out. As he approached the metal side door a Cessna began to head along the runway, finally lifting from the ground and clawing skywards. He'd glimpsed the words Peninsula Aerial Photography Services stencilled on the fuselage, and that meant that Kitty had landed and parked her Kittyhawk and taken off again in her Cessna. She made a bread-and-butter income from the cameras fixed to the underside of the Cessna, taking low-altitude shots of farmhouses to be laminated and later hung on study walls, high-altitude shots for the shire's planners and surveyors, and oblique shots of the coastline for publication on postcards and calendars.

Challis stepped into the hangar, making for a partitioned corner that had been set aside for the restoration of old aeroplanes. His 1935 Dragon Rapide was at the far end. He had to pass a wrecked Wirraway, Kitty's latest project, to get to it. Everyone called her Kitty because of the Kittyhawk. Her real name was Janet Casement, and although Challis had a companionable relationship with her they were not close in any sense. There was an air of solitariness about her. Tinged with loneliness? Unlikely, given that she'd got married only six months ago. Perhaps he was reading his own loneliness into her.

He pulled on a pair of overalls, found an FM station on the greasy transistor radio that was strapped to a rusty hook on the wall, and went to work. He didn't mind working alone. He too was guilty of solitary habits and intentions.

Six years earlier he'd found the Rapide lying in pieces in a barn north of Toowoomba, bought it and had it trucked down to Waterloo. So far he'd replaced the splintered, rotted and worm-eaten sections of the airframe and rebuilt one of the motors. He rarely had time to work on the Dragon, but believed that time didn't matter when you were restoring something of beauty. He admired the way the Dragon sat there with its flimsy upper and lower wings outspread and its questing, rounded snout testing the air.

Today he'd work in the cockpit. Most of the instruments needed to be replaced or recalibrated. This was better than gardening or cleaning ditches, and his mind began to sift and refine the clutter of his life, bringing him by degrees to the Floater again.

Specifically, the Rolex watch. Frozen at ten o'clock on the second of the month. Morning or afternoon? He stopped suddenly, screwdriver poised in one hand. Why was he getting bogged down in questions of time? Perhaps he should be considering the watch itself. How rare was the Rolex? Could it be traced?

Challis pondered this as he unscrewed the back plate of the airspeed indicator in order to clean it and replace the cracked glass, and as he worked he grew aware of two distinct sounds outside the hangar: an aeroplane was throttling back as it made its approach, and a noisy vehicle had entered the aerodrome and was roaring past the hangars toward the landing strip.

Then there was a shout, the brap of a horn and a squeal of tyres. Challis raced outside. The Land Rover that had been parked on the track outside the perimeter fence was now at the far end of the airstrip, gathering speed and heading straight for Kitty's Cessna, which had just touched down. He watched helplessly. So did a handful of weekend pilots, mechanics and aerodrome staff. Kitty swerved left. The Land Rover swerved, cutting it off. Kitty swerved right; the Land Rover leaned hard in anticipation, tipping dangerously, leaving commas of rubber on the landing strip. Finally Kitty took the only avenue available to her: she opened the throttle, waited for lift, and skipped over the Land Rover, clipping it with her tailwheel. But she hadn't the speed to sustain a takeoff, and bounced onto the strip again, the tailwheel breaking away and sending the Cessna into a twitching skid past a row of Aero Club planes parked on an asphalt apron between a hangar and the perimeter fence. Finally it skewed around, halted, leaned, and Kitty got out shakily. She stood bent over for a moment, her hands on her knees as though gasping for breath. Then she straightened her back, gazed at Challis and the others, stuck her thumb in the air. A ragged cheer went up around the airfield.

CHAPTER **EIGHT**

'He must've been drunk or something.'

Now that she'd walked twice around her wrecked Cessna and noted the damage, Kitty looked drained suddenly, pupils dilated, features pale, a slight tremble in her hands and voice. She pushed both fists into the pockets of the old suede jacket she wore whenever she flew, and began to bump her upper thigh against the fuselage. Then she jerked into action again, retrieving a film canister from the nose-mounted camera.

'Kitty.'

Challis said it a little sharply, to gain her attention. A gaggle of other pilots and mechanics was converging on them. 'Kitty,' he said, 'do you know who it was?'

She shrank inside her jacket. 'I've no idea.'

'Did you get a clear look at the vehicle or the driver?'

'Not really.'

'Did you recognise the vehicle from anywhere?'

'No.'

'Kitty, it seemed deliberate to me. Is there anyone you—'

But then they were surrounded by others, who were full of noise and curiosity, shaking their heads on her behalf. They took over cheerily, wheeling the Cessna around, hooking it to a tractor and towing it off the landing strip before Challis could think to tell them they might have been interfering with a crime scene. But then he thought that it didn't matter. They'd all seen what had happened. He took their names one by one, asking: 'Do you know who it was?'

They all said no.

'Know any reason why someone would want to hurt Kitty?'

'No,' they all said. And echoed Kitty: 'The guy must've been drunk.'

Then Challis led Kitty to the hangar and gestured for her to sit on a packing case next to her workbench. 'Tea? Coffee?'

'Actually, Hal, there's a shoebox full of mini-bar bottles under the sink.'

Challis gave her a brief, lopsided grin and hunted in the damp shadows for the shoebox, which was soft and warped and broke apart as he lifted it out. 'We have scotch, brandy, gin.'

'Brandy. Have one with me.'

'Scotch.'

They drank from the flimsy plastic cups that came with the coffee dispensing machine. The brandy seemed to burn through the tense muscles that had forced Kitty's features into an unbending mask, heightening her colour and giving her back her nerve. Her eyes, dark and enlarged by fatigue, sorrow or fear, flashed a little. 'I could have been killed.'

'Tell me what happened,' Challis said.

'Well, I took Rita for a spin'—Rita, for Rita Hayworth, her long legs and name stencilled on the nose of the Kittyhawk by an American pilot based in Darwin in 1942— 'then came back and loaded film in the Cessna and took off again,' Kitty said. She glanced at him. 'Real estate firm in Red Hill hired me to take some shots.'

Challis nodded. 'Go on.'

'The rest you know. I finished the job, came in to land, and this big . . .' She looked at him inquiringly.

'It was a Land Rover,' he said.

'Land Rover comes racing in off the entry road and drives straight at me. Hits the undercarriage and part of the fuselage.'

She went motionless and distant. Challis knew to be patient. She was still a little unhinged. 'Kitty' was a curiously apt name for her, although 'Janet' suited her, too. Her movements were slow, economical, almost sleepy—like a cat's—but hinting at barely contained energy. He saw her push both hands back through her hair, tucking the ends behind her ears, and then she blinked in an effort to focus her attention on him again.

'Sorry, Hal, it's starting to get to me. If you don't mind I'd like to ring my husband.'

Then she lifted up both hands and looked at them in wonderment. 'Look, I'm shaking.'

'I'll ring him for you,' Challis said, taking out his mobile phone. 'What's his name?'

'Rex.'

'He'll be at home?'

She nodded. 'He's always at home. He generally likes to stay at home and play the stockmarket on the Internet.' She looked faintly embarrassed, as though a husband should have an out-and-about sort of job. 'I actually taught him to fly, but he's not really interested.'

She was prattling, a sign of rattled nerves, so Challis smiled and gently, firmly, asked for her home phone number and dialled it.

Five rings and then the answering machine, Rex Casement's voice, a clipped English accent: 'You have reached the number for Rex and Janet Casement. You may leave a message after the tone.'

Challis said, 'It's Detective Inspector Challis, Mr Casement. Don't be alarmed, your wife's okay, but there's been an incident here at Waterloo aerodrome and your wife would like you to collect her. Please call me,' he finished, giving his mobile number.

'Not there?' Kitty said.

'No.'

'I bet he was there. He gets on the Net and ignores the phone. After a while he'll play back the message.'

They waited, sipping their drinks. Kitty looked forlorn suddenly, as though aware of her mortality. She glanced up at every noise outside, as if expecting her husband to appear. Challis was about to suggest that he call back and leave a message to say that he would take her home when the mobile phone in Kitty's pocket started to ring.

She snatched it out. 'Yes . . . Yes, sweetie, I'm all right. No, nothing like that . . . Yes, but I feel a bit shaken . . .' She laughed fondly. 'I *knew* you were on the Net. Sure. I'll be here. Bye.'

She closed the phone. 'He'll come straight here. You needn't hang around, Hal.'

'It's all right.'

She smiled gratefully, but clearly didn't want to talk. Challis sat and glanced around at the hangar as if seeing it for the first time. Spare parts, tools, workbenches, the Dragon Rapide he was restoring, a director's chair with a rotting canvas seat, Kitty's work area with its chewed-looking pinboard, filing cabinet, manila folders leaking letters and receipts, flying regulation books and navigation tables stacked on a shelf. Business cards, aerial photographs and a commercial pilot's licence thumbtacked to the pinboard.

Challis said suddenly, 'Did you owe money to anyone?'

She looked startled, then offended. 'Certainly not.'

'Must have cost you money to set up the business.'

She said coldly, 'I had money of my own.'

Challis said nothing, showed nothing. It was a tactic honed over the years to elicit reactions, but how fair was it in this case? He felt drawn to Kitty. They'd shared hangar space and supported each other with labour time, contacts and companionable small talk at the ends of long afternoons. Companions. But that had shifted during the past hour, almost without his being aware of it. There was the badness with Tessa Kane, and with his wife, complicated by his witnessing what appeared to have been an attempt on Kitty's life. She was shaken, vulnerable, in need of comfort. Yet he was close to bullying her with these questions about enemies and money owed. Where did he stand, exactly? What was he here, now—policeman or friend?

Stupid. She had a husband. She wanted and needed her husband, not an inquisitive cop. A door began to close inside Challis.

He said gently, 'Does your husband have any enemies?'

'Rex sits in his study and trades shares on the Internet and makes a packet from it. So, no, he doesn't.'

But her voice was tinged with neglect, and Challis imagined the lonely hours she might spend in a house with a husband who chose to shut himself away. He decided to drop the matter. He touched her forearm.

'Routine questions,' he assured her. 'Forget I asked. We'll see if we can find the Land Rover and whoever was driving it and with any luck you're right, he was drunk or stoned.'

Her head was bowed. She nodded numbly, and began to tremble. He got to his feet, crossed the grimy patch of concrete, and stood beside her, letting her rest her shoulder against his waist while he placed his hand comfortingly on her head.

They were posed like that when the husband bustled in, full of concern. Challis stiffened in embarrassment but Rex Casement gave him a quick, shy smile of thanks and took over, murmuring, 'It's all right, I'm here now, it's all right,' as Kitty stood and flung herself against him. Casement wore a pair of old, belted cords and a blue polo shirt, sunglasses pushed back to nestle in fading red hair shot through with

CHAPTER **NINE**

Easter Monday. Two days since the lovers' lane arrest and her daughter's party, and Ellen Destry was still bone-tired. She wasn't obliged to work today but had paperwork to catch up on, so she'd driven in to Waterloo after breakfast and now she regretted it. She'd found nothing on Carl Lister beyond the fact that he was new to the Peninsula. She swivelled in her ergonomic chair and leafed moodily through some new cases. A dangerous driving incident at the Waterloo airfield, involving a friend of Hal Challis. A break-in at the chainsaw and ride-on mower place out at the industrial estate. And a spate of incidents related to the new detention centre: two inmates on the run, a broad daylight assault on two Malaysian students, who'd had their headcoverings torn off, the words 'Bomb Moslems back to the stone age' spraypainted across the 'Keep Out' sign on the razor-wired cyclone fence around the centre.

She sighed and shoved the files to the other side of her desk. Refugees, asylum seekers, queue jumpers, fanatics, terrorists: the inmates of the detention centre were called many things and were hated and feared, but to Ellen they were starved-looking, psychologically frail wretches. The good locals had been outraged when the old Navy barracks were converted, even as the Chamber of Commerce welcomed a shot of federal money and renewed life for the worthless, empty buildings on the piece of marshland beside a mangrove swamp on Westernport Bay. As far as Ellen could see, the detention centre had provided only half a dozen jobs for the locals, lined the pockets of the American corrections company that operated it, and stirred up the local bigots. It had brought no joy to anyone.

She worked desultorily through the morning, breaking for coffee she made using Challis's espresso pot and stock of Lavazza grounds. Plenty of burglaries and a couple of robberies at ATMs; the thing was, they could be traced back to drugs, to the income needed to feed a drug habit, and they were on the rise, which to her was further evidence of increased drug activity on the Peninsula. She made notes, wondering if they would ever be useful: for example, ecstasy tablets had brand names, the preferred brand was the Euro Dollar, everyone said the Snoopy was no good.

Around midday, discouraged, she wandered down across the railway line to the High Street shops, looking for something to eat. Most of the shops had shut for the Easter break. There were one or two more empty shop windows, with 'Support Your Local Traders' pasted across the glass. A new $2 bargain shop had opened, making three in two blocks.

Café Laconic was open, three women at an outdoor table talking raucously over the squalls and complaints of half a dozen toddlers and babies. As Ellen passed them, a two year old climbed into his mother's lap, undid her buttons and latched on to one of her breasts. The mother shifted automatically to improve his access to her nipple and kept on talking, scarcely registering that he was there.

Ellen crossed to the other side of the street. The bakery was open. Next to a rubbish bin outside it was a wood and metal seat, occupied by a gaggle of teenage girls dipping into potato cakes wrapped in butcher's paper. Just then a lowered Valiant crawled by, teenage boys inside, headbanging music detonating in Ellen's ears.

The car stopped. The boys pressed a pornographic magazine against the rear passenger-side window, a gynaecological close-up pasted to the glass.

The girls tittered, hid their smiles behind fistfuls of greasy chips, and called out to the boys.

Not a good look. Those girls would fall pregnant at seventeen to no-hopers like Brad Pike and end up grieving like Lisa Tully, or sitting around like slovenly cows in the main street.

Ellen sighed. She was being unfair. What was happening to her? What was happening to the Peninsula? Maybe the reminder of Lisa Tully's missing daughter was getting her down. Some cases affect you more than others. When it was a little kid it hollowed you out. You don't forget them but reflect on them at odd moments—in the car, at dinner, with your own kid, watching TV. When a kid is raped or murdered it turns everything around. All the goodness leaks away. In fact, you almost stop believing in goodness.

Scobie Sutton was at home with Beth and Roslyn that day, combing nits out of Roslyn's hair. The TV was on to keep his daughter calm while he did it.

The best way was to use hair conditioner, really slapping it on like axle grease, then run a special nit comb through it, wiping the gunk off onto tissues. You had to do it several times. You were after not only the lice themselves but also the eggs, which clustered at the roots, often behind the ears or at the back of the neck.

Roslyn had been infected four times now. It meant that Scobie and his wife had to wash and treat everything each

time—towels, bedding, clothing, their own hair. They were
fed up. They did the right thing, treated their kid and didn't
send her back to school if there was any doubt, but still she
got infected. Got infected because the other parents couldn't
believe that their own precious little darlings could have nits.
Couldn't believe that clean, wholesome families such as theirs
could have nits. *Dirty* people got infected with lice, not them.
Well, have I got news for you, Scobie thought, wiping the
comb onto a sodden tissue.

It was worse with girls. They had long hair and liked to
lean forward over their little classroom tables, their heads
resting against one another's companionably, the lice cheerfully
jumping from one little head to the next.

He wondered who kept reinfecting his daughter. Someone
from a slapdash, hard-pressed or ignorant family. Like the
Pearce kid, or the youngest Munro kid. Roslyn played with
them at school, shared a desk with them, had them over after
school. Strange, troubled kids. The Munro kid lived on a farm,
the daughter of a bully. The Pearce kid's father kept a ferret.
Somehow, it seemed to Sutton, both sets of home circumstances suggested neglect, and therefore head lice.

He paused for a few minutes, caught by an animated
character on TV. Why was it that British children's television
was obsessed with vehicles that talked and *adult* characters
like Bob the Builder, Postman Pat and Fireman Sam? And
what did the dully decent, lower middle-class, nice-cup-of-
tea, socks-and-sandals *tone* of British children's television have
to do with childhood?

'Dad? Daddy?'

'Mmm?'

'Daddy?'

'Mmm.'

'Daddy?'

'I said yes.'

'No you didn't.'

Scobie breathed out. 'Sweetheart, tell me what you want.'

'Who do you go for?'

Scobie didn't understand. 'What?'

'Jessie Pearce goes for the Bombers,' his daughter said. Her voice rose, growing anxious. 'I don't know who to go for. Who do you go for?'

She's talking about *football*, Scobie realised. He loathed football, knew nothing about it, was relieved when a daughter and not a son had been born to him. But now this. 'If Jessie goes for the Bombers,' he said, 'you could too.'

She absorbed this. She didn't seem satisfied, as though she wanted guidance from him, not Jessie Pearce. Then: 'Can Jessie come over to play?'

Scobie thought of the strange, silent child of the ferret man and said, 'Sorry, sweetheart, not today.'

Easter Monday and John Tankard had to fucking work. They were short-staffed because it was Easter, so he was cruising the streets of Waterloo alone, feeling stiff and sore, giving the local hoons the evil eye from the driver's seat of the divisional van.

He was making short forays into the housing estates and industrial park and down High Street—where he saw Sergeant Destry; now, she had a good set of tits on her—but mostly he kept close to the Fiddler's Creek pub, (a) because he had an arrangement with the bottle-shop manager for one slab of beer a week, and (b) because he'd seen Bradley Pike's car in the carpark.

He tried to picture it but couldn't. Everyone hated Pike. Who would want to sit with him? Who would want to drink with him? Everyone knew he'd offed his girlfriend's kid and hidden the body. Probably raped the poor little brat as well.

Tankard intended to follow Pike when he came out, stick hard on his tail all day, thoroughly rattle the useless prick till he made a mistake, broke the law and could be arrested.

But the next time Tankard swung by the pub, Pike's car was gone. And it was a different guy working the bottle shop. Fuck it all. Tankard slammed his fist on the dashboard in frustration. At times like this he knew why men went bananas with a gun.

He was driving along a rutted lane behind the industrial estate when he found a Land Rover, doors open, tinted windows, loose wires hanging underneath the dash.

Pam Murphy had Easter Monday to herself. She could have gone to Point Leo to surf but the buses were infrequent because of the holiday and the surf beach would have been packed with maniacs, so she stayed in Penzance Beach. Anyway, she didn't like the look of the sky. Squally wind, darkening clouds, pretty choppy out on the water.

Tomorrow with any luck the cheque from Lister Financial Services would clear and she'd have access to $30 000. One of the community policing officers at Waterloo was selling a Subaru Forester with roof rack, air-con, power steering, genuine 50 000 km on the clock. No more taking the bus to surf beaches.

Except she had a problem with money. A problem holding on to money. The police credit union had turned her down for a loan and so had a couple of banks, so she'd gone to Lister Financial Services and borrowed thirty grand. Fifteen per cent interest instead of the ten per cent a bank would have charged for a personal loan, so not too bad, could have been worse. The trouble was, she'd agreed to weekly repayments and, even though the loan cheque was still to clear, she'd signed the papers last Thursday, so the first repayment was almost due.

Time to manage herself better. For example, she could cut down on buying something each time she went to Ikea or Freedom, stop flying to places like Bali for holidays, stop buying CDs and books for a while.

. . .

The Meddler, Mostyn Pearce, walked along Ian Munro's fenceline to see if the starving sheep were still there. They were. He hoped the RSPCA would get their act together soon. Its being Easter shouldn't stop them from investigating.

He made to go on but two things changed his mind. First, the electronic bird-repelling gun was booming about once every two minutes in the orchard at the bottom corner of Ian Munro's property, and it was getting on his nerves. Two, there was a small car parked by the road, a man and a woman with plastic buckets walking head down beneath the pine trees on either side of the road. They were ethnics. Somewhere from Europe, judging by their features and the shape of their heads. Suddenly the woman stooped, flashed a knife and straightened holding a pine mushroom, which she dropped into her bucket. That figured.

So he turned and went back down Five Furlong Road, passing the estate where he lived and heading toward an intersection where Five Furlong Road met four other roads. One curved downhill into Penzance Beach, one went to Waterloo, one to Mornington and the other was a dirt lane that skirted farmland and gave rear access to Upper Penzance.

It was a bad intersection. It needed a roundabout. Pearce liked to stand there sometimes and watch the idiots endanger themselves through careless driving or failing to heed the give-way signs.

He was there for five minutes when the car coming down the track from behind Upper Penzance swerved and instead of slowing for the give-way sign actually skittled it, snapping it off at the base and running right over it, the sign bashing and scraping against the underside of the car.

Then it braked violently and a man he recognised from one of the big houses in Upper Penzance tumbled out of the driver's seat, brushing agitatedly at his clothing.

The Meddler was close enough to see the spider fly off and land in the grass. A big one, too. Probably dropped onto the guy's lap from behind the sun visor.

Then the car drove off again and Pearce took out his pad, noted the time, date, registration number and other details. He'd go to that big house and get the guy's name from his letter box or the mail in the box itself. Then he'd write a letter to the shire—which must, he thought, spend thousands of ratepayers' dollars each year replacing signs because it never knew who to fine.

He was halfway home and the driver's face kept swimming into his consciousness. He was sure he'd seen him in another context recently. The face was a bit different and it was in connection with something dark or unpleasant.

Then he remembered where. On that 'International Most Wanted' program he'd taped on pay TV.

An Easter Monday afternoon in early autumn. Early *fall*.

Challis watched a red persimmon leaf fall to the grass like a clumsy butterfly. On the tree they glowed like paintings but on the ground or pasted to his gumboots they merely looked lifeless. He glanced around his yard. Buttery sunlight, the air drowsy and still, but an autumn storm was brewing and this morning when he'd gone to collect the paper from his mailbox he'd seen strips of bark all over the road.

He put away the rake. He drove to the aerodrome at Waterloo, wondering at his motives.

Kitty wasn't there.

In fact, as he was working on the instrument panel of the Dragon a man and a teenage girl wandered in, asking where they could find 'the lady who gives joyrides'.

'We had an arrangement,' the man said, his face shiny, hard, stubborn. 'My daughter turns sixteen today.'

'Sorry,' Challis said, 'but she had a bad scare yesterday, and her plane's been damaged. She probably won't be coming in today.'

No gasps of concern. No is-she-all-right? Just irritation.

'But I paid a deposit. I want a refund.'

'Try calling her next week.'

'We came down here from Dandenong special,' the man said.

Challis shrugged, wiped his hands on a rag. 'Sorry.'

The man glowered. After a while he fished in his wallet and said, 'This is my card. Could you give it to her, ask her to call me?'

Challis didn't want to climb out of the cockpit of the Dragon so nodded his head toward Kitty's workbench on the other side of the hangar. 'Leave it over there,' he said, and went back to work.

When next he looked he was alone again and the man's business card had fallen onto the oily floor.

Challis sighed, climbed down and retrieved the card. Kitty had always pinned invoices, business cards, brochures and photographs to the pinboard above her bench. He looked for an unused thumbtack and his eye was drawn to a cluster of aerial photographs that Kitty had taken for one of her clients. They were curled and dusty and poorly composed. Presumably they'd been rejected by the client.

But one photograph in particular attracted a closer look. It showed a patchwork of pine plantation, open farmland, dam and vineyard, stitched together with roads and tracks. A typical Peninsula landscape, in fact.

Except for the cannabis plants, showing deeply and richly green under a dun-coloured canopy of eucalyptus trees.

CHAPTER **TEN**

Tuesday. School and work again for most people. The morning school-run served to anchor Scobie Sutton, reminding him that he was more than a CIB detective. He was one of the other parents, a citizen of the district and, most importantly, Roslyn's dad. He'd sing along to a Hi-5 tape with her as they drove to school, walk her to the Prep I classroom ('I' for Inger, Roslyn's prep teacher), natter with the other parents, make sure that Roslyn recognised the hook for her blue, surely-too-big backpack, then exchange a hug and kiss with her and a cheery goodbye with the other parents before returning to his car and the drive to Waterloo.

The other parents. Mums, mostly. April now, relatively early in the year, and they were still sussing him out. Scobie forced them to acknowledge him. He learnt their names, made sure they knew his (though not that he was a copper), made eye contact with them and engaged them in conversation. Most were thawing to him, but they still had unvoiced questions for him. He could read it in their faces. Are you a single father? If so, why? Why aren't you at work? Are you unemployed? A male parent, alone with a female child. Is it safe to let *my* daughter go to your house to play with *your* daughter after school?

58

He'd got to the school early one morning and a classmate of Roslyn's had said, 'Come and see the koala.' So they'd made their way along the path, red-brick pavers winding between tan-bark islands, shrubs, gumtrees and classrooms, to a solitary gum beside the After School Care room. There was a pink hair tie at the base of the tree, a dewy school windcheater draped over a pine rail nearby.

Scobie looked up. Sure enough, there was a koala halfway up the tree. And sure enough, the mother of the other child was soon hoofing it toward him, darting suspicious looks at him, as though he might spirit her kid away.

Scobie wanted to say nastily, 'Is there a problem?' but felt small and mean. That mother—*any* mother—was right to be wary. Even so, he was in no hurry to inform them that he did have a wife, and if not for her job up in the city, which obliged her to leave home at seven-thirty am and get home at six-thirty pm, she'd gladly be sharing the school run with him.

You didn't usually get fathers making the school run but one was there this morning, Mostyn Pearce, a thin, narrow-faced, agitated-looking individual, dressed in jeans, trainers and a Collingwood football jumper. His daughter, Jessie, pale, weedy, undernourished-looking, stood clutching his leg, ducking her face away when Scobie caught her eye. In any other child it might have been an appealingly shy gesture, but by some twist of heredity it was unappealing in Jessie Pearce.

Leaning against the man's other leg was a ferret on a lead. The child and the ferret were perfect reproductions of the man: slight, edgy, sly, quick, a mass of nerve endings.

The other children were drawn to but afraid of the ferret, and stood watching in a cluster some distance away. Scobie heard Pearce say, 'It's all right, he won't bite.' There was impatience in his tone, as though he spent his life explaining things to people who were slow, obtuse or careless. His gaze skittered over Scobie's, taking in everything, settling on nothing.

Scobie stood alone for a few minutes, smiling and nodding as mothers arrived with their children. He said a breezy hello half a dozen times, but no one approached him. Eight-fifty am . . . Inger would be opening the classroom door soon. Older children raced past, yelling. It was a cheerful, nourishing sort of school, but there were no black or Asian faces, no round veiled faces, and—judging by the tone of the weekly newsletter and other take-home notices—no sign that a feminist perspective had reached this far south.

He listened to the conversations around him. Did you go away for Easter? Footie season soon. The kids dragged their heels this morning. How would the blooming mayor feel if *he* had a detention centre on his doorstep, that's what I'd like to know . . .

And then Scobie saw Aileen Munro. She seemed to sidle in and stood well back, a bulky presence along the serpentine path leading to Prep I. As Scobie watched, she bobbed to kiss her two older children goodbye, watched them race to their respective classrooms, then stood with her youngest daughter, scarcely daring to meet the eyes of the other parents. Then, apparently sensing his scrutiny, she looked up and her gaze locked on Scobie's, anguished and beseeching.

She knew who he was. She'd known for the past eighteen months that he was a CIB detective based at Waterloo. She was embarrassed to know him, embarrassed that he'd had cause to visit and question her in her farmhouse kitchen on Five Furlong Road.

Her husband, Ian Munro, had been suspected of sending a padded envelope containing a .303 bullet to a bank official in Waterloo. The bank had earlier threatened to foreclose on a loan taken out by Munro. When Munro sold off a parcel of land to repay the loan, the matter was dropped, but there had been a series of other incidents since then. Munro had apparently brandished a rifle at repossession agents, run the tyres of his ute over the toes of the council sheriff, and punched a process server who was attempting to deliver a legal document. He'd been abusive to shire officers and suspected of placing gelignite on the driver's seat of the bank loan officer's car.

Scobie had investigated, and urged people to press charges, but Munro was a bully, stocky, cold and unremitting, and the locals knew better than to come forward.

Scobie watched Aileen Munro edge through the other parents until she was able to murmur in his ear, 'I'm worried about Ian.'

Scobie jerked his head. They moved away from inquisitive ears. 'Tell me,' he said.

Aileen Munro's lined face looked up at him. 'He's all hyper. It's like he's going to explode.'

Aileen's daughter was clinging to her mother's dry, bony fingers, gazing at Scobie. There was a cut across her nose, a hint of bruising beneath one eye. Then she scratched her scalp and his gaze went to her hair and he shuddered to think of lice crawling there.

He turned to Aileen. 'Has Ian been violent with you or the kids?'

'Ian? No, never.'

'How did Shannon cut her face?'

'Fell off the trampoline,' Aileen said, her expression saying that was her story and she was sticking to it.

'All right,' Scobie said, sighing. 'So, what's wrong with Ian?'

'Like I said, he's all wound up.'

'About anything in particular?'

'Money. It's always money. It was all right till he took out that loan. Now he's in too deep and not paying the bills. The government this, the government that. He's letting the place run down.'

'I thought he'd paid off the loan.'

'This is a new loan.'

The banks have a lot to answer for, Scobie thought. 'I don't see there's much the police can do at this point,' he said. 'If you like I could talk to him, but—'

'Oh, no,' Aileen said, horrified. 'He's already had a row with a man from the RSPCA. He'd throw a real wobbly if he thought I'd been talking about him to the police, going behind his back.'

'Have you talked to the bank? They could tailor the repayments to suit your income.'

'Yeah, right, you know what he thinks of banks.'

'Then I don't see what I can do.'

'I just want you to know, that's all. Be prepared, kind of thing,' Aileen Munro said as the siren sounded for the beginning of classes.

She paused. 'I don't know if I can hack it any longer. He's got guns, you know.'

CHAPTER **ELEVEN**

Challis slept badly and woke early on Tuesday morning. To clear his head he walked for an hour, pumping his arms and striding out in order to stir his sluggish blood. It seemed to work, and by seven-thirty he'd showered and dressed and was drinking coffee on his deck, which faced the healing early sun through leaves on the turn.

By seven-fifty he was heading for Waterloo, where a temporary office had been allocated to him ten months earlier for the investigation into the disappearance of the Tully child. That case had dragged on and after a time he'd had to attend to more pressing but less interesting homicides—mostly domestics—elsewhere on the Peninsula; but then the Flinders Floater had been found and he'd returned to Waterloo, where the little office was still available. Then that case had gone stale but this time he stayed on, electing to use Waterloo as his base. It was a recent Force Command initiative, allocating a senior Homicide Squad officer to each of the main non-metropolitan regions. The old system of sending a team of Melbourne detectives long distances to remote regions had been inefficient and the cause of local resentment. Challis liked Waterloo. The staff were easygoing and it was close to home.

He parked the Triumph, entered through the back door and went upstairs to the CIB office, a large, open-plan room with partitioned cubicles along the walls. His office was in one corner and overlooked the carpark. He happened to glance down and saw Ellen Destry park her car and enter the building. No sign of Scobie Sutton's car.

There were message slips on his desk. A Land Rover had been found. It bore dents and scratches on the passenger-side wing. The owner had reported it stolen at about the time Constable Tankard had found it while on patrol.

Challis stared at the phone. His hand reached out, collapsed on the desk again. He didn't want to call the prison and see how his wife was doing; he also ought not to use police time and resources. But a call from work would somehow make him feel less intimate and committed than a call from his home.

He made the call. His wife was back in her cell, on suicide watch. Did the inspector wish to talk to her? It might help her. No, Challis said. Tell her I called.

Then he went to the poky kitchen and brewed coffee, wondering who'd been at his packet of Lavazza. He'd learnt a long time ago always to provide his own tea and coffee. Police station coffee tended to come in a Maxwell House tin the size of a fuel drum and no one had ever heard of weak tea, let alone peppermint.

Finally, with a mug of coffee at his elbow, he opened the *Progress*, printed overnight and hot off the press. There was the Meddler's letter, and Tessa's column about the wanker with the ferret, and her sharper, more contentious observations about the asylum seekers and the detention centre. He could practically hear her spitting as she wrote that she'd found it necessary to point out to the worthy citizens of Waterloo that her objection to the local detention centre was not to *that* detention centre on *that* bit of land but to the notion of incarceration of asylum seekers in the first place.

No doubt she'd lose some advertising now, and the coppers of Waterloo police station would glance at him sideways and wonder about his relationship with the ratbag, leftist, pinko editor of the local rag.

He threw the newspaper into a bin and took out the Floater file. Not for the first time, he wondered about the thousands who go missing each year, unreported and apparently unloved and untraceable. Surely someone loved them? Surely someone remembered them? Here's a man prosperous enough to own a Rolex watch: surely he left a trace somewhere?

On an impulse, Challis reached for the local yellow pages and under the heading 'watchmakers' found a young woman who told him that the figures etched into the case of the Floater's Rolex were service marks. She jotted them down and said she'd make a few calls and let him know in a day or two who had serviced the watch.

So that was progress. Next Challis examined Kitty Casement's aerial photograph of the cannabis crop. There was a topographical map of the Peninsula on his wall but he was unable to match the tiny patch of coastline represented in the photograph to any part of the map.

A job for CIB and after that the Drug Squad, so he went in search of Ellen Destry. She was not in her cubicle. He walked downstairs and into a throng of uniformed and plain-clothes police, some cramming breakfast hamburgers from the fast-food joint across the street into their mouths.

Challis shuddered, saw Pam Murphy and edged toward her. 'What's going on?'

She blushed faintly, as if surprised that he knew her or would want to talk to her. In fact, Challis rated highly her detection abilities and knew she wanted to move on from uniformed work. 'The Monday talk, except it's on Tuesday this week.'

She pointed to a typed notice on the wall of the corridor. Challis read that Senior Sergeant Kellock would be addressing staff on 'Self-Selection and the Criminal Mind', starting at nine am, finishing at nine-forty. Kellock had scrawled at the bottom: 'All staff are urged to attend'.

Not for me, Challis thought, but then Ellen entered the corridor and tugged at his sleeve. 'Come on, Hal, you might learn something.'

He let her lead him into the main conference room and found himself leaning on the back wall with her, looking over a sea of heads to a table and a whiteboard at the front of the room.

'Scobie not here yet?'

Ellen shook her head. 'School run.'

Kellock was aptly named. It suggested a bullock, and the man was constructed of a thick pelt and a heavy super-structure of chest and shoulder bones and muscles. Waterloo was his station. He ran a tight ship. He also used to say that his door was always open, but last year someone had swiped the keys to the drugs safe and now the words were more metaphoric than literal.

'As you know,' he said, swinging his massive head about, 'I've been in the States and Europe on a Churchill Fellowship.'

'And pretty darned pleased with myself,' murmured Ellen in Challis's ear. Challis grinned.

'The topic of today's chat is a very useful finding made by criminologists in the UK,' Kellock said. 'I mean, it's so obvious and simple, all you can do is shake your head in wonder.'

He looked at them expectantly, waiting for them to bite, but the air in that little room was too warm, too stale, too overburdened with yawns and settling stomachs and aftershave and scented soaps and shampoos for that.

So he said, 'Simply put, your bad guy self-selects.'

He waited.

Nothing.

'What do I mean by that? Well, your criminal type tends not to let himself be bound by everyday laws and conventions. He'll park illegally, for example. He'll think nothing of speeding, running a red light, driving an unregistered and unroadworthy vehicle. And so on. There's a serial killer case in the States that was solved only because the killer was pulled over for driving with bald tyres. They opened the boot of his car and found his latest victim inside.'

Challis, like the others, looked at him attentively, wondering where this was going.

Frustration showing through for the first time, Kellock said, 'So, one of the best places to find a criminal is in the disabled-parking bay at your local supermarket.'

He referred to his notes. 'In a six months' study in Huddersfield in the north of England, it was found that *one-third* of illegal parkers had criminal records, *half* had committed previous road traffic offences, and *a fifth* were of immediate police interest owing to suspected connections with unsolved crimes.' His big head looked out at the room again. 'Those are significant figures, ladies and gentlemen. Furthermore, one in ten of the cars illegally parked by these characters was found to be unroadworthy and *a fifth* had a direct or indirect link to various criminal offences: getaway vehicle, transportation of stolen goods, etcetera, etcetera.'

The audience shifted, murmured. Ellen muttered to Challis, 'So what are we supposed to do, check out every disabled-parking spot?'

'So what I want you to do,' Kellock said, 'in the normal course of your duties, is run an immediate numberplate check on any car you see parked illegally. I want to test the Huddersfield study here on the Peninsula. If I'm not mistaken, the results will duplicate the Huddersfield results. Any questions?'

John Tankard was scowling. 'Sarge, why can't the traffic wardens do that? We've got enough on our plates as it is.'

CHAPTER **TWELVE**

When Challis and Ellen went upstairs afterwards they found Scobie Sutton at the water cooler, staring into space, his long, mournful face heavy with thought.

'Penny for them,' Ellen said.

He came out of his trance. 'It's just . . . sometimes you're reminded how precious and vulnerable children are, and how precarious everything is, and how hard it is for some people.'

Sutton could be overly sentimental sometimes, but that was probably not a bad thing, Challis thought. It didn't make Sutton a worse copper—probably the opposite. In fact, Challis believed that his own sentimentality was leaking away and he wondered whether he'd have to chuck the job in when it was gone.

Meanwhile he said nothing. Scobie Sutton could be an earbasher on the subject of his little daughter. To avoid that, Challis said, 'Could I have a word with both of you?'

'Sure, boss,' Sutton said.

Ellen took off her jacket. 'What about?'

'Two things, but they're both linked to the one person.'

He ushered them into his office and shut the door. The flimsy wall shook.

'A woman called Janet Casement operates a flying business out at the aerodrome. Some charter work, aerial photography, joyrides—'

'The one you call Kitty?'

'That's right.'

'Someone rammed her plane on the weekend,' Ellen said.

'Yes.'

They looked at him expectantly. He said, 'John Tankard found the Land Rover on patrol yesterday. I'd like to question the owner.' He held the palm of his hand out toward them, as though to forestall objections. 'I know it's not strictly my area, but maybe it was *attempted* murder. Also, I know Kitty, and saw the incident, so I have a personal interest.'

Ellen looked at Scobie for confirmation. He nodded and she said, 'Fine by us, Hal.'

'Next matter.' He showed them Kitty Casement's aerial photograph. 'I found this pinned to a noticeboard in the hangar where she works.'

He watched them lean forward to peer at it. Scobie's hair was thinning, he noticed. Ellen's was neatly parted down the centre of her scalp, short fair hairs standing up here and there amongst the longer ones, and he felt an absurd, everyday connection with her, and remembered his childhood and playing with his sister on the sitting-room floor.

'What are we looking at?' Scobie said.

Ellen knew. Her long thin forefinger tapped the area of dark green under the washed-out eucalyptus tones. 'Marijuana crop,' she said. 'Mature plants, ready for harvesting by the look of it.' The finger moved. 'Irrigation pipes here and here, leading down from this dam. Pump housing. This could be the curing shed.' She looked up at Challis. 'Where was this taken?'

He shrugged.

Scobie said, 'Is she involved?'

'I don't know,' Challis said. 'People commission her to take aerial photographs all the time. We can't be sure she knows what's in this photograph.'

'Does she know you're with the police?'

'Yes.'

'Then she'd be a mug to leave it out where you can see it, wouldn't she?'

'That's what I was thinking,' Challis said.

'But either way,' Ellen said, 'we have to talk to her. At least find out where this place is.'

'I'll come with you,' Challis said.

Feeling a twinge of guilt, he called the admin office of the aerodrome and learnt that, yes, Kitty had come in to work. She was with air safety investigators, examining her damaged Cessna. Did Challis want to leave a message?

'No, that's okay.'

He turned to the others. 'Let's go.'

Sutton drove the unmarked CIB sedan, Ellen in the passenger seat, Challis behind her. Sutton often drove and, not for the first time, Challis wondered why they let him. Sutton tended to be inattentive and restless, always shifting to get comfortable, sighing, suddenly swigging from a water bottle, slowing right down whenever he contributed to a conversation. Ellen liked to say that Scobie Sutton was the most un-still person she'd ever met.

Now, as he wound the car past a housing estate and then marshy paddocks and an orchard, the pear trees turning gnarled and spindly as the wind whipped away the dying leaves, Sutton turned around to glance at Challis in the back seat. 'In California, marijuana is the second most valuable cash crop after corn.'

'For God's sake, Scobie, watch the road,' Ellen said.

He swung away, gripping the wheel. 'I was reading up on the sinsemilla variety the other day. It was developed in California. What they do is uproot the male plant and this causes the female plant to put out richer and larger buds in an effort to get fertilised. You can have plants up to three-and-a-half metres high, with sixty heads. What I'm getting at,' he added hastily, as though sensing their impatience, 'is that big cannabis crops can mean booby traps and gangs ripping one another off.'

Challis nodded, on the one hand reminded of the booby traps he'd encountered when he'd worked briefly in the Drug Squad a few years earlier, the trip wires tied to shotguns at knee height, the steel wire nooses, the fishhooks and grenades filled with shrapnel, and on the other thinking that maybe the plane-ramming incident was related to the drug crop in the photograph.

'How do we do this, Hal?' Ellen asked.

'You take the lead,' he said. 'Concentrate on the photograph rather than the ramming incident. If the photo seems to be related, then I'll have some questions for her. But until then I'll simply observe. But let me put her at ease first, okay?'

Ellen nodded.

They arrived in time to see a small mobile crane carrying the fuselage of the Cessna from a grassy corner of the field to one of the hangars. The wings—one of them badly crumpled—had been removed from the fuselage and waited in the grass for the crane to return. They found Kitty in the hangar, supervising the unloading of the fuselage. A handful of mechanics and men with clipboards waited nearby.

She was so absorbed that she jumped when Challis said in her ear, 'Could we have a word?'

She glanced at him, glanced at Ellen Destry and Scobie Sutton, then returned her gaze to the punctured fuselage of her Cessna. 'It's not really a good time,' she said, faintly irritated. 'And I don't think I can add anything to what I've already told you.'

'We're opening up another line of inquiry, Mrs Casement,' Ellen said.

Kitty blinked at her distractedly, wanting to be polite but drawn to her aeroplane as it thumped softly onto the concrete floor and the holding straps settled around it. Challis stepped in, touching her upper arm to gain her attention, then introducing Ellen and Scobie, adding, 'We'll be as quick as we can.'

'Time is money right now, Hal. I have to get in the air again as soon as possible.'

'I understand.'

She sighed. 'All right, where do you want to do this?'

'Your work area will do.'

She led them to her bench in the hanger where Challis was restoring his Dragon Rapide. Ellen had been there before but not Sutton, and he gazed around him with a low whistle. 'So this is where it all happens.'

They ignored him. Kitty stood leaning against the workbench, her arms folded, frowning a little at Challis, who nodded to Ellen to begin.

Ellen took the photograph from a folder. 'Mrs Casement, is this one of your photographs?'

Kitty gestured shyly. 'Call me Kitty. Everyone else does.' She leaned over to look. 'Yes, I took this. In fact'— she glanced around at her noticeboard —'it used to be pinned right there. How did you . . . ?'

'Could you tell us when you took it?'

Kitty shrugged. 'It was left over from a job I did for someone.'

'But when did you take it?'

'Year ago? Six months? I can't remember.'

'It's clearly not a year ago,' Scobie said. 'Look at the orchard in the top right-hand corner. The trees have still got all their leaves.'

'Honestly, I can't remember when.'

'How about who hired you?'

Kitty took the photograph and gazed at it intently, then looked into the distance. A moment later her face cleared and Challis was certain that the change was genuine, not staged in any way.

'Now I remember,' she said, and stopped.

'Yes?' Ellen prompted.

'It was a promotion thing.'

'A promotion?' Scobie said.

'You know, I was looking for business,' Kitty said. 'I spent a few days flying over the Peninsula—select areas like Red Hill, Merricks North, Flinders—taking photographs. Some were generic coastline shots at a medium altitude, others were low-level shots of individual properties, houses, gardens, nearby paddocks, that kind of thing. I remember I numbered each shot on a topographical map so I'd be able to match them to specific addresses, then I went knocking on doors trying to sell photos.'

'And?'

'Did quite well. People were intrigued, flattered. I showed them examples of frame sizes, matt or glossy finishes, and took orders. Or I sold them the sample photos on the spot.'

They gazed at her. Challis was inclined to believe her and so, he sensed, were the others. Ellen indicated the photograph in Kitty's hand and said, 'Perhaps you could search your records and tell us which part of the Peninsula is depicted here.'

At once Kitty lifted the photograph and examined it intently. 'Why? What's it show?'

Challis wondered how Ellen would respond to that. There were good reasons why she shouldn't reveal too much, but he was pleased when she replied, 'It shows a marijuana crop.'

Now all three were watching Kitty closely, gauging her reaction.

'God. Where?'

Ellen pointed. 'Here.'

Kitty peered at it doubtfully. 'It could be anything as far as I'm concerned. I wouldn't know a marijuana plant if I fell over it.'

'If you could just search your records . . . ?'

Kitty turned to her filing cabinet, four drawers of greasy, dented grey metal, pulled out a chart and spread it over her workbench. Challis could see names and numbers pencilled along the coastline. He heard Kitty murmur to herself and then snap her forefinger onto the chart.

'Here.'

They looked. A farm along Five Furlong Road, just before the costly houses of Upper Penzance, and a scrawled name: Ian Munro.

Ellen gave Challis a brief, unobtrusive nod, and he stepped forward. 'Do you remember visiting the Munro farm?'

'No. But I would have gone there.'

'So you don't recall anything? Was there anyone at home? Did you have to call back? Did you see Munro himself or someone else who lives there? Did they buy the photo? If not, how come you have a copy?'

She cocked her head at him. 'An awful lot of questions. I'll have to check, it's all here somewhere. But the reason I have another copy is that I sometimes took several of the one area. Sometimes there'd be a cloud shadow or a sunburst at the wrong moment. Or a car entering the shot.'

He nodded.

She looked troubled as she returned to her filing cabinet and took out another file. 'I keep a record,' she said, 'of where and when I take each photo, and when I went knocking on doors last year I made a note of visits and return visits and who bought what. Here we are. I spoke to Ian and Aileen Munro. They bought two shots: a close-up of their house and a larger area shot like this one. Oh,' she said, concern filling her face, 'his cheque bounced.'

Challis went tense. 'Did you chase it up?'

Kitty shook her head. 'There was no point. I hate aggravation and I didn't have the time or the resources to do anything about it. I just paid the bank fee and forgot about it. The photos only came to fifty dollars, not worth the hassle. Besides, it was all done on spec anyway. Only about thirty per cent of people I doorknocked actually bought anything, so it wasn't as if I really lost out.'

Ellen said, 'You didn't follow it up at all? Didn't offer to take more photos at other times of the year? Didn't discuss aspects of the photo itself with the Munros?'

'Not that I recall.' She went pale. 'You don't think it was him, do you? In the Land Rover?'

Challis gazed at her evenly and said, 'That's what we intend to find out.'

CHAPTER **THIRTEEN**

Pam Murphy was driving this time, but only because she'd beaten Tank to the keys and the driver's door. There was a corner—admittedly a pretty wide corner—of John Tankard that didn't hold with women drivers or women's driving ability. She kept her eyes on the road while beside her he stamped on an imaginary brake and braced his meaty hands against the padded dash. She edged up the speed a little, threw the van around the curves that would take them toward the Waterloo hospital. He must have forgotten that she'd driven pursuit cars at her last station and passed all of the advanced driving courses they'd thrown at her.

Then they were off the main road and on streets too narrow and curved to risk putting the wind up John Tankard, so she settled into a gentler pace and rhythm. She felt him begin to relax. Then his overheated gaze settled on her.

'You've got your pointy bra on today.'

'Careful you don't impale yourself on it,' she said.

Impale. He didn't like it. He knew what it meant but it wasn't an everyday word and she knew he took it as a subtle put-down of his intellect. 'Get off my case,' he said.

They drove on in silence. She had a sense of his mind working overtime, trying for a way to flatter and charm her, put her onside. To steer him away from that she said, 'Do you think Kellock's right?'

'About what?'

She resisted saying about what he was talking to us about not five minutes ago, and said, 'Do the bad guys self-select?'

'Sounded like bullshit to me.'

'I think he had a point,' Pam said.

There was a primary school on one side of the road, a church on the other. She slowed for a speed hump and the school crossing. 'I mean,' she went on, 'if you pull someone over for a broken brake light, ten-to-one he's also drunk or doped to the eyeballs or hasn't got a licence or his car's unroadworthy or he hasn't paid a swag of parking fines. As far as he's concerned, things like speed limits and working lights don't apply to him.'

'Yeah,' Tankard said. 'He's stupid.'

'I think it's more than that,' Pam said, but before she could expand on it, Tankard stretched elaborately and managed to drape his arm along the top of her seat. The next best thing to embracing her. She could feel his arm there, a pinkish hairy slab, millimetres from her neck and shoulders.

She said dangerously, 'Don't.'

'What?' he said, full of false innocence, but removed his arm anyway, turning the gesture into one long, getting-comfortable pantomime.

'That's better.'

'What is?'

She changed the subject. 'Know anything about this Munro character?'

He shrugged. 'Nup.'

She could never be sure how much John Tankard took in during the briefings at the start of every shift. According to Sergeant van Alphen, an RSPCA inspector had been investigating a report of distressed sheep on a farm up near Upper Penzance. There was a suspicion that the farmer, Ian Munro, had assaulted the inspector and put him in hospital.

'Check out the inspector's story,' van Alphen had said, 'see if he wants to press charges, then have a word with Munro.'

There hadn't been time to run Munro's name through the computer, but one or two of the other uniforms in the briefing room clearly knew Munro, and had said to Pam, their voices full of mock direness, 'Well, good luck,' as though she was going to need more than luck on her side.

'A thankless job,' she said now.

'Being a cop?'

'Well, that too, but I meant it'd be thankless being an RSPCA inspector.'

'How come?'

Why did John Tankard never engage with a topic? Why wasn't he musing over her remark right now and responding to it one way or the other? She wanted to say think about it, but they had reached the entrance to the hospital and she was forced to brake for an old man in an elderly Holden, nothing showing but his hat and his hands clutching the wheel as he contemplated his next move in the exact centre of the gate pillars.

'Dozy old bugger,' she said, intending Tankard to see himself as ending up like that dozy old bugger one day.

He said nothing. Then, as if to assert his masculinity, said, 'Footie season starts next Saturday.'

She knew that he barracked for Essendon and had a head-banging regard for the game. So did she, for that matter. Hawthorn, of course, owing to where she'd more or less grown up. And the fact that she loved football in the first place owed plenty to the type of family in which she'd grown up: remote, university-intellectual father and brothers who had no time for athletic achievements—*her* achievements, to some degree. Her father was especially scathing about 'footie

professors', particularly professors of Australian history, who
liked to think they were at one with ordinary people but
were in fact effete poseurs. She shook off the memory—she,
for one, loved footie—and settled into a vigorous argument
with John Tankard.

Then they were inside the hospital grounds and parking
in a 'visiting surgeons' bay and walking through glass doors
into air scented with new paint, carpeting, concrete and steel.
A woman at the reception desk directed them upstairs to a
ward overlooking the carpark. Here the air was hot, sluggish,
medicated, and Pam wanted to curl up and sleep.

Clive Fenwick lay glumly looking at the pink venetian
blinds on his sun-struck window. There were no cards or
flowers, nothing to cheer him or his nurses or visiting police
officers. He turned his head stiffly, saw their uniforms through
glasses too big for his face, and closed and opened his eyes.

The disapproving face of a born inspector, Pam thought.
His hair had bunched up from hours of lying on a hospital
pillow and he looked profoundly aggrieved and disappointed.
She introduced Tankard and herself, and said, 'We'd just like
to ask you a few questions regarding the incident at Ian
Munro's farm, Mr Fenwick.'

Fenwick closed his eyes. His forehead was cut and bruised;
one arm and one ankle were in plaster. A broad strip of cotton
bandage showed at the collar of his pyjamas, as though his
ribs had been tightly bound.

'Munro really laid into you, old son,' Tankard said.

Fenwick shook his head and croaked, 'No.'

'No?'

'Accident.'

'You want to wake up to yourself, mate,' Tankard said,
ignoring Pam, who glared at him to tone it down. 'You went
to check on this guy's starving sheep and he flattened you.'

'Crashed my car.'

Pam cocked her head at Fenwick in doubt. 'You told the doctor who treated you that you'd been beaten up.'

'Misunderstanding.'

'Yeah, sure,' Tankard said. 'Munro went ballistic, right?'

Fenwick closed his eyes. If his face hadn't been so stiff and sore, he'd have pursed his disapproving mouth, Pam thought. 'Mr Fenwick, tell us what happened. Start at the beginning.'

'Anonymous call,' Fenwick said. 'Starving sheep, no water in the paddock. I drove out to the address given. It was borderline. The sheep had been shorn, so they looked skinny. And there was water for them, in a trough in the far corner that couldn't be seen clearly from the road. The paddock slopes,' he explained, looking fully at Pam for the first time. 'But I wasn't entirely happy. The sheep were hungry, though you could see where hay had been spread for them a few days earlier.'

'What did you do?'

'Went to the house, said who I was—'

'Who did you speak to?'

'Mrs Munro.'

'And?'

'Then her husband comes charging over from one of the sheds, shouting abuse at me. He thought I was from his bank or the shire or something.'

'Go on.'

'When I said I was from the RSPCA it was like the last straw,' Fenwick said, more animated now. 'I've heard it all in my time, but this was shocking, absolutely shocking. I feel sorry for the wife, quite frankly.'

'Mr Fenwick,' Pam said, 'how did you get the injuries?'

Fenwick looked away. 'Accident.'

'How?'

'Rolled my car at the bottom of the hill.'

'So Mr Munro didn't touch you?'

In a voice she could scarcely hear, he said, 'Kicked me.'

'He kicked you? Where?'

Fenwick wouldn't look at her. 'Seat of my pants,' he said, as if he couldn't bring himself to say 'buttocks', or wanted to downplay the incident.

'So he *did* assault you,' Tankard stated.

Fenwick said hurriedly, 'I don't want to press charges.'

Pam gazed at him. In her mind's eye she saw the way it had played out, the chain of events that put Clive Fenwick in Waterloo hospital.

The visit to the property. Munro, beside himself with fury at the intrusion by another bureaucrat. Worse, a bureaucrat who has come to investigate his farming practices, based on an anonymous tip-off. Fenwick sent packing with a kick up the bum. Deserved, at one level, because he's such a tightarse. Fenwick drives away, badly panicked, and rolls his car. Is hospitalised. Frightened, outraged, ashamed, he declares his injuries to be the result of an assault. Then reconsiders, not wanting a man like Munro to come gunning for him.

He's telling the truth now, Pam thought—or some of it, leaving out the panicky drive down the hill and rolling his car on the first bend.

Still, Munro warranted a hard talking to before he caused serious harm to somebody.

CHAPTER **FOURTEEN**

Today the Meddler was driven more than usually by sourness. Not that the day had started badly. He was on the four pm to midnight shift this week, leaving the mornings free to take Jessica to school, and yesterday and today he'd thought it would be good to have the ferret with him, watch the kids jostle nervously, wanting to touch but fearful of sharp teeth. He'd even dared them a little. He got a kick out of it—their fear, his difference from the other parents: drones, most of them.

Then he'd gone home via the bakery, where he'd grabbed milk, escargot and the local paper, the *Progress*, and settled with a milky coffee on the front verandah, overlooking bracken and blackberry canes and across to the strangled peppermint gums on Five Furlong Road. Sipped his coffee and chewed his escargot—stale, probably yesterday's—and flipped through the paper, stopping to read his weekly letter, the one they called The Meddler Report, getting a little glow and rekindling his general outrage. He moved on to Tessa Kane's own weekly column, right next to his. Read a few lines and a deep shame settled in him. Nothing like it in his life before.

The bitch had seen him walking the ferret that time in Rosebud and here she was writing about it, calling him a wanker. He thought he'd got a few funny looks at the school this morning. Clearly some people had already seen the article and put two and two together.

The general mirth at his expense. The fingerpointing behind his back: *wanker.* Mostyn Pearce burned. 'Wanker'. 'Meddler'. His skin was superheated with embarrassment and he could scarcely breathe.

He stumbled away from the house, along the Crescent and then onto Five Furlong Road, where he walked like a zombie, burning, burning. How could he deflect or defuse the sneering? Never be seen with the ferret again, obviously. God, he'd like to sort her out, that Kane bitch. What kind of name was that? Jewish? God, what a bitch. One part of him had always wanted her to know who he was, what his real name was, this man she called the Meddler and published every week. But if he made himself known she'd recognise him as the man with the ferret, the wanker, and his weekly raging at shire ineptitude and nose-thumbing citizenry would lose all force. She'd chortle, point her finger and say, '*You're* the Meddler?' and stop publishing him.

He stomped down the centre of the road feeling powerless. The dead gums formed a web of twisted grey fingers over his head. There was an old orchard on the other side of the blackberry-choked fence, the leaves yellowing. Half a kilometre ahead of him was Upper Penzance, like a gated community without the gate, smug on its hilltop. To his left was Ian Munro's place. No sign of the distressed sheep this morning. Had the RSPCA investigated? Bet they hadn't. Nobody gave a stuff about anything anymore.

He came abreast of the American-style letter box. Unbelievable. The little red flag was up. Pearce flicked it to the down position.

Just then he heard a soft motor behind him and the growl of tyres and then a brief brap of a horn. He stepped off the road into dead grass. A police van, a female cop in the passenger seat giving him the evil eye, like she thought he was up to no good just because he was walking and wasn't a cop.

Well fuck you, he thought. It might interest you to know that I'm in law enforcement myself and always have been. Kind of.

Pearce had been a physical education teacher for years, a strict disciplinarian until that business where they said he'd been too rough. Now he was a corrections officer for Ameri-Pen, the private company that had won the contract for the Westernport Detention Centre. Designed to hold five hundred detainees, there were almost eight hundred and the numbers were growing. You had four to six men in two-man cells. That was a problem, the overcrowding. You immediately thought of unnatural practices of a kind your Arab type condoned. Plus they were would-be terrorists, half of them. You saw them huddled, their dark liquid eyes watching you, their hawk noses sniffing you out. The other half were just depressed. You saw them beating their heads against brick walls, rocking and wailing on their haunches, crying inconsolably.

Well, what did they expect? They should have thought of that before they tried to enter the country illegally. Send them back to Afghanistan, Iran, Iraq, Pakistan, wherever. It was not your Middle Eastern kind of climate in this part of Australia anyway. Pearce doubted that the escapees would last long on the outside. Damp, coolish—they were used to dry heat and sandy wastes.

What Ameri-Pen did to keep them in line was remove all of the cell doors and hang dense black plastic sheeting over the windows. Everyone in bed by ten pm, and you left the cell and corridor lights on all night. You'd never want to leave them in darkness. God knows what they'd get up to. Partly because of that, partly suicide watch and partly to keep them rattled, you went around every thirty minutes during the night to pull the sheets and blankets back and shine a torch in their faces. There was a kind of satisfaction in doing that. Kind of akin to putting fear of the ferret into the kids at Jessie's school.

The ferret. Mostyn Pearce burned with shame.

So his mind returned to the matter that had had him staring thoughtfully at the bedroom ceiling last night while his wife snored softly beside him. Before going to bed he'd watched his videotape of last weekend's 'International Most Wanted' again, congratulating himself for having subscribed to pay TV, and confirmed that, yes, he did recognise that face. A grainy black-and-white shot, taken some time ago, the hair longer and thicker back then, but still recognisably the face of a man who now lived not a million miles away from here.

There was a driveway ahead of him. It wound up through a wooded slope to a fussy weatherboard house, all gables, turrets and fancy timber pointings on the dormers, the work of a Mornington architect. You saw his places all over the Peninsula, anything from gingerbread cottages to Tyrolean Cape Cods. Pearce hated them and was looking for a way to channel that into his Meddler column for the *Progress*.

Everything reminded him of his shame this morning, so when the elderly couple emerged from the driveway in their Audi—typical, a classy, imported kind of car, but not too over the top—and gave him a look of wonderment and consternation as they accelerated toward Waterloo, his bitterness increased tenfold. He thought he recognised that look on their stupid old faces. It was a look that said, oh dear, who is that man and why is he walking along the road by himself and what if he robs our house while we're at the shops?

So Pearce watched the Audi disappear over the first rise— the stupid old fool driving painfully slowly as he craned his neck at the rear-view mirror—and concealed himself behind a big roadside pine.

Twenty to one the old couple would fall into a heap and turn around and drive back to their house as though they'd forgotten something. They'd come back over the rise and not see him anywhere and fall further into a heap.

Sure enough, half a minute later the Audi reappeared. Pearce crouched behind the trunk of the tree, feeling bitter satisfaction deep inside himself. They'd be wondering where he'd disappeared to. They'd be clutching each other, going, oh dear, he must have gone onto our property, what shall we do?

While this was going on he heard a car behind him, coming down from Upper Penzance. That cop car again. He didn't know or care whether or not he'd been spotted. He was having fun watching the Audi—everything about its movements spelling fear and trepidation—turn in to its driveway.

And the lift to his spirits helped him to work out exactly what he was going to do about the wanted man on his videotape. It was time he profited from his vigilance. Direct action this time, no more letters to the shire. He would confront the guy, take the shotgun with him for a bit of extra leverage.

CHAPTER **FIFTEEN**

'Your hair's still fairly blonde from summer,' John Tankard said.

They were climbing the winding road out of Penzance Beach and through farmland to Ian Munro's farm, Tankard driving this time. Pam ignored him, just looked out at the dusty blackberry canes and bracken that choked the ground between the roadside gums and pines. Not a good walking road, she thought, glancing at the man who'd stepped off the gravel onto the grassy verge to let the divvie van pass. But then she supposed that there wasn't a lot of traffic, so you could safely stroll along the centre of the road and enjoy the view across Ian Munro's paddocks to the sea and Phillip Island.

But what about snakes? Snakes in the grass, she thought, and wondered why. Maybe the man standing in the grass made her think of 'snake'. Something quick and flickering about him. A hint of snake in the way his tongue-tip rested on his upper lip and his neat shaved head had watched her. Where was his dog? Somehow you expected a dog when you saw a solitary figure walking along an unsealed road.

'I notice the way your hair goes lighter in the sun,' Tankard said.

Pam wanted to call him a try-hard, but thought that any response at all would encourage another clumsy overture.

It was hot in the van. The sleety winds of Easter had given way to an Indian summer. A top of twenty-eight degrees expected today. She wound down her window. A turbulence composed of grassy odours, dust and heat swirled past her face. A tendril of hair escaped from her clip and pasted itself to her damp neck. The way Tankard had been talking about her hair lately, he probably imagined it spread like a fan over his meaty thighs and stomach. Vomit.

Too bad he'd had to see her in her black bra at the stakeout on Saturday night. He'd been generally inflamed ever since.

'Must've spent a lot of time at the beach this summer,' he went on.

She could turn this to her advantage. 'Surfing,' she said, and added: 'With my boyfriend.'

He seemed to rock back in the driver's seat and went mercifully quiet. Her boyfriend. In fact, the kid who taught her surfing at Point Leo. Eighteen years old. Seventeen to her twenty-seven when they first had sex. Young enough to bring a frown to certain faces. Maybe a disciplinary charge. So she'd kept quiet about it, knowing it wouldn't last—and it hadn't. She pointed suddenly. 'There. Hang a left.'

The name Munro was carved out in big rounded letters on a stained pinewood signpost. A driveway entrance marked by white-painted wagon wheels, three on either side of a stock ramp.

Tankard steered onto a narrow, blue-gravelled track that wound between fences, past a dam and an ancient apple orchard, down to a clearing and a weatherboard farmhouse, silent and dark beneath huge pine trees. Someone had painted the house white a long time ago, but pollen, salty sea winds and the prevailing damp and lack of direct sunlight had turned the boards greenish-black. The gutters hadn't been cleaned in a while and grew rust and tufts of grass. Pine needles carpeted the ground. Pam got out and felt how closed-in the place was. The light was dim and the pine needles deadened her footsteps. Even the pink Barbie bike propped against a verandah post looked cheerless.

'This way,' Tankard said, walking toward a door in the screened-in back porch.

'Please,' a voice said suddenly, 'leave us alone.'

A woman was standing in the doorway. Pam had encountered Scobie Sutton in the carpark earlier and told him about Munro, and he'd described Munro's wife as looking 'worn out'. More than worn out, Pam thought, peering at Munro's wife through the grimy screen door. Defeated. Waiting for the inevitable, whatever that might be.

'Mrs Munro?' Tankard said. 'We need to speak to your husband.'

Her voice was flat. 'Can't you leave us alone?'

'Just a quick word.'

'He's got a lot on his plate at the moment.'

'This won't take long.'

The woman's voice changed in tone, becoming shrill and accusatory. 'You people just can't let up, can you? You just push and deny and quote regulations this and regulations that until the ordinary person has lost everything, including their dignity.'

Pam wondered if these were Aileen Munro's words or her husband's. 'We won't take up much of Mr Munro's time,' she said. 'Just a couple of quick questions.'

'If it's about the RSPCA inspector—'

'An allegation has been made,' Tankard said. 'You know the drill: save yourself some grief and just tell us where he is.'

Pam placed her hand warningly on his arm. Short sleeves. The flesh was moist. She jerked her hand away again and said, 'Perhaps you could ask him to come to the police station in Waterloo?'

'It's okay, love, I'll talk to them.'

Ian Munro had been standing in the gloom behind his wife all along. His face, hands and shirt front were damp, as though he'd come in for morning tea and thrown handfuls of water over himself to sluice away farmyard grime. At first glance he didn't necessarily look like the kind of man you couldn't turn your back on. He had a pleasant, forty-year-old weatherbeaten farmer's face and looked a lot healthier and better adjusted than his wife. His body was a neat package of muscles and tendons, contained and fit and graceful, like a large, sleek dog. Pam was attracted and repelled.

He'd shaved scrupulously, leaving neat sideburns that ended level with the bottoms of his ears. He wore half-moon specs, the frames thick and chewed-looking, the lenses a little scratched or scorched, as though he wore them for close work, like wielding a grease gun under a farm implement, or welding a metal gate.

But he was staring at Pam over the lenses and there was definitely something unhinged in the gaze—strong feelings of antagonism barely held in check, a quickness to take offence, a contempt for officialdom. It was there briefly, and gone again, as though she'd imagined it.

'May we come in, sir?'

'No.'

'Perhaps we could talk out here then,' Pam suggested.

'All right.'

He came out, passing close to Pam so that she could smell him, a not-unpleasant mix of the morning's shampoo and shaving cream, perspiration, diesel fuel and something familiar yet harder to place. Some kind of oil?

She froze. Gun oil.

'What's this about?' he said mildly.

'An RSPCA inspector by the name of Clive Fenwick alleges that you assaulted him,' Tankard said.

'No he doesn't. And I didn't,' Munro said. Then he smiled, a dismissive half-smile, showing more gums than teeth, waiting as if he had all the time in the world.

'But you did threaten him?' Pam said.

'His word against mine. Little jumped-up office clerk.'

'You kicked him,' Tankard said.

'Look,' Munro said, glancing at his watch. 'I'm busy. If there's nothing more . . .'

'Booted him in the arse.'

'Did he own up to that? A grown man?'

They were getting nowhere. 'Sir,' Pam said, 'a kick is a kick. It can be construed as assault. Did you or didn't you—'

'Is the prick pressing charges?'

'Well, no, but that's not the point. Did—'

'Goodbye,' Munro said, and he walked calmly, economically, back through his screen door and into the inner darkness.

They returned to Waterloo, passing the snake in the grass again. This time he seemed to be pissing against a tree. Then the radio was squawking. Something about the library and pornography, and would they deal with it.

CHAPTER **SIXTEEN**

Scobie drove them from the aerodrome back to Waterloo. 'So what next?'

'We search Munro's farm,' Ellen said. 'The whole kit and caboodle—paddocks, sheds, house, motor vehicles, the works.'

Scobie nodded. 'With armed backup.'

From his seat in the rear of the car, Challis leaned into the gap between the front seats. 'Why? Do we know him?'

Scobie nodded. 'Threatening behaviour, a couple of minor assaults, brandishing a weapon, mostly against bank officials and shire inspectors.'

'What kind of weapon?'

'Shotgun.'

They fell silent.

Then Ellen took out her mobile phone and called ahead to get the paperwork started on a search warrant. She finished with a call to Kellock. It was a long conversation and Challis tuned out until she angrily shut and pocketed the phone, saying, 'Pompous prick.'

'What did he say?'

'He can *probably* let us have Tankard and Murphy. He asked how long before we called on Munro. I said as long as it took to get a warrant and work out a plan of action. He said how long would that be. I said as soon as possible—an hour, two hours. He said Tankard and Murphy are working on a job at the moment and get off at four today. I said have you got anyone working later than four today? He said no. I said we'll try to finish before four. He said, and I quote: "It would be only fair on my officers if you did." *His* officers. *They* can't stand the man.' She paused. 'Actually, he said that Tankard and Murphy were at Munro's a short time ago. Something about an assault on an RSPCA inspector.' She glanced at Scobie. 'So that fits in with what you told us.'

'Let's hope they didn't get Munro's back up,' Challis said. 'Do we know where they are now?'

'Gone to the library.'

'Library?'

'Someone's been logging on to porn sites.'

Challis saw Scobie Sutton shake his head. He guessed what the detective was thinking: there are traps for children around every corner and how can you possibly anticipate them?

He yawned. With the warmth and motion of the CIB car, he gazed sleepily through the window and began to wool-gather. He could see the BHP smokestacks in the distance, furniture barns and muffler shops closer to. But Waterloo always threw up incongruities. There was an inner-city style delicatessen in the main street and just now they were passing a showroom full of beautifully crafted blackwood, teak, jarrah and Huon pine tables, chairs and sideboards. And just last week he'd met an installer of solar-heated swimming pools who was in demand all over Australia.

So who had tried to kill Kitty, and why? Assuming it *was* attempted murder and not a drunken or doped-up or deranged stranger acting on impulse.

There had been a time early in his career when Challis found it uncanny the way two or three CIB detectives will find themselves thinking unconsciously along the same lines or about the same thing. But now he took it for granted, and was not surprised to hear Scobie Sutton say: 'If Munro wanted to kill the Casement woman, why wait all this time?'

And not surprised to hear Ellen reply, as though she'd been waiting for the question: 'He bought a photo from her, so maybe he thought he had the only copy. Then he learnt that she had an extra one or started asking himself what if she *did* have an extra one.'

'How would he know she had an extra copy unless he saw it on her pinboard? And if he did, why not take it and burn it? Unless he feared that would draw attention to it.'

'I don't know,' Ellen said. 'Is he someone likely to visit the airfield?'

Scobie shook his head. 'Not the Munro I know of.'

Ellen turned, leaning to peer at Challis between the seats. 'Hal? Any thoughts?'

'Perhaps when he bought the photo from her last year he did so because it showed the cannabis crop and he didn't want anyone else to see it. Kitty presumably *seemed* to be unaware of what it showed and so he thought he was safe. But then he started having second thoughts. Asked himself what if she kept the negatives for clients who wanted further copies, for example.'

'Intending to kill her is a bit drastic, though, unless he really had something to fear from her.'

Challis nodded. 'I know. We can't discount the possibility that she recently recognised what was in the photo and made contact with him, or that she's known all along and has held it over him all this time.'

'Blackmail?'

Challis shrugged. 'Or she wanted a share of the action.'

'She's your friend, Hal.'

'So?'

'Do you want to be involved?'

'It's your case at present, Ells.'

'Or,' she said, 'someone else tried to kill her, if that's what it was.'

They were silent for a time and then Challis said carefully, 'Scobe, would an ordinary farmer like Munro have the means to grow, harvest, dry, package, transport and distribute marijuana?'

Sutton shook his head. 'Not the Munro I know. But he's struggling financially and could have been receptive to the idea of growing marijuana. There's big money to be made. One hydroponic plant can produce five hundred grams of cannabis worth four thousand dollars or more. Ten plants producing three or four times a year would bring in up to a hundred and sixty thousand.'

Challis nodded. He knew the profiles: there were the 'ferals', who grew a few plants on crown land for their own use; the more organised who grew up to one hundred plants per season to supplement their incomes; big-time growers who used the income to finance legitimate businesses; and struggling, erstwhile property owners who harvested larger plots to supplement struggling farm incomes.

He said, 'Surely Munro would be too well known to sell it locally, so who's helping him? And is he distributing further afield, like the city? Does he have contacts there? And what does he do if a crop gets diseased? It wouldn't be the first time that a grower has used an ex-CSIRO botanist to doctor a struggling crop. These are some of the questions we have to answer.'

'True.'

Challis glanced at Ellen. 'Sorry if I seem to be telling you your job.'

Ellen shrugged offhandedly. 'Doesn't bother me. The more heads working on this the better I like it. There's plenty of anecdotal evidence of increased drug activity, not necessarily marijuana. I blame South Australia.'

Challis knew what she meant. Owing to the relatively relaxed marijuana laws, South Australia had become a mecca for hydroponic marijuana crops. But this meant extensive trafficking routes out of that state and into Victoria and New South Wales via cars, buses, aircraft, long-haul trucks. Now the police were stopping and searching interstate traffic more intensively, threatening the supply routes, so dealers in Victoria and New South Wales were forced to depend on local suppliers.

And that's where the matter stood. They mulled it over for another kilometre and then Ellen froze in her seat. 'It's Venn. Look. Walking around large as life.'

'The lovers' lanes rapist?' Challis asked.

'None other.'

Challis searched faces in a knot of people entering the McDonald's on the roundabout at the end of High Street. After a moment he picked out Dwayne Venn and the Tully sisters.

'I heard he got bail.'

Ellen said in disgust, 'They should have thrown away the key.'

'Don't be hard on him, Ells,' Challis said. 'He's just an average disenchanted bloke, made a mistake, like we all do. We shouldn't condemn him for it.'

'A model citizen by modern standards,' Scobie Sutton said, picking up on Challis's tone.

Challis pointed a finger at Ellen. 'All he did was rape and assault and terrify three defenceless women. Who are you to condemn and harass the poor guy and treat him like a criminal?'

'It's not as if he's murdered anyone,' Scobie said.

'Even if he has,' Challis said, 'there was probably a good reason for it.'

Ellen was grinning by now. 'Like what?'

'Like someone made fun of him when he was little.'

Ellen looked away and sighed.

Challis turned serious. 'Who dobbed him in?'

'Pam Murphy heard a whisper and told me. She's reluctant to reveal her source.'

'She's a good officer,' Challis said.

'She is.'

In the carpark at the rear of the Waterloo police station Challis said, 'It's one o'clock now. Let's meet back here at two-thirty. That should give you enough time to do the paperwork and brief Murphy and Tankard, and me time enough to talk to the owner of that Land Rover.'

CHAPTER **SEVENTEEN**

They were in an unmarked car this time, not the divisional van, and in T-shirts and jeans, not their uniforms, a quick change into plain clothes for this library stakeout. But first Pam asked Tank to pull over so that she could check her account balance at the automatic teller machine outside the Commonwealth Bank in Main Street.

Good, the thirty grand from Lister Financial Services had gone into her account. She still didn't quite believe that her application had been approved, but there had been no questions from Carl Lister. 'A member of the police? No problem, girlie.'

Girlie. She was almost thirty, but got 'girlie' a hundred times a day, from work colleagues, civilians, even her father. Maybe when she'd bought her car and no longer took the bus they'd all stop calling her 'girlie'.

Constable Murphy to you, arsehole.

A bit of spending money wouldn't go astray. She keyed in $100 and while the machine counted it out she glanced at her watch. Would she have time to pay for and collect the car later? Maybe tomorrow, Wednesday. But then it would be Thursday and her first loan repayment would be due, and no salary going into her account until Thursday fortnight. She felt the first, faint stirrings of panic and returned to the unmarked police car, John Tankard watching how the seatbelt bisected and defined her breasts inside the Riptide T-shirt as she buckled up. 'Satisfied, Tank?'

'Never,' Tankard said, in his pinkish, dampish, beer-bellied, faintly bovine way. He pulled into the traffic without signalling, drove to the library and parked hard against the box-hedge border.

'I can't open my door,' Pam said.

But he was already crossing to the front steps of the library. She slid across to the driver's seat—it was unpleasantly heated by him; she pictured his hairy arse and shuddered—and got out and locked the car. A breeze was blowing in from the bay. There was a small circus on the foreshore grassland, lingering after the Easter break.

She climbed the steps and entered the library. Clearly the librarians hadn't expected perverts when they'd gone on-line, for they hadn't given much thought to the positioning of the computers or the moral sickness of the local punters. According to Sergeant van Alphen, who briefed them quickly before they went out, someone had downloaded child pornography onto a hard drive. Someone else had left behind a screenful of fellatio thumbnails. It was impossible for the librarians to monitor everyone, so they'd called in the police.

'Sarge, I don't know much about the Internet,' Tankard had complained at the briefing.

'No big deal,' van Alphen said. 'Just sit and read, wander around a bit, browse the shelves, but keep an eye on who logs on and what they're downloading, without being too obvious about it. And leave your radios in the car. Use the library phone if you have to.'

Pam had managed not to smirk: the thought of John Tankard in a library. 'Good exercise for the beer arm, Tank, raising a few hardcovers.'

'That's enough, Constable,' van Alphen had said.

Pam reached the library doors just as they slid open and Tank came hurrying out. He was in the grip of a glittering, mouth-twisting, fist-against-the-palm emotion.

'Case solved,' he said.

'What?'

'It's Brad Pike.'

Pam glanced past his big torso but Pike was concealed by the inner doors, the loans desk and a quarter-acre of shelved books. 'What's he doing?'

'Sitting at a computer.'

'Yes, Tank, but what's he doing?'

'Take a wild guess.'

And so Pam took a reasoned guess, mentally linking Internet pornography with that day, ten months ago, when Bradley Pike, aged twenty-two, unemployed and unemployable, had been babysitting his defacto's two-year-old daughter, Jasmine Tully. It had been a Saturday, and to settle Jasmine for her afternoon nap he'd driven around with her in his car. When she was asleep he slipped into a milk bar for cigarettes. 'I was gone five minutes,' he said. 'No, three minutes. Three minutes tops.' When he got back, the child was missing. He hadn't bothered to lock the car. The car hadn't yielded forensic evidence except what you'd expect from a car shared by people like Bradley Pike and Lisa Tully. They were young, poor, badly educated, neglectful and stupid. Lisa Tully had taken the train to Frankston with her sister Donna that day, and when she got back to Waterloo, smelling of perfume samples and rattling with shoplifted aerosols, and found her child missing, she'd started spitting and screaming. 'You done it, Brad, I know you done it.'

The police were of a similar view and had searched the house and garden. Nothing. They grilled Pike for days on end and search teams had scoured the Peninsula: culverts, rock pools, bracken thickets, rubbish tips and farmland. The child was never found. Pike was never tried.

Like a moron, Pam thought, Pike had stayed on in Waterloo. And just to show how fucked-up some people are, he could still be seen with Lisa from time to time, although the rest of the district would have nothing to do with him.

'You know what it is, don't you?' Tankard demanded. 'No one will fuck him anymore so he gets off on pornography.'

It could be true, Pam thought. The latest in Pike's on-again, off-again relationship with Lisa Tully was the restraining order that Lisa had taken out on him, claiming harassment. Before that she'd had a change of heart and said she no longer believed he'd been behind her daughter's disappearance. Before that she'd been adamant that he *had* been responsible. Pike was challenging the restraining order—because no one else was stupid enough to fuck him, the town said, and he needed her back again. Pam knew that the restraining order didn't mean much. It kept Lisa and Donna Tully in the public eye, though.

'I'd like to flatten the little cunt,' Tankard said now, clenching his fist.

Pam nodded absently. They'd have to get into the library unobserved and try to see what Pike was doing on the computer. That was their main concern. Unfortunately, Pike knew both their faces. After all, they'd had plenty of contact with him ten months ago. Since then he'd been beaten up a couple of times. And there was the night he'd gone to hospital with minor scorches to his face and hands after siphoning petrol from an abandoned car and using a cigarette lighter for illumination. He'd also come into the police station in an outrage one day because the marijuana plant he'd been cultivating in a pot on his back verandah had been nicked. Then just the other day, when she'd seen him on the street and he'd told her about Venn being the lovers' lane rapist, he'd claimed that he was being stalked. Pam shook her head. Not real bright, our Bradley.

'How are we going to do this?'

'For all we know, he's doing research on his car, not downloading kiddie porn.'

Pike drove an unroadworthy Torana.

'Simple. We just go over and hassle him. I'm looking forward to this. We might get lucky.'

Pam knew all about Tankard's approach to crime: hassle offenders and suspected offenders until they commit a crime, then arrest them. She shrugged. 'Okay, go for it.'

They went in, Tankard heading like a bull on heat across the room to a partitioned corner. Pam followed, threading her way around a scattering of tables filled with Year 12 kids doing research projects, elderly men reading the daily papers in armchairs, a photocopy machine, a portable noticeboard displaying breast cancer posters.

She reached the computers in time to see Pike's screen go blank as Tankard grabbed—too late—at Pike's mouse hand. Pike, expressing indignation, began to shout, 'Leave us alone, I'm being stalked, okay? I'm just doing research on stalking, okay?'

'Still on about that, Brad?' Pam said, cocking her head and looking at his emaciated face, sunken chest and unwashed hair worn mullet style. God knew what Lisa Tully had ever seen in him.

Just then a librarian stopped them. 'Excuse me, you're wanted on the telephone,' she said, eyeing Pike with mingled apprehension and glee.

Pam took the call. It was Sergeant Destry, saying drop everything, CIB wanted her and Tank to help with a search of Ian Munro's farm. 'I'll see you at the station in five minutes for a briefing.'

'Yes, Sarge,' Pam said.

'Your lucky day, Bradley,' she told Pike as they left.

CHAPTER **EIGHTEEN**

It was nerve-wracking, sure, but somehow liberating at the same time. The old Meddler would have made an anonymous call, tipping off the police to see justice done, but receiving none of the glory and certainly not profiting in any way.

Like cash in hand.

Stung by the 'wanker with the ferret' article, Mostyn Pearce was shaking off the old Meddler. No more lurking in the bushes or selflessly standing by. The meek shall inherit the earth? Fuck that for a joke. The *strong* shall inherit the earth. The strong take action. The strong *take*.

So, before going to work that afternoon, Pearce grabbed his shotgun, fully licensed, no problems with the paperwork given that he worked in law enforcement, and knocked on the guy's front door.

The guy opened the door and saw the shotgun and the Meddler saw a flicker in the guy's eyes, no mistake. Fear? Acknowledgement that the Meddler wasn't to be trifled with? Resignation? All of the above.

Anyway, he had the guy's immediate attention, and said, without preamble: 'I know who you really are.'

The guy said nothing.

'Your real name is Michael Trigg.'

No reaction.

'I was thinking a one-off payment of a hundred grand,' the Meddler said.

Nothing.

Then: 'You'd better come in,' the guy said.

After his run-in with the cops in the library, Bradley Pike walked back up High Street via Coolart Computers. Last week they'd had a second-hand trade-in there. Five hundred bucks got you a PC with a monitor, internal modem, sound card, speakers, keyboard, a couple of gigs on the hard drive, Windows 95 already installed. Surf the Web in the privacy of your own home.

Better than some easily shocked sheila peering over your shoulder in the library and dobbing you in to the cops.

Except he didn't have five hundred bucks. Went via the shop anyway and discovered they'd sold the trade-in and didn't have another.

'But keep dropping in,' they told him.

Or the young guy serving said it. He didn't know Brad Pike from a bar of soap. But the manager of the shop recognised Pike, and Pike could tell from the dirty look that he, like the rest of the good citizens of Waterloo, thought that Bradley Pike was guilty of murdering Lisa Tully's little girl.

So on the way out of the shop, Pike made a point of getting in the manager's face and saying, 'Charges were dropped, okay?'

Without batting an eyelid the manager replied, 'That's not the same as being found not guilty, though, is it?'

That hurt Pike and he continued up High Street punching his fist into his palm.

And saw Dwayne Venn and the Tully sisters on the other side of the street. His first thought was to run and hide. But then he realised that would look bad. He had to tough it out like he'd toughed out the past few months in this town, all the whispers and slights and bad-mouthing he'd had to endure.

Besides, if he ran now it would look suspicious. It was he who'd tipped off that female cop, Murphy, about Venn and the lovers' lane rapes. Venn had been doped to the eyeballs around at the Tully sisters' house, bragging about this sheila he'd done over in the Stony Point carpark one night and flashing this matchbox full of pubic hair. Genuine blonde, too.

The Tully sisters—also on dope and giggling—getting a kick out of hearing the sicko brag about it.

It was an on-again, off-again thing, Pike's relationship with Lisa Tully. Sometimes she'd let him visit, other times she'd scream at him, '*I know you killed my baby, you bastard,*' and not let him through the door. So that was another reason why he couldn't run and hide. He wanted to keep sweet with her.

He crossed the street breezily and said hello and tried to gauge from their faces whether or not he'd made a big mistake.

'So I usually cut her nails when she's asleep,' Scobie Sutton said.

'Uh-huh.'

'I mean, she's into clothes and hair and makeup, traditional female stuff, you'd think she'd take an interest in her finger-nails, let me trim them for her, but no way, José. Toenails are even worse.'

They were climbing the stairs to CIB, Ellen beside him with an armful of files.

'Was Larrayne like that as a kid?'

'Like what?'

'Interested in clothes and hair,' Sutton said.

'Not particularly.'

'Is she now?'

Ellen had been distracted, but now mention of her daughter snapped her out of it. 'She's got a boyfriend so, yes, she's into clothes and hair and makeup.'

That reminded Scobie of another of his daughter's quirks and he laughed and said, 'Apparently Roslyn's the main pusher of stick-on earrings in Prep.'

'Uh-huh.'

Scobie Sutton knew that he sometimes bored the others with his stories of his daughter. It was just that she was the biggest thing to have happened to him, and she was endlessly new, an endless revelation. He could sense Ellen drifting away so he tried a different tack, asked for advice.

'I don't know how to help her cope with this triangular relationship she has with two other little girls,' he said. 'She can't bear to be separated from them even though they sometimes gang up on her.'

But Ellen's mobile rang as they entered CIB and she motioned him away and went into her cubicle to take the call.

'DS Destry.'

An immature male voice said, 'Mrs Destry?'

'Yes.'

'It's Skip.'

'Hello, Skip.'

'I just wanted to thank you for returning my jacket. Sorry I wasn't home.'

'That's okay, Skip.'

He paused, then said slowly, 'I'm sorry I vomited and everything.'

'These things happen,' Ellen said, wanting to ask him about ecstasy tablets and amphetamines and whatever else he might have taken at Larrayne's party, or even been pushing to her friends.

'And if my father was a pain I'm also sorry about that.'

Skip seemed decent, plausible, and Larrayne was clearly fond of him, so Ellen wished she could tell him not to burden himself with guilt for what his father had done. Instead she asked if he'd like to come to dinner. There was a pause, then he said yes in a rush and hung up.

She sighed, poured herself a mug of coffee and called to see if the search warrant for Ian Munro's farm was ready.

Tessa Kane had seen the unmarked police car leave the Waterloo aerodrome, Challis in the back seat, Ellen Destry and Scobie Sutton in the front. They'd been conversing animatedly and failed to see her or recognise her car. It had given her a quite peculiar feeling to see Challis like that, unexpectedly, with his colleagues, working, talking about the things he talked about when he worked. When last she'd seen him he hadn't been animated but miserable-looking. Her fault, kind of.

And kind of not her fault. It wasn't as if she wanted to move in with him or anything. She wasn't putting pressure on him. She was simply tired of the baggage he carried around with him, that's all. It seemed to make him a degree or two remote from her when they were together, and she was tired of it. Though God knows it wasn't simple baggage he was carrying around. His own wife had connived with her lover to murder him, after all, and it had almost happened. He was trying to put it behind him but had a way to go yet. She was prepared to wait, but only up to a point.

All in all, she felt put upon today. Just before she'd left the office there'd been an angry caller who'd said he'd been the man with the ferret and until then a loyal friend to the *Progress*, but now it was no holds barred and she'd better watch her step. It could come at any time, day or night, but it would come, and it wouldn't be pretty. She'd flung the phone down as if it had bitten her.

And more flack about her asylum seekers article. In part she'd been arguing about the power of labels to create and channel public opinion. When an 'asylum seeker' became a 'terrorist', a 'queue jumper', an 'illegal immigrant' or a 'fanatic' he was no longer seeking shelter but an opportunity to destroy, undermine or cheat. He didn't deserve pity but fear and hatred. And now she was learning about labels at first hand. Just a few months ago she'd been an admired critic of the authorities' inability to jail Bradley Pike, a 'seeker-out of the truth', a 'champion' of the Peninsula. Now she was a 'traitor', a 'do-gooding bitch', a 'dyke', a 'fucking intellectual' and too big for her boots.

However, a couple of friends—not Challis, or not yet—had called to say she was 'fearless', so that was all right, though being fearless had nothing to do with it. She was just doing what was right, that's all.

But at the forefront of her mind now, as she drove away from the aerodrome, was the interesting deviation her taped interview with Janet Casement had taken. She'd been after a simple human interest story about a local woman whose plane had unaccountably been rammed by a drunken maniac, putting said woman's life in danger, and at the end, out of nowhere, had come the remark: 'It's not as if I even *know* this Munro character.'

And then she'd clammed up.

Anne Jeffries lived on two acres of dog kennels on a back road inland of Penzance Beach. It took Challis ten minutes to drive there from the Waterloo police station, and he found himself in familiar territory, a dirt road full of potholes and erupted tree roots. Even with his window up he could hear the kennelled dogs, an ever-present yip and yelp and deeper barking. He pulled up at a box hedge and got out. The property was in an airless hollow and the smell of caged dogs hung heavily around him. He stretched his back. He could see the distant ridge that was Upper Penzance, and orchards, vines and grazing cattle in the middle distance.

In the foreground was Anne Jeffries, coming through an old paint-caked wire gate in the hedge.

'You must be Inspector Challis.'

They shook hands. She was aged about sixty, weather-beaten, white-haired, in overalls, rubber boots and an army surplus forage hat. He couldn't see her eyes, for she wore Anti-Cancer Council wraparound sunglasses with very dark, almost black, lenses.

Then, as if she'd read his mind, she removed the sunglasses, wiped pink-rimmed watery eyes with a handkerchief, and hid behind the lenses again.

'Trouble with the old eyes,' she said. 'Can't stand bright lights of any kind.'

Challis nodded. He had an answer now for the dark tint that had been applied to all of the Land Rover's windows. Convenient for whoever had rammed Kitty's Cessna, he thought. No way of knowing if it had been a man or a woman or even someone known to Kitty.

He got down to business. It didn't take long. Anne Jeffries was in the habit of never locking the Land Rover.

'I mean, this is the Peninsula,' she explained.

Challis wanted to tell her that the old Peninsula was long gone.

She'd gone to bed on Saturday night, heard nothing, woken to find the Land Rover gone.

Hadn't reported it because she tended to be forgetful. Might have left it somewhere and taken a taxi home. Wouldn't have been the first time. Last month she'd parked it at the Bittern railway station and taken a train to Frankston and from there up to the city, and on the way back had got off in Frankston and taken the bus home. 'I'm a silly old moo,' she said. 'Short-term memory all over the place.'

'The dogs didn't alert you?'

She put her head to one side and regarded Challis amusedly, as if to say: use your noggin, Inspector. 'The flaming dogs bark twenty-four hours a day,' she said.

That was all. He drove back to Waterloo.

CHAPTER **NINETEEN**

This wasn't a homicide, so what was Challis doing there? That's what Ellen Destry read in the faces of Pam Murphy and John Tankard as the two police vehicles met at the entrance to Ian Munro's farm. They were only uniformed constables, so it wasn't a question she was obliged to answer, but it was a useful reminder to her that this was her case and Challis was along for the ride.

The driveway, a narrow track between fenced paddocks, opened onto a broad, flat area scattered with gumtrees, hedges and farm outbuildings. The house itself was set further back in the dank, gloomy shade of massive pine trees. The driveway was the only apparent exit, so Ellen directed John Tankard to seal it off with the divisional van.

Scobie Sutton knocked on the screen door. The man who opened it had the coiled look that many men get when cornered. He eyed them assessingly, his gaze flicking from one to the other then resting on Challis as the senior man. 'What do you want and why send in an army?'

Ellen saw Challis shake his head and step to one side. She took over. 'Ian Munro?'

Munro ignored her. He turned to Pam Murphy and John Tankard and said, 'Let me guess—you two stuffed up earlier, so your bosses had to come along and show you how it's done.'

'Are you Ian Munro?' Ellen said.

He shifted his gaze to her with an air of weariness and contempt for her gender. 'So what if I am?'

'I have here a warrant to search your property. That includes all—'

He plucked it from her hands, screwed in into a ball and tossed it underhand to John Tankard. 'Catch, fat boy.'

Ellen stiffened. She didn't want Munro to take control or distract her in any way. She said, 'You have been properly served with a copy of the warrant and now my officers and I will search your property. Do you understand?'

But she felt a tightness inside her and perhaps they all did, for Munro was lithe and full of barely contained power. His eyes glittered, looking for the core of her and easily dismissing it. She read a kind of animal intelligence in him and knew she shouldn't trust or attempt to outguess him.

He grinned. And, grinning, stepped back into the house, slamming the screen door in their faces.

Ellen immediately turned to the others. 'Take out your weapons. He may have a gun in the house. Pam, stay here with Inspector Challis. Tank, around the back. Scobie, come with me.'

She opened the screen door. The interior of the house smelt closed-in and stale. No sun ever penetrated the windows and the walls and linoleum floors looked dingy. No dirt anywhere, just an atmosphere of unhappy use and disappointment. No toys or childish crayons displayed, though she knew there were children in the family. Ellen scoped the front room on the right, Scobie the one on the left, and they met in the hallway again with brief headshakes before proceeding in the dim light to other empty rooms. In the kitchen they found a tired-looking woman who was slumped at the table like a sackful of river stones, moodily playing with a cup of tea and a cigarette in an ashtray. She barely registered their presence.

'Mrs Munro, where did your husband go?'

She didn't answer. She was rawboned and sullen and stared at the window above the sink. An incongruously brand new Miele dishwasher sat white and gleaming under the bench. The benchtop was a dark, pitted laminate, scarcely visible in the weak light coming through the window above the sink. Pine needles hung here and there in the insect screen.

'We know he's somewhere inside. Is he armed?'

Then Ellen heard a shout somewhere at the rear of the house.

It was an old place, the style reminding Ellen of her childhood. The back door opened onto a screened porch, with sleepout bedrooms at either end behind fibro walls. A screen door on a return spring opened onto a couple of mossy concrete steps and a back yard choked with oleander bushes. It was the kind of backroads farmhouse that needed bulldozing, and the Peninsula was full of them.

But what mattered right now was John Tankard. He lay curled up on the ground, gasping for breath.

Ellen crouched with Scobie. 'Tank? You all right?'

'The bastard come at me with a shotgun. Never saw him coming.'

'He shot you?'

'Clubbed me in the guts with it.'

Ellen glanced up and across the yard, trying to spot Munro. A rickety hayshed, an implement shed, a chook shed, a bulk-fuel tank on steel legs, a rusting truck cabin, splintered pallets, bricks, empty apple crates, an incinerator, two bony, chained dogs hurling themselves at her on their chains across the ravaged yard.

Her gaze returned to the implement shed and a hint of movement from the shadowy reaches inside it. A starter motor ground once, twice, and a heavy engine snarled into life.

A Toyota traytop utility fishtailed out of the shed, solid-looking, its heavy steel tray swinging as the big tyres bit into the dirt. An empty drum bounced on the tray and toppled out, and in watching it Ellen almost lost her life, for Munro held the shotgun out of the open window with one hand and fired it at her.

There was nothing they could do. The Toyota disappeared around the front of the house, there was a grinding crash and then another crash, and when Ellen got there and began mentally preparing for a manhunt, she found that the divisional van had been rammed and pushed against the fence.

CHAPTER **TWENTY**

Ellen got home late, roast dinner warming on a covered plate in the oven, her husband shut away with his books and notes, her daughter and Skip Lister at opposite ends of the sofa as if they'd spun apart when they heard her car in the driveway. The TV was on. After a while Ellen realised that they were watching the 'Movie Show' on SBS, of all things. In this household, that was a first.

She stood there for a while, watching from the doorway, her meal getting cold on the kitchen table behind her. Sensing her interest, Skip said, half apologetically, 'I wanted to see what they had to say about the latest Todd Solondz.'

Never heard of him, Ellen thought. She fetched her plate of congealed roast chicken and vegetables, and a glass of white wine, and perched on the armchair next to the sofa. Skip and Larrayne, she noticed, had edged a little closer to each other. Well, good, she didn't want them to be afraid of her.

'Are you a film buff, Skip?'

'Is he ever, Mum,' Larrayne said warmly. 'Aren't you?' she said, turning her knees toward Skip and touching his wrist fleetingly.

Go on, Ellen urged, cuddle up to him, I don't mind.

Then she saw that Skip was wearing short-legged cargo pants, revealing his shins and a series of bruises. Knocking into things? Falling down? Falling down stoned, or drunk? Beaten by his father, maybe?

At least the 'Movie Show' had him absorbed, his habitual edginess at bay. He was leaning forward, lips slightly apart, and Ellen found herself thinking that Larrayne needed a boy who had a passion about something. She continued to watch him, musing: Skip, I hope you straighten out; I hope you don't let her down or lead her astray.

When the 'Movie Show' was over and Skip had flicked off the TV, she told them about Ian Munro and the arrival of Special Operations police from the city. 'It's in their hands now.'

Skip closed his eyes briefly. Ellen felt an absurd desire to hug him and make everything better, whatever it was, the poor, motherless kid.

Where was the mother, incidentally?

She discovered the answer sooner than she'd expected to. An innocuous question did it. She said, 'Some people at work are going to the opening of the footie season. I can get tickets, if you're interested. Skip?'

He shook his head violently. 'I hate the game.'

And that's when it came out, a much-loved older brother, running around with an undetected heart defect, dies playing football. 'Mum blamed Dad, Dad blamed Mum, they weren't getting on anyway, so she cleared out on us.'

He was nine years old. 'I see her once or twice a year.'

And clearly believed that she'd let him down. Larrayne, overcome, hearing the story for the first time, scooted across the sofa and held him tightly.

And the thought crept into Ellen's head: are Skip and

Larrayne close because they feel neglected, taken for granted, loved only absent-mindedly?

To change the subject she poured them each a glass of wine and asked Skip as non-pointedly as possible what he intended to do when he graduated. Chemical engineer, he said, eyes alert suddenly, as though she'd given him a conversational opening. Soon they were talking about drugs and she had some old war stories for them, crimes she'd worked on where drugs were involved. Skip was all ears, a good audience, full of questions, and seemed not to notice the gentle warning she was trying to impart in everything she said: don't buy, don't sell, don't use.

'The better rave parties,' she found herself saying, 'have plenty of water on hand.'

'Yeah, Mum,' Larrayne said scornfully, 'at three dollars a bottle. Some kids can't afford that and when they're high on ecstasy they feel so good they forget to drink water anyway.'

Glancing out of the corner of her eye at Skip, Ellen wondered if rave parties had once been his scene, but he was putting that behind him now. It was something about the way he was nodding sagely as Larrayne talked, Larrayne well and truly worked up.

'The conversations, God, they're so banal,' she was saying. Adopting a dopehead pose and accent, she said: 'I'm so off my face . . . Yeah, me too, I'm so, like, wasted . . . '

They laughed.

Encouraged, she went on: 'This kid at school, a dealer offered her five hundred dollars to take ecstasy into a rave party for him—get this, *in her knickers.*'

They laughed again. The wine was mellow and the outside world far away. Ellen had turned off the ceiling light and in the dim glow of a floor lamp watched her daughter add: 'The security guard wouldn't let the dealer in and he was desperate, had all these clients lined up inside.'

'What did your friend do?'

'She said no.'

Ellen wondered about all the ones who'd say yes and all the security guards who'd turn a blind eye.

CHAPTER **TWENTY-ONE**

When Pam Murphy arrived for work at eight on Wednesday morning the air was taut with purpose. Special Operations police had reached Waterloo from Melbourne in the fading light on Tuesday, uncommunicative and faintly ludicrous in their square-jawed grimness and brisk, clattering boots—almost, she thought, as though they thought they were in a Mel Gibson film. She passed a couple of them as she walked through the station and wondered how it went. Did the officer in charge of outfitting the different sections of the police force go to see the latest Hollywood cop film and come back with ideas? 'What we need, sir, are those cool baseball-style caps and . . .'

She attended the morning's roll-call and learnt that she and Tank would not be required to help in the hunt for Ian Munro. They'd been questioned brusquely by the Special Operations commander last night but now it was clear to everyone that the local coppers were expected to return to their small-town, backwoods concerns. Don't call us; we'll call you.

So Sergeant van Alphen assigned her to work the phones and Tank to drive around in the patrol car.

But first she slipped into the canteen, found the guy selling the Subaru, and paid a deposit of one thousand dollars. A new battery fitted, the crack in the windshield repaired, and the car would be hers. Probably later today, all right?

Then to the phones.

The first call came at ten am.

'Waterloo Police Station, Constable Murphy speaking.'

'Is this the cop shop?'

Pam said again, 'Waterloo Police Station. How can I help you?'

'I've just shot my wife and now I'm gonna shoot myself.'

Pam reached for the switch that activated the digital recording. 'Your name and address, please, sir?'

The voice had begun feverishly; now it was manic. 'Didn't you hear what I said? I shot my wife and now I'm gonna shoot myself.'

When they played the tape back later, they heard Pam Murphy pause. You'd be weighing up your options, too. If you tell the guy to calm down, you risk inflaming him. If you go by the book, name and address before anything else, ditto. Treat it like a hoax call, ditto again.

So Pam tried all three approaches at once, saying, 'Come on, sir, take it easy, tell us who you are and we'll sort it out one way or the other.'

It worked. 'The name's Pearce, all right? I live on the estate up near Upper Penzance. Just off Five Furlong Road.'

He gave her his street and number. Pam scribbled furiously, passing it to another dispatcher, adding the words: 'suspected shooting'.

Then she said, 'Sir, Mr Pearce, the gun. Where is it now?'

'In my hand. Where do you fucking think it is?'

'Sir, why don't you put it down somewhere. Take it outside, then go back inside and wait. Someone will be with you shortly. Are there friends or family you could call?'

Later, listening to the tape, someone would note how sustained Pearce's hysteria was, when sudden mood shifts might have been expected. And the list of grievances was too pat: 'Fuck that! The wife tells me she's walking out on me, she's spent all my savings, I'm in a shit job. I've had enough.'

'Don't be hasty, Mr Pearce. Now, how badly hurt is your wife? Perhaps she needs an ambulance?'

The voice was incredulous. 'An *ambulance*? Sweetheart, I've just blown her fucking head off.'

Then the phone went dead.

After that it was out of her hands. CIB were dealing with it—Challis, Sutton and Destry. Pam handled a couple more calls—a lost wallet; kids reported on the railway line—took a tea break and generally daydreamed about her new car. She hoped she could afford the repayments.

The second call came at eleven-twenty. A frail, elderly woman's voice. 'Is that the police station?'

'It is. How can I help you?'

Pam detected embarrassment now. 'It sounds absurd, I know, but I've just had a strange conversation with a little girl.'

Thinking flasher or molester, Pam said carefully, 'I see.'

'On the telephone,' the woman said. 'About an hour and a half ago.'

'The telephone. I don't quite see—'

'I was going to let it pass,' the old woman went on, 'but the more I thought about it the more it seemed that something was wrong.'

'Start at the beginning,' Pam said, tapping the end of her pen on the desk.

'Well, as I said, just before ten this morning the phone rang. I answered and a little voice said, "Hi, Gran, it's me, Clare." And she talked and talked and talked.'

'Yes?'

'I don't have a grandchild called Clare.'

'You don't?'

'No. This little voice says thank you for the birthday present, Gran, I'm looking forward to my party on Saturday, but I've got ballet first, do you want to come and watch me? On and on she went, the dear little thing.'

Pam said, 'Sounds to me like an innocent mistake. She dialled the wrong number, that's all. Heard your voice and assumed you were her gran.'

A note of impatience entered the caller's voice. 'Let me finish. You didn't let me finish. The child went on to say that she wished her father would hurry up and get out of bed. She'd gone into his bedroom several times and given him a good shake but he wouldn't wake up. Then she said she thought he might need a doctor because there was blood on his pillow.'

That got Pam's attention. 'Why didn't you report this straightaway?'

'Because the child didn't seem alarmed and I thought there might be all kinds of reasons why her father was in bed with blood on his pillow. Maybe he's a drunk and had been in a fight and had passed out.' She paused. 'But you're right, I should have called earlier.'

'You've called now,' Pam said warmly, 'that's the main thing. Did you ask if the child's mother was there?'

'Yes. I had my marbles about me to that extent, at least. She told me her mother always left early for work and some-times stayed away overnight. Perhaps she works up in the city. A lot of people do, you know. They commute every day.'

'Yes. What else can you tell me? Anything at all to help us locate the house or who these people are.'

'That's all, I'm afraid.'

'Perhaps if you gave me your phone number . . .'

Pam scrawled it on her pad as the woman recited it. 'That's Penzance Beach,' she said. 'That's where I live.'

'Do you, dear? You must be one of the few young ones. The place is full of old ducks like me.'

'The kid probably transposed a couple of digits or pressed an incorrect key,' Pam said. 'I'll try dialling a few permutations. I might get lucky.'

The old woman chuckled. 'Just don't call my number again. Well, dear, I'm keeping my fingers crossed that you get lucky sooner rather than later.'

Pam got lucky thirty minutes and nineteen calls later. Another quavering grandmotherly voice, confirmed that, yes, she had a granddaughter called Clare, and demanded to know what it was about.

CHAPTER **TWENTY-TWO**

Two uniforms had investigated the murder-suicide call, reported back breathlessly that there were two bodies, massive wounds, a lot of blood, and now Challis was standing in the sitting-room doorway of a small house that smelt metallically of that blood tinged with burnt cordite and something more ingrained, as though the place housed animals. Even now, after years on the job, a murder scene still had the power to distress him. He tucked in his tie—this wouldn't be the first time he'd vomited over it—and walked in.

Two bodies. The woman was jammed between a sofa and a coffee table, her face and shoulders sprawled over a magazine open on the table, her rump on the outer edge of the sofa, her knees on the carpet. She'd taken a blast to the back of the head. Blood, bone and brain matter had fanned out ahead of her across the coffee table and beyond that to the floor.

As for the man, he was in an armchair opposite the woman, the twin barrels of a shotgun propped under his chin. He'd apparently reached down with his right hand and used his thumb to trigger the shot. Most of his head was missing.

'You'd have to be dedicated to do that,' Sutton said.

Challis ignored him. A kind of secret, humming satisfaction had settled in him. This was a double murder and the only rules that applied now were: assume nothing, trust no one, check everything.

He guided Sutton wordlessly out of the house, pausing to tell the uniformed constable at the front gate, 'I want this place sealed off. Authorised personnel only, and they must be wearing crime-scene gear.'

He meant white sterile overalls, overshoes, gloves and hoods. There were spare sets in the CIB Falcon and he and Sutton dressed hurriedly before returning to the sitting room.

First Challis circled the bodies at a distance, occasionally crouching, occasionally gauging sightlines. Now that this was a crime scene, a perimeter would be established, especially in regard to the media and the ranges of their lenses and microphones, and the culprit's entry and exit routes would have to be determined, for they would be secondary crime scenes. Meanwhile the room would be sketched, videotaped and photographed by crime-scene technicians, and the pathologist would make a preliminary investigation into the apparent cause and time of death, and whether any of the observable injuries were ante- or post-mortem. And contaminants to the crime scene would have to be identified: suspects, the weather, relatives of the victims, animals (there was that smell again), and any person there officially—himself, other cops, ambulance officers, the pathologist. But now Challis was doing *his* job, mapping and absorbing the scene.

Then he crouched and felt the man's pockets. There was a set of keys in the left pocket. He compared the man's hands without touching them. The right hand bore fewer day-to-day cuts, grazes and calluses than the left, and was marginally smaller.

He stood and said, 'I want the room and bodies checked for prints and the hands bagged.'

'Boss?' Scobie frowned.

'Maybe they scratched the killer. Maybe the killer touched them.'

'But it's a murder-suicide. You heard the tape.'

'First,' Challis said, 'the husband is left-handed, not right-handed,' and he explained about the keys in the pocket, the comparable wear-and-tear on the hands themselves.

Scobie began to nod slowly, and then to focus on the room. Challis saw it happen, and waited.

Finally Scobie pointed. 'There's a bit of blood and grey matter on the guy's trouser cuffs. It's not his, the shot that killed him was fired upwards, so it must be from his wife. If he stood behind her and shot her in the back of the head before sitting down and shooting himself, how did his cuffs get sprayed by her blood? So someone else shot her while he was sitting there. He might even have been shot first. I doubt he'd just sit there and watch his wife get shot.'

You'd be surprised, thought Challis. Many a man facing death will happily let someone else get killed ahead of him.

But Challis didn't say any of this. 'We need a toxicology report,' he said, 'in case they were drugged first. But I'm betting they were bludgeoned first. With any luck the pathologist will find something, unless the shotgun blasts destroyed any evidence of that.'

He turned to gaze at the bodies. 'As for the shotgun, we need to know if it belonged here or was brought here.'

'How come no one heard anything?' Scobie asked pensively.

Challis shrugged. 'It's the end house, the neighbours are at work, there's that electronic gun thing going off in the vineyards every so often.'

Then the crime scene technicians arrived and went to work. Challis retreated to the doorway and watched for a while. They dusted the main surfaces for prints, occasionally shooting first with a Polaroid CU-5 fixed-focus camera before trying to retrieve prints that risked being destroyed when lifted. Challis didn't think they'd find prints from the killer. He—or she—surely wore gloves. And he doubted they'd find prints on the bodies, even if the killer hadn't worn gloves when he killed them. Latent prints on living flesh maintain their integrity for no more than ninety minutes. Prints on a corpse were determined by atmospheric conditions, the state of the skin and other prevailing factors.

Sutton murmured in his ear, 'So who made the emergency call? Was the husband forced to, maybe?'

Challis had played the tape before leaving the station. He tried to recall it now. Had the man's voice sounded fearful, as if he'd been forced to act against his will? Not really. Agitated. *Faked* agitation.

'The killer,' he said.

He eyed the telephone, and when it had been dusted for prints he walked across to it, picked up the receiver and pressed the redial key. He heard eight beeps and then a woman's voice: 'Waterloo Police Station, Constable—'

He hung up. There was a card Blu-tacked to the wall near the phone. Local emergency numbers. The killer had read the number from the card.

Anyone else in an agitated state would simply have dialled triple zero. He sighed and returned to the hallway. Where was the pathologist? He heard Scobie Sutton clattering about in the kitchen. Just then Ellen Destry appeared from a room further along the hall.

'I've been searching the study,' she said.

'And?'

'His name's Mostyn Pearce. Wife's name is Karen. They have a kid of school age called Jessica—who could be at school, she's not here.'

Sutton heard that. He joined them, saying, 'My daughter goes to school with a Jessie Pearce.'

Ellen showed him a photograph in a pewter frame. 'Are these the parents?'

Scobie nodded. 'God, who's going to tell the kid?'

'There's a Rolodex in the study. Maybe the grandparents are listed.'

Challis was peering over her shoulder. 'Is that a ferret?'

'Yep. It's tied up in the back yard at the moment.'

He saw a family portrait, against a hedge, a ferret in the grass at their feet. Challis concentrated on the man's face. No sunglasses. The man he'd seen walking a ferret in Rosebud had been wearing shades. It was probably the same man, though. Then Sutton was saying, 'Pearce worked at the detention centre. He gave everyone the creeps. Whenever he took his kid to school he'd bring the ferret with him. Walk it on a lead like it was a dog.'

Challis thought of Tessa Kane and her article and the laughter they'd shared. Pearce had been a figure of fun but hadn't deserved to die like this.

'So what do we know about the Pearces?'

The common features of a crime like this were: victim, culprit, motive, evidence, weapon. They had the victims and the weapon—unless there was also a blunt instrument lying around somewhere. They had some limited evidence, but possibly no evidence at all that would help them identify the culprit. And they didn't have a motive.

'A very interesting scrapbook in the study,' Ellen said.

They followed her. 'Study' was a convenient word for a room that contained one tiny, heavily lacquered bookcase, a desk with a computer and printer, a sewing machine in one corner, an exercise bike in another.

The scrapbook lay on its side in the bookcase. Ellen spread it open on the desk, and Challis found himself reading clippings of the Meddler's letters to the *Progress*, together with handwritten drafts of irate letters to shire councillors, the police, Vic Roads, the mayor, the Federal and State Members of Parliament, all meticulously dated and annotated.

'Pearce is the Meddler?'

'Looks like it.'

Challis groaned. 'A man who's offended dozens of people in the past two years.'

Ellen flipped forward through the scrapbook. 'Here's a letter he drafted yesterday.'

Challis read a line or so: 'On Easter Sunday I phoned in a report of poorly treated sheep on the property of Ian Munro—' He didn't read on, but gazed quizzically at Ellen.

She said, 'Munro's property is only a kilometre or so from here. I even saw Pearce walking past it the other day. Given that he likes to dob people in to the authorities, maybe he'd had a run-in with Munro in the past, and maybe Munro decided to get even with him.'

'Bit drastic,' Sutton said.

'Well, he *is* unhinged.'

'True.'

Challis stared past them, staring into space, thinking it through. Coincidences did happen in murder inquiries, and so did things that were hard to credit, but he knew enough always to search for the simple answer, the most likely answer, first.

Pearce had offended someone. Munro? Would Munro stage something as elaborate as this—or simply walk through the door, blasting away with his shotgun? That's if he would do something so over the top to begin with.

'Check it out,' he said. 'Meanwhile Munro crossed swords with bank managers, lawyers and shire officials. We'd better make a list and start warning them. I also need to know whether or not the Pearces owned a shotgun. It could be Munro's, of course—according to his wife, two shotguns and a rifle are missing.'

Then Pam Murphy was calling him on his mobile, saying that she had another murder for him.

CHAPTER **TWENTY-THREE**

Pam Murphy stood in a house in Tyabb, numbly watching the pathologist. Inspector Challis and his crew had been and gone, Challis shaking his head and saying, 'Looks like our boy's been busy.' Apparently Challis, Scobie Sutton and Sergeant Destry had spent the morning at another shooting, a married couple shotgunned to death over near Upper Penzance, and now this one. The word was, Ian Munro was settling scores.

Challis had praised her for taking the time to check the old woman's story and finding the body. 'Good detective work,' he said.

She wasn't a detective, merely a uniformed constable, but she'd glowed to hear him say it. Now she was reminded of the everyday shit you see in police work. A shotgun shooting. Her first. Thank God the child hadn't seen it happen—and hadn't herself been shot.

John Tankard had collected Pam from outside the police station and driven her to the house. The real grandmother had arrived just as they were getting out of the car. Her name was Margaret Seigert and she'd tapped on the front door and the child, a very collected and precise little girl, had been clear about the fact that her daddy wouldn't wake up and there was a bit of blood on his pillow.

A bit of blood. While John Tankard, the child and the grandmother remained out in the corridor, Pam had gone in and seen the dead man, on his back in a queen-sized bed, doona up to his chin. Fortunately the child hadn't pulled back the doona and seen her father's chest: massive shotgun wound, the torso a pulpy mess, the mattress soaked in blood.

Then Tank had demanded a look, and she had taken his place in the corridor. When Tank came out again he appeared shocked, pale, sweaty, as though aware for the first time what a shotgun could do to you, aware that he'd been a very lucky man yesterday, outside Ian Munro's back door.

CIB were convinced that Munro had done this. According to a thick folder of correspondence found in a filing cabinet, the victim, David Seigert, had once represented Ian Munro in various legal and civil matters, including a court appearance on a charge of threatening behaviour in which Munro had been fined $875.

Seigert had a wife, but she taught at a university up in the city and often stayed away overnight. Pam had phoned her, the worst call she'd ever had to make, and the woman had returned immediately to this house in Tyabb and, with the grandmother in tow, had whisked the child away.

Shotgun killing. Only there was no shotgun at the scene.

According to Inspector Challis, the double shooting he'd just attended had also been a murder but staged to look like a murder-suicide and so the gun was there at the scene. The Seigert shooting was different, he told her. No gun and no shell casing.

Pam knew that even if he found the gun it wouldn't tell him much. Given that a shotgun fires pellets rather than a solid slug, and the inside of a shotgun barrel isn't rifled, it's more or less impossible to link the pellets from a victim to a particular gun—unless the shell casing is found at the scene, for it will bear characteristic imprints from the firing pin and the loading process. Sometimes a commercial wadding (paper or plastic) can help to trace a shell's manufacturer, but that kind of knowledge hardly puts you closer to the killer. Sometimes shotgun shooters make their own shells, but there was no way of knowing if that was the case with the Seigert shooting. There was no gun and no empty shell.

And now it was the pathologist's turn. Presumably she'd come straight from Challis's double murder. Freya Berg her name was, and she wore white coveralls, paper slip-ons over her shoes, a hairnet. She had a narrow, expressive face and long, quick fingers. Pam remembered her from an earlier case Challis had been involved in. A case in which Pam had also shown initiative and been praised by him.

It was interesting, watching the woman work. Tankard should be watching this, Pam thought. But Tankard was outside, ostensibly keeping nosy parkers away from the house but in reality trying to get his nerve back. 'What a way to die,' he'd said, more than once.

Dr Berg would be performing an autopsy later at the morgue, but right now she was examining the body, speaking into a micro-cassette recorder.

'The apparent cause of death is a massive wound to the chest, probably caused by a shotgun fired at close range. Materials found in the wound itself would suggest that the gun was pressed against the doona and fired through it.' She pushed the pause button and glanced at Pam. 'If that is the case, it might have been done to suppress the sound of the blast.'

Pam nodded. She watched as Dr Berg released the pause button, grabbed each foot and manipulated the ankles before lifting each leg and watching it bend at the knee. Laying each leg onto the sodden mattress again, she pressed down on the abdomen and appeared to watch the surface of the murdered man's skin.

'Room temperature is eighteen degrees Celsius, slightly cooler than the outside temperature of twenty-two degrees Celsius. There is still good movement in the extremities but the stomach is beginning to show signs of rigor mortis.'

Pam knew from her studies that the body cools at three degrees per hour at first. Later, the rate is one degree or less per hour. Rigor works from the head through the body to the extremities, so presumably Dr Berg would test the head last.

Sure enough, the pathologist hoisted herself onto the bed, manoeuvred herself until she was at the bedhead looking down the body, lifted the skull gently off the pillow and attempted to turn it. 'The head is pretty well locked,' she said.

Finally Dr Berg pressed the end of her ballpoint pen against the bottom side of the torso, repeating the action from near the armpit to the waist.

'There is no blanching, the blood appears to be fully clotted.'

She swung off the bed again and began to remove her latex gloves, saying, 'The deceased has been dead for between six and eight hours.'

Pam glanced at her watch. It was midday now. The child, and the victim, would have been sound asleep at four or six that morning, when Ian Munro came in blasting. She was nearly going to say *dead to the world*.

The pathologist was speaking to her.

'Constable?'

'Sorry, yes?'

'If you could tell Inspector Challis?'

'Sorry, what?'

A note of gentle patience. 'It's never easy; it never gets easier, Pam.' Berg paused. 'Just tell the inspector that I'll try to do the autopsy later this afternoon or first thing tomorrow morning. Tell him I put the time of death at between four and six this morning, okay?'

Pam nodded.

'Where is he, anyway? He usually sticks around.'

Pam tried to clear her throat. 'We think the person who did this also shot those people over near Five Furlong Road, so Inspector Challis has gone to have a word with the Special Operations commander.'

'Never rains but it pours,' the pathologist said, grabbing her bag and leaving Pam there to her thoughts and the odour of the blood.

CHAPTER **TWENTY-FOUR**

Special Operations police and their tracker dogs were searching open ground near both crime scenes, uniforms from Waterloo were doorknocking the neighbours, and Scobie Sutton had returned to the Munro farm. That left Upper Penzance for Challis and Ellen. The residents would have to be advised. They might also have seen something or somebody. After all, the miserable estate where the Pearces had been shot lay less than two kilometres downhill from Upper Penzance.

Ellen drove. As they approached Upper Penzance she said, 'Larrayne's been going out with a boy who lives up here.'

Challis shifted in his seat. This was small talk and required a response. 'How's she been since . . .'

He meant to say since her experience at the hands of that abductor last year, but found his voice trailing away. Ellen knew what he meant. She said, 'Fine, thanks. A lot quieter, though: more serious about things.'

Challis heard doubt in Ellen's voice and chided himself for thinking that she was engaged in small talk. There were things she needed to air, and so he prompted her. 'Except . . . ?'

Ellen flashed him a glance, then returned her gaze to the twisting road. 'The boy she's been seeing is called Skip Lister, though his actual name is Simon. His father's name is Carl.'

Her tone was interrogative. Challis shook his head. 'The name doesn't ring a bell.'

'There's nothing on him,' Ellen said, meaning that she'd checked the national computer and asked around without result.

'But your antenna's up,' Challis said.

'My antenna is up.'

Challis watched her and waited. Gravel pinged against the underside of the car and Ellen braked once or twice for pigeons that flew into her path from the bracken at the sides of the road. She was a good driver, mindful of the possibility of oncoming vehicles beyond the blind corners, eyes flicking from the rear-view mirror to the road ahead and rarely glancing his way.

Eventually she said: 'For a start, Carl Lister is a bully. I don't mean physically, I mean in manner. He doesn't seem to care much what Skip gets up to. At Larrayne's party last weekend we discovered Skip passed out in the back yard. He could have choked to death on his own vomit if we hadn't found him. I rang his father, who implied that it wasn't his problem.' She went silent.

'Anything else?' Challis said, knowing there would be. Ahead of them was the first driveway, a stone outer wall with a locked gate and intercom grille on a brick pillar beside it. Ellen slowed the car and turned off the road, saying, 'He's the kind of man, you ask what he does for a living, he says "business". You ask what kind, he says "this and that" or "buying and selling". You never get a straight answer, so naturally you ask why not.'

'You think he's bent.'

'In a word.'

Ellen put the car into neutral and climbed out to announce herself through the intercom system. When there was no response she fished for a card, scribbled on the back of it and slotted it in the gate where it could be seen. She got behind the wheel again and buckled herself in, sighing, 'The joys of doorknocking. If it's not a weekender and therefore un-inhabited, it's going to be empty because the owners are at work.'

Challis nodded. 'Maybe this Lister character will be home, so I can give him the once-over for you.'

'Your famous instincts at work.'

'Exactly.'

There was no answer at the next two houses, and then they came to a set of brick pillars and the name 'Costa del Sol' picked out on a board in chips of coloured glass and pottery, and Ellen said, 'The home of the Listers, father and son.'

'The mother?'

'Doesn't live with them anymore.'

Ellen got out and spoke into the intercom. Challis heard a crackling voice and a few minutes later a kid emerged from the distant house and came down the driveway toward them.

Ellen turned to Challis from her position near the gate and mouthed the word, 'Skip.'

Challis got out and stood to one side, intending to watch and listen. The afternoon sun had some autumn heat in it now, and as he stood there a sea breeze sprang up, stirring the leaves and chasing away some of the odours that subcon-sciously he'd been trying to identify: rotting vegetation, blood-and-bone mix from a nearby farm or garden, and something slighter and more fleeting, now gone even as he almost had it pinned down.

'Hello, Skip.'

'Mrs Destry.'

The boy was thin, nervous, untidy, unshaven, and therefore no different from a hundred thousand other male students in their late teens. Cargo pants, square-toed shoes and short-sleeved shirt worn loose, all in black. Chopped-about short hair with blonde tips. Nicotine on his fingers. Hollow cheeks, a hint of facial sores, restless: maybe genes, maybe the effects of long-term ecstasy use. Or maybe he's simply freaking out about his university work, Challis thought. And he remembered his own late teens, the mutual wariness and sizing-up between himself and the parents of the young women he dated.

It would have been worse if any of those parents had been coppers. Poor Skip Lister had a *pair* of coppers to contend with, so a little edginess was excusable.

'Anything wrong?' Challis heard him say.

'I'm afraid so,' Ellen replied, and the boy froze.

'Nothing to do with you,' Ellen hastened to add. 'Is your dad home?'

That seemed to make it worse. Skip Lister swallowed and glanced back along the driveway to the big house. 'Er, no, he's at work.'

So Ellen told Skip about Ian Munro. 'Call your father and let him know,' she went on. 'I'm sure there's nothing to worry about, but don't let anyone in, and call the police if you see anyone roaming around or signs that anyone's broken into one of the outbuildings. Better keep your doors locked at all times.'

Skip Lister's face cleared, as though a burden had been lifted from his shoulders rather than dropped onto them. 'No dramas,' he said. 'We've been careful anyway—you know, those escapees from the detention centre.' And then he was backing away from her, waving and turning to hurry back to his house.

'He's a nice enough kid,' Ellen said a moment later as she strapped herself in. 'He comes around a couple of times a week, often stays for a meal. Lonely, I'd say.' She sat there, one hand poised to turn the ignition key. 'Pearce worked at the detention centre. Do we know how he treated the inmates?'

'A bully, you mean? This was a revenge killing?'

Ellen nodded.

Challis said, 'We have to check it out, obviously, but it doesn't seem likely, surely?'

'I agree. But once the media starts to put two and two together—Pearce's job, two escapees from the detention centre still at large—they'll start to speculate and everyone will go into a panic.'

Challis knew she didn't mean Tessa Kane. 'I'll have a word with our public relations people,' he said.

The next two properties were unoccupied, and then they came to a driveway with the name 'Casement' stencilled on a milk-churn mailbox. No wall or locked gate or intercom system this time. 'Kitty's place,' Ellen said, glancing at Challis and stopping the car.

He nodded.

'You don't want her to be mixed up in anything,' Ellen went on. It was a statement, not a query.

'Are you questioning my judgement?'

Ellen smiled and shook her head. She seemed reluctant to drive in but kept the motor idling. Then she said offhandedly, 'Have you met the husband?'

'Yes.'

Challis read many things into the question and tone of voice. Ellen Destry had a normal curiosity about his love life—or lack of it—but also cared enough to want him to be happy. The unspoken questions were: do you fancy Kitty Casement? Is that because you've fallen out with Tessa Kane? Is your mad wife keeping you from committing yourself? Are you falling for Kitty Casement because it's a safe thing to do, because she's married and therefore unattainable, yet you're incapable of committing yourself to her anyway?

He saw Ellen shift in her seat. They exchanged a long, complicated glance that asked and evaded all of these questions. She sighed and accelerated slowly along the driveway. 'Hal, we're going to have to push a little harder on her connection with Munro.'

'Yes.'

'You don't mind?'

'It's our job,' Challis said.

The Casements lived in an old but well-kept weatherboard farmhouse—one of the original houses along the ridge above Penzance Beach, Challis guessed. It was painted a vivid white and set amongst weeping willows, umbrella trees and small flowering gums. They parked behind Kitty's Mercedes and got out. A winding stone-chip path lined with herbs and lavender led them to a glossy blue front door and a gleaming brass knocker.

Kitty answered. She seemed puzzled and mildly flustered to see them but stepped back with a smile to usher them into a huge kitchen. It had been renovated: stainless steel benchtops and appliances, waxed hardwood floor, an old freestanding chopping block, copper-bottomed pots and pans on hooks. The late-afternoon sun streamed in and lit the room and Kitty's hair, and the hair on her forearms, and for a moment Challis felt an appalling need to reach out and stroke her bare skin.

'Tea? Coffee? Something stronger? Beer? Gin and tonic?'

The atmosphere in that bright kitchen was friendly and Challis, smiling disarmingly, said, 'I think we could manage a small gin and tonic.'

Ellen shot him an amused look and said, 'Sounds lovely.'

Kitty went out and came back with her husband and a bottle of gin. Rex Casement looked sleepy and dazed, and stretched hugely before shaking their hands and joining them around the table. He wore a tracksuit and Nike running shoes but was otherwise neat and trim where another man might not have bothered to shave or comb his hair if he shut himself at home in front of a computer screen all day.

'Been on the Net,' he said. 'Sometimes I forget what hour it is.'

'What *day* it is,' Kitty said.

'That too.'

Challis was watching Kitty carefully. Her face and manner were flat and neutral: there was not the indulgent smile of the put-upon but loving wife, nor the scowl of the neglected one. He glanced away.

When the drinks were poured, Kitty said, 'I don't think I can add anything to what I've already told you.'

Ellen glanced at Challis. He nodded for her to start.

'Actually, that's only partly why we're here,' she said, and briefly told Kitty and her husband about the murders and the incident at Munro's farm.

Challis was watching, and saw Kitty's eyes widen in alarm, her hands go to her face. 'Oh no.'

Rex Casement swallowed, looked stricken. He turned to Kitty and rubbed her back, his palm audible against the fabric of her shirt. 'It's all right, sweetie,' he said lamely.

'Is he coming after me?'

Ellen cocked her head. 'Do you think he might be?'

All of Kitty's gestures were extravagant. She flung out her hands. 'How should I know? I only met the man once. I've had nothing to do with him since. Did you question him about the marijuana crop?'

'Yes.'

'Marijuana crop?' her husband said.

She glanced at him apologetically. 'It's complicated. You were on-line so I didn't get around to telling you.'

'Telling me what?'

She placed her hand over his in a manner that was warm but firm. 'I'll tell you in a moment,' she said, then glanced at Challis. 'Does Munro think I told you about the marijuana? Is he going to come after me?'

'We don't know. He's heavily armed and he did fire a shotgun at us.'

'Shotgun,' Rex Casement said, staring at the table in bafflement and shaking his head.

After a day on the Internet, a healthy dose of reality is what you need, Challis thought. It was a small and churlish thought, but he didn't retract it.

'So keep your doors locked and eyes open,' Ellen said.

'Sweetheart, what marijuana crop?' Casement asked.

Kitty told him.

'Oh.' He thought about it, then took in Challis and Ellen with a glance around the table. 'You think this guy first tried to silence her by ramming her plane, and now might try to shoot her because he thinks she went to the police?'

Challis shrugged. 'We're keeping an open mind. We don't know what he's thinking or what he's got planned.'

Casement sat there, shaking his head.

CHAPTER **TWENTY-FIVE**

Tessa Kane had tried to interview the director and staff of the detention centre for material on Mostyn Pearce—was there any truth in the rumour that Pearce bullied the inmates?—but didn't get past the front gate, and when she approached a table of Ameri-Pen guards in the Fiddler's Creek pub, she was thrown out.

But she heard running footsteps behind her as she made for her car afterwards, and a woman who introduced herself as a receptionist at the detention centre said, 'I'll have to be quick, they think I've gone to the loo. Look, if the detainees were going to kill anyone it wouldn't have been Pearce. He was a creep, but not a bully in the sense that some of the other guards are. I just can't see it, myself.'

Tessa thanked the woman and drove to the dismal housing estate where Pearce lived. As so often happened, she found herself going over ground trodden by Hal Challis. She didn't have many reporters on the payroll and this story was big, two separate murder incidents following hard on the heels of the manhunt for Ian Munro—and in fact possibly committed by him—and so she was doing a door-to-door along the ugly crescent where the Pearces had lived, and kept meeting people who'd been interviewed by the police and seen the tall, dark-haired, sad-faced homicide inspector coming and going.

Now she was knocking at the home directly opposite. A brisk, cheerful but harried woman with grey hair answered, listened to Tessa's opening remark, and said, 'I was in the middle of something, so come in and we can talk in the kitchen.'

Tessa followed her down a short hallway to a kitchen as neat as a pin, full of natural light, nothing like another kitchen she'd seen only hours earlier, through a grimy window—Aileen Munro's, Aileen ordering her off the property just as a call had come on the mobile, the switchboard operator at the *Progress* telling her about the murders.

'Cup of tea?'

In fact, a cup of tea was just what she wanted. 'Thanks. Weak black.'

It was one pm by the clock on the electric oven, and a grey-haired man shuffled into the kitchen, looked in bewilderment at her and then in faint irritation at his wife, and said querulously, 'What's for lunch?'

The woman, reaching for teabags in an overhead cupboard, threw Tessa a look and turned to her husband. 'Water,' she said, pointing at the tap over the sink.

Then at the bread crock: 'White sliced bread.'

And the refrigerator: 'Cheese, sliced ham, gherkins, tomatoes.'

His face went sulky. He wore slippers, a white business shirt and the trousers of a grey suit.

'And while you're at it,' the woman went on, 'make me a sandwich too. And if our young visitor . . . ?'

Tessa smiled. 'No thanks.'

'Or,' the woman said to her husband, 'you could take me somewhere nice for lunch.'

Grumbling, he wandered off to another part of the house. 'He retired recently,' the woman explained, 'and he doesn't know what to do with his time. Never had to do anything for himself. He'll be dead within five years,' she added, in exasperation and not a little sadness.

Tessa found herself thinking about Hal Challis and what he'd be like when he retired. God, that was twenty-five years away. Would she still be in the picture? At least he knew how to fend for himself domestically and he had outside interests, his bloody aeroplane. Obscurely reassured, and quite unable to see Challis as old or frail but forever young and lithe in her mind's eye, she began to ask the woman about the couple who lived across the way, their awful deaths.

She learnt little but the tea was refreshing and the woman bright, wry company.

'He worked at the detention centre, you know.'

Tessa stiffened inwardly. 'Yes.'

'My husband thinks those escapees shot Mr Pearce and his wife.'

'I see.'

The woman cocked her head and examined Tessa. Tessa waited, expecting a tirade of nasty opinions, but the woman said, 'Absolute nonsense, of course.' She leant forward across the little kitchen table and clasped Tessa's wrist. 'You keep up the good work, dear. We're a community of narrow minds and empty hearts and shallow pockets where the asylum seekers are concerned.'

Tessa went away thinking that the world wasn't all bad and what a great line that was about minds, hearts and pockets, she should use it, a way of acknowledging and thanking the woman with the grey hair.

CHAPTER **TWENTY-SIX**

On Wednesday the Displan—Disaster Plan—room had been commandeered for the Munro manhunt, so on Thursday morning Challis met Scobie, Ellen and a couple of other CIB detectives in a small conference room. No extra computers, phone lines or staff.

'So it's just us,' he said. 'But we've been offered *in principle* support from the uniforms.'

He exchanged a lopsided grin with them. They could picture Kellock's disobliging, by-the-book response to Challis's request.

'Meanwhile,' he went on, 'we have three people shot-gunned to death at two separate locations: a lawyer named Seigert who was apparently shot in his sleep in the early hours of yesterday morning, and a married couple, Mostyn and Karen Pearce, gunned down sometime later.'

He sighed and touched his fingers to his temple in a sudden gesture of fatigue. 'Both cases are complicated by the fact of the hunt for Ian Munro. Seigert was once his lawyer, the Pearces were his neighbours, and there's evidence to suggest that Pearce reported him to the RSPCA for the condition of some sheep. The RSPCA inspector who investigated the report was threatened by Munro and so two constables paid him a visit. Now, this is a man who has a short fuse, is chronically in debt, and apparently has been growing marijuana, so when he gets *another* visit by the police on the same day, this time with a search warrant, he flips out.'

Challis paused, gathering the strands of his account. 'It's natural to assume that he then set out to settle old scores— first the lawyer—'

'Why him, boss?' one of the detectives said.

'He represented Munro against the banks and the shire a couple of years ago. Munro accused him of caving in to them.'

The detective nodded, satisfied.

'Then Munro apparently went after Pearce, who may have been a thorn in his side for years, reporting him to the authorities over all kinds of matters. We've discovered that Pearce was notorious for doing that.

'Also,' Challis went on, 'Munro owns two shotguns and a rifle that we know about, and fired a shotgun at us when we called with the search warrant. All in all, Ian Munro is in the frame for all three murders.'

'However,' said Ellen Destry dryly.

'However,' Challis agreed. He paused, thinking how best to frame his next remarks. 'I spoke to Superintendent McQuarrie this morning and told him of my concerns, that there are sufficient differences between the two murder scenes to suggest two killers. I'll come to that in a minute. Basically the super gave good, solid, standard detective-school advice: why look for a complicated explanation when there's a perfectly simple and logical one available?'

Challis glanced around at them one by one. 'But *I'm* saying keep an open mind. That should be the first rule of police work. We gather the evidence, analyse it and follow where it leads us.

'Now, the differences between the two murders. The lawyer was asleep in his bed at about four in the morning when someone came in and shot him at point-blank range. The only other occupant was a small child, who presumably was deeply asleep, but may not have heard much anyway, given that the shooting was muffled and she slept at the other end of the house.'

He paused. 'Let's suppose it was Munro. After a gap of several hours he walks in on the Pearces who live just a kilometre or so from where he lives and where he'd taken a potshot at police the previous afternoon—and where police are conducting an ongoing search for evidence that he was growing marijuana, incidentally. They're alone, their kid's at school. Munro takes them into the sitting room and conks the husband on the head.'

Scobie Sutton broke in. 'You know that for a fact?'

'The pathologist confirmed it. She found skull fragments showing an indentation consistent with a heavy blow from something like a fireplace poker.'

Ellen frowned. 'What's the wife doing all this time?'

Challis shrugged. 'Paralysed by fear? Had a gun aimed at her? In any event, she's made to sit on the sofa and the killer then goes around behind her and shoots her in the back of the head—with Mostyn Pearce's own shotgun, incidentally, as we've now confirmed. Finally he shoots the husband, hoping the pellets will obliterate any sign of his being bashed by the poker, and then stages it to look like a suicide, finally calling it in as a murder-suicide.'

Challis stopped and leaned forward so that his palms were on the table. 'An awful lot of trouble to go to for a man who's on a mission of revenge and had earlier walked in and calmly shotgunned someone in his bed without any elaboration. Why should he care about covering up the murder of the Pearces?'

'And what was he doing between four and ten in the morning?' Ellen said.

'Exactly,' Challis said.

He straightened his back, moved away from the table and began to pace. 'And so we're treating these as separate killings, and acting as if Ian Munro doesn't exist. If we find evidence linking him to either or both killings—an eyewitness would be nice; a fingerprint; a confession—well and good, but meanwhile I want you to keep open minds, do more door-knocking in both areas, check bank accounts, go through their desks and computers, find out if they had any enemies or shady acquaintances. Pearce worked at the detention centre. If he was a bully, maybe an escapee did him in. You know what to do.'

'There *is* someone else,' Ellen said. 'A long shot.'

Challis cocked his head at her.

'Dwayne Venn,' she said. 'He's vicious enough.'

'Explain.'

'Venn and the Tully sisters apparently dumped some rubbish at the side of Five Furlong Road, up near the estate where the Pearces lived. Someone—presumably Pearce—found the rubbish, sorted through it and discovered a letter addressed to Dwayne Venn and Donna Tully. The shire was notified, they investigated, and Venn was fined for dumping rubbish. He threatened to kill the shire officer who served the notice on him.'

'But how would Venn have known it was Pearce?' Sutton asked. 'For that matter, how would *Ian Munro* have known that Pearce dobbed him in to the RSPCA?'

Challis smiled broadly at him. 'Exactly. Maybe he didn't know. Maybe Pearce rubbed someone else up the wrong way.'

They sat moodily for a while. Ellen said, 'And there's the matter of Janet Casement.'

Challis put his hands up, as if to tell her to back off. 'Let's put that on the back burner for the moment.'

'She's been warned that Munro's on the loose?' Scobie asked.

'Yes. We've warned everyone we can think of. Now, updating the Floater. Scobie, you took a call from a jeweller for me?'

Sutton glanced at his notebook. 'The Rolex was serviced by a firm called Timepiece, on Collins Street, up in the city.'

Challis nodded. 'I'll pay them a visit sometime.'

'One other thing, boss. The anchor that weighed down the body's gone missing from the property room.'

Someone had light fingers, or someone had been careless. 'Terrific,' Challis said. 'You know the drill—put the word out at trash-and-treasure markets, second-hand dealers . . .'

'Boss.'

Later that morning, Challis went to see Seigert's widow. She was red-eyed, her grief raw. Ostensibly he was there to ask her some gentle questions, but he learnt nothing new and hadn't expected to; visiting and comforting the bereaved was the other side of a murder investigation. Waves of misery and anger can spread from a single act of homicide and swamp a family and its friends. Challis represented order. Where things were falling apart for the bereaved, he was competent, professional, focused, and familiar with a bewildering system.

Sometimes his relationships with bereaved families and individuals lasted years. His was a shoulder to cry on; he was a link to the beloved victim; he represented the investigation itself and so offered hope and justice. He'd provide his phone number and find himself talking calmly, patiently, at the darkest hours of the night, and visiting from time to time, and taking people who'd almost lost heart into the squad room and showing them the desks, the computers, the photo arrays—the sense of justice at work. It often meant a lot and the flow was two-way, for as the bereaved felt valued and encouraged, so did he.

Afterwards he returned to Waterloo and read interview statements. Privately, he was certain that Munro had shot Seigert and a person or persons unknown had shot the Meddler and his wife. That was as far as he'd got when a civilian clerk came around with a message slip and a fax that caused him to mutter, 'Blast from the past.'

'Sorry?' the clerk said.

He smiled at her. 'Nothing. Thinking aloud, that's all.'

She went out. The fax was from the Home Office in London. The HOLMES computer had failed to find any link between the Flinders Floater and anyone known to the authorities in Great Britain.

The message slip was from Tessa Kane. She was writing about the murders for the next edition of the paper and wanted to interview him. She could come to him or he to her, or they could meet on neutral ground, whatever would suit him best.

Challis called her. 'Meet me here.'

'Here' was a small conference room next to the front desk. The double-glazed window looked over a gum tree with scaly bark, and they were seated at a solid metal table, sipping coffee, not bothering with the chipped plate of stale biscuits.

'Fire away,' Challis said.

Tessa pounded her small fists on the table and said, 'Hal.'

'What?' he said—though he knew. She'd put the Easter walk fiasco behind her, wanted warmth between them again, and here he was being clipped, professional.

'Chill out,' she said.

He gazed at her, not wanting to be unkind but finding that the old configuration of Tessa Kane was gone. There had been a time—it seemed like years ago—when she'd step unbidden into his mind and he'd feel himself stir, wanting her badly. He'd picture her naked and replay their love-making. Now she was sitting opposite him like a vaguely familiar stranger and he didn't want her.

Why? Because he could never have her while his mad wife continued to step between them? Because Kitty Casement now filled his head?

'Sorry,' he said, bringing warmth into his voice and face and in fact *feeling* real warmth for Tessa. He saw her respond, a flash of gratitude and longing. Was it that easy? Was he fickle? Did his affections and desires mean anything, or had they been warped by what his wife had done to him?

He reached out and rested his hand over hers. She flexed her knuckles and he might have been sheltering a warm small creature there.

'I haven't seen you for days,' she said. It was a way of telling him that he needn't have gone cool and distant on her, that she'd been mad at him for a while but it had blown over, just as it always blew over with her, and he should have known that about her, or at least given her the benefit of the doubt.

Challis nodded, squeezing her fingers hard and wanting her again.

'A bit of decorum, Inspector,' Tessa said, reading his eyes and wryly pulling away from him.

Then the questions: who found the bodies in both cases? Were there any similarities between them? Differences? Did the police have a suspect? Were the shootings linked in any way to the manhunt for Ian Munro? How was that going, incidentally? Was Munro still believed to be hiding out in the Westernport area? Did Challis place any credence in the fact that Munro had been sighted as far afield as Geelong, Sydney and the Gold Coast?

More often than not Challis gave her his half-smile and head-shake, saying, 'You know I can't divulge that kind of information.'

And the more she questioned him the more she stopped being Tessa Kane, his sometime bedmate, and his mind drifted again.

CHAPTER **TWENTY-SEVEN**

It was always the same with a door-to-door inquiry. Half the time there was no one home and you had to follow it up later. The other half of the time the occupant would come to the door showing wariness, guilt, anxiety—some reflection of whatever was uppermost in their minds or lives at that time. Never innocence or warmth.

Of course, no one had ever seen or knew anything. But once they realised that the knock on the door didn't relate to them, they'd be all helpful and start filling the air with a stream of useless information. Or if they didn't like the cops you'd see it in their faces, an expression that said you were on your own and good riddance.

With this in mind that Thursday, Pam Murphy door-knocked up and down the streets adjacent to the home of the lawyer Seigert, asking if anyone knew anything about his murder. But no one knew anything and after a while it became automatic, the doorknock, the handful of questions, the polite goodbye and the short walk to the next house, and her thoughts returned to what was uppermost in *her* mind.

Money. Or rather, how taking out a loan for thirty thousand dollars hadn't given her the liquidity she'd sought or been promised. 'This will free you up,' Carl Lister had said when he'd co-signed the contract and given her his oily smile, except she'd forgotten about the quarterly bills—phone, electricity, gas—and the on-road costs for the Subaru, and then there was rent to pay every fortnight, and she'd done a stupid thing and booked a holiday in Bali for when she got time off in September. Throwing money around like she had stacks of it.

Now she saw clearly that the thirty thousand *wasn't* hers—or rather, not hers to keep. It was *borrowed*. It had to be paid back. And not paid back just when she felt like it but *weekly*, in instalments. She should have chosen monthly. And now there was *no* money. It was all accounted for. And this week's instalment was due but her salary was *not* due. Not till next week.

How could she have been so stupid? Maybe she could go back and renegotiate the loan. Ask for a grace period maybe, or lower instalments, or monthly or quarterly instalments. Except that Lister had warned her, told her this was a high-interest loan with stringent conditions. 'I lay everything out for my clients, fair and square so there are no misunderstandings,' he'd said. Implying by his words and manner that she was lucky to get this loan and she'd better not abuse it.

'Pardon?'

Pam blinked. She found herself on a front verandah, talking to herself while the householder, an elderly man with a watering can, was watching her from a nearby outcrop of potted ferns. 'My name is Constable Murphy,' she said automatically, 'and I'm investigating . . .'

John Tankard was doorknocking the Pearce murders, driving up and down the housing estate and wider, into the backroads beneath Upper Penzance. Uppermost in his mind was the replica of the Sig Sauer pistol he'd seen advertised in *Sidearm News.*

He was really sold on this Internet thing. The other day he'd found himself forking out five hundred bucks in Coolart Computers for a used PC. They also signed him up with a local service provider and last night he'd surfed the Web and found a handful of excellent sites devoted to handguns, rifles and accoutrements. Crystal-clear images, descriptions, price lists. And your American sites didn't beat about the bush. They knew what a handgun was for—to protect, to fight back with. Forget about shooting at cardboard targets.

One site even had a tutorial link. Click on and you were in a virtual street, gangbangers, hold-up men and raghead terrorists behind every rubbish bin and power pole.

'Pow,' Tankard would go, a Sig Sauer or a Glock virtually there in his grasp, a classic two-handed stance, snapping shots. Snapping shots at Ian Munro. Always Munro's knowing, sneering face there on the monitor of John Tankard's home computer. Popping Munro right between the eyes. Blood, bone and grey matter spurting from the back of Munro's skull, John Tankard getting the drop on Munro this time.

'If it isn't Bradley Pike.'

Brad Pike waited on the doorstep of the Tully sisters' house, watching Donna Tully's face. She made no move to let him in.

'Lisa home?' he said.

Donna shrugged.

Behind her Lisa called, 'Who is it?'

Donna yelled over her shoulder, 'Lover boy.'

A moment of silence and then Lisa was there with Donna. 'Hi.'

'Hi,' Pike said.

He waited, and then the Tully sisters turned their backs and disappeared, leaving the door open, so he followed. He caught up with them in the sitting room, Donna already on the sofa lighting up a cigarette, Lisa beside her, flipping through a Myer catalogue. Clearly no one had ever taught them good manners and Pike felt a flash of anger go through him.

But he swallowed it. 'Can I bot a smoke off yous?'

Donna shrugged but let her packet of smokes sit there on the glass coffee table, so he helped himself. She didn't snap out her arm and smack his hand away, so that was progress. This time a couple of weeks ago he wouldn't have been allowed through the front door.

'Dwayne in?'

That shrug again. Lisa ignored him, bending her head suddenly at something in the catalogue. 'Interest free for the first six months,' she said.

'What?' Donna said, animated at last.

'DVD and TV package,' Lisa said.

'Gis a look,' Pike said, wanting to be part of this, crouching beside her. The carpet was sticky. He let his arm brush hers. She didn't retreat from the contact. Together they gazed at the catalogue, and he found himself saying, 'If yous are interested, I'll buy it for ya.'

He blew smoke out of the side of his mouth and dared to watch Lisa's face. He saw it soften. 'Brad, that's so sweet,' she said.

Brad Pike grinned. In like Flynn.

He didn't know how he was going to pay for the DVD and TV package. He didn't even know if he'd *have* to. He was in with Lisa again and he could always distract her if she started on about it.

That evening Skip Lister was there when Ellen got home. That made it three times since Easter. Apparently Skip and

Larrayne had been to a four o'clock session at the cinema in Rosebud.

Ellen did what she always did now and glanced keenly at his face, watching his movements and listening to his voice. She didn't know if he'd been doped to the eyeballs on the evening of Larrayne's party, or simply drunk, but whatever it was he'd been clean since that time.

'Hello, Mrs Destry.'

'Hello, Skip.'

Larrayne was hanging on to Skip's arm. Fortunately there was nothing mooning, goofy or melting about the gesture so Ellen grinned at the pair of them and said something about rustling up some dinner.

'Take a load off, Mrs Destry,' Skip said. 'It's all taken care of.'

'You cooked?'

'Yep,' he said proudly.

There was a third ring in one of his ears. She wondered when he'd had it done. 'That's very kind of you.' She paused, testing the air. 'I *thought* I smelt something delicious when I came through the door.'

'Ready when you are, Mum,' Larrayne said, and Ellen gazed at them, at their unaffected love and their youthfulness and wondered what would happen to that if Skip's father proved to be dirty and she was obliged to arrest him for it.

Scobie Sutton got home in time to give Roslyn her bedtime bath. Afterwards she curled up in his lap, soft and sweet smelling in her pyjamas. Scobie was overcome: he missed this closeness, and found himself burying his nose into the gap between her collar and her neck, breathing her in, and examining the perfect whorl of her ear. Before long they were examining each other's fingers for splinters, and fortunately he had one at the edge of his right thumb, a souvenir of the search for Ian Munro's marijuana operation, and she fetched the tweezers and more or less pulled it out. Then it was time for her story and finally he sank into the sofa, dinner on his lap, glass of beer on the coffee table.

'You look tired,' his wife said, dressmaker's pins in her mouth.

She was in her armchair, a gooseneck lamp casting a cone of harsh light on a lapful of unravelling hems. He recognised a couple of Roslyn's dresses and his old pair of cords.

'I am,' he said. 'It's these murders,' and he went on to talk about his day. He told her everything. He had always done so. It was a rule of thumb that you should not tell your loved ones anything, but there were gossipy loved ones and unsympathetic loved ones, and Scobie Sutton's wife was neither.

'The worst thing was this morning,' he said, describing the school run. Aileen Munro hadn't been there with her children. He doubted if he'd see them there ever again. The school was a small, fingerpointing community. And of course, the Pearce kid hadn't been there. Senior Sergeant Kellock had tracked down a set of grandparents who'd whisked the child away. Another he wouldn't see at the school again.

He imagined their pain, and said it: 'Imagine their pain.'

His wife shook her head and clicked her tongue. She couldn't imagine the pain. He, on the other hand, imagined everyone's pain, and that was one reason why he'd never make a top-flight copper.

He'd have expected the demands of the job to cure that, for that's what had happened to every cop he knew, but it hadn't happened to him. He swallowed. He tried not to let the tears begin or think of Roslyn all alone in the world, but how can a decent person shake off those sorts of pictures once they've crept into your head?

CHAPTER **TWENTY-EIGHT**

On Thursday night Munro's battered Toyota was found in a pub carpark from which a Ford F100 pickup had been stolen, and so on Friday morning Challis and Sutton drove to the farm to question Aileen Munro. Challis was tiring of Sutton a little but Sutton knew Aileen Munro; his presence there would help to ease what was bound to be a fraught situation.

Aileen took them through to the sitting room, the carpet and upholstery oppressively floral in styles that had disappeared from every corner of the world except backroad farmhouses. A wedge of grimy sunlight illuminated one corner of the floor; otherwise the light was dim. But there were incongruous touches here and there: a massive entertainment unit in one corner housed a flatscreen television set, VCR and sound system, and the torso of a Barbie doll peeked from beneath the nest of tables under the window. A CD case cracked faintly behind a cushion when Challis sank into the sofa. He fished it out. *Strawberry Kisses* by Nikki Webster. It meant nothing to him beyond the fact of the Munro children reaching for life beyond this lifeless house.

Aileen Munro sat heavily in an armchair opposite Challis. Scobie Sutton sat beside him. Challis didn't like the arrangement, for it reinforced a sense of two ranged against one, but it was too late to change that now. He relaxed, tried to look unobtrusive, and let Sutton begin.

'First, Aileen, I'm really sorry this has happened.'

Aileen Munro's gaze darted from Sutton to Challis and back again. She opened and closed her mouth as though to moisten it. 'Thank you,' she muttered.

'It must he hard for you.'

'Yes.' Barely a whisper.

'Remember, if there's anything I can do . . .'

A tinge of hysteria this time. 'You can get those reporters off my back!'

John Tankard had been at the front gate when Challis and Sutton arrived. He was there to keep the media away from the house and looked sour about it. 'They'll lose interest after a while,' Sutton assured her.

Tessa Kane hadn't been in the media pack, or not that Challis could see. She hadn't contacted him for another follow-up, but would do so. She'd have Munro's photo by now, one taken when he was arrested for assault two years ago, and passed out to the media by the public relations clerk.

'Meanwhile, I'm afraid we have to ask you some questions,' Sutton said gently.

A curt nod.

'First, have you had a chance to think of likely places where your husband might be?'

'No.'

'Any buildings or scrubland on the Peninsula that he knew well, or once owned, or was fond of visiting?'

Her voice when it came was shrill. 'You say he shot three people dead. Do you really think he'd just hang around the district? He's long gone.'

'But where, Mrs Munro?' Challis interrupted. His voice was low and calm but Aileen Munro was still agitated.

'How should I know? We never went anywhere. We always stayed at home—or I did, anyway. How should I know where he's gone?'

Challis nodded. Sutton said, 'As you know, we think Ian was growing marijuana over in the far corner of the farm last year. There's no crop there now, and we've found nothing in any of the sheds to suggest he was cultivating it—no plants drying, no packets of dried leaf—but perhaps you could tell us who he—'

She brought her fists down hard on her lap. 'I don't know anything about that. Why don't you listen?'

Challis believed her. She looked genuinely perplexed. He said, 'Did Ian have anything to do with the Pearces, Aileen?'

'No. Far as I know, he never knew them, never talked to them.'

'He didn't say anything about getting even with Pearce for reporting him to the RSPCA?'

Aileen Munro gasped. 'It was him?'

'We have reason to believe he called them anonymously.'

'But how would Ian know it was Pearce who dobbed him in if it was anonymous?'

Good point, Challis thought.

'And the lawyer?' he asked gently.

Aileen scowled and looked away. 'Ian had business with him in the past. Hated his guts. He used to talk about getting even with him for letting him down.'

They were silent. Challis noticed for the first time that Aileen Munro's cardigan was buttoned crookedly, the buttons themselves a mismatched array of shapes and colours.

Scobie cleared his throat. 'Anyone else your husband disliked, Aileen?'

She looked at him with contempt—contempt for the situation, not Sutton himself—and said, 'Give me a name, any name. Ten-to-one my husband had something against him. He was a good hater. *Is* a good hater.'

'Getting back to the marijuana, Aileen, I—'

'I told you, I don't know anything about that. I wouldn't know a marijuana bush if I fell over one.'

'I believe you,' Challis said. 'But presumably your husband harvested the crop and sold it. Who did he get the seeds or seedlings from? Who bought the crop? Were there any unusual visitors at any time? Phone calls? Letters? Mysterious trips away?'

She shrugged. 'No one visits.' Her voice grew hollow. 'People used to visit us once upon a time. Not anymore.' She glanced in the direction of the front gate and the reporters gathered there. 'Now we've got hundreds of visitors, only not the kind you'd want. Bloody vultures, I can't hack it anymore.'

Challis grew aware of the ticking silence of the house. 'Mrs Munro, where are your children?'

She looked at him in surprise. 'In their rooms. The kids at school . . .' She grew hard. 'You're not asking them questions. No way.'

'No, no,' Challis said. He paused. 'Do they know what's happened?'

'Leave them alone.'

'They're very quiet,' Challis said, and a stillness settled in him. He glanced at Sutton, got up, and swiftly left the room.

He heard Aileen wail behind him, 'Where's he going?'

'He'll be back in a moment, Aileen,' Sutton said soothingly.

Challis found the children in a large room, three beds against the walls. The older two were playing a computer game in furious silence, only their breathing and the clack of keys betraying them. The youngest was sitting quietly, drawing. But she glanced up cringingly when Challis stepped through the door. Who beat her, disciplined her? Challis wondered. Had she thought for a moment that it was her father filling the doorway?

Conscious of his size, Challis crossed to the little girl, sat on the bed and tried a smile. 'Hello. My name's Hal. Do you know Mr Sutton? Scobie? He's Roslyn's dad. Roslyn's in your class at school, I think.'

She nodded. 'I see him in the mornings,' she said in a high, thin voice.

'That's right. He's here with me at the moment. We're talking to your mum.'

The girl sorted through her crayons. Most were greasy stubs, and several bore bite marks. She selected one and unconvincingly ran it back and forth across the page of her sketchbook. Challis said, 'Is your dad home today?'

After a moment, the child shook her head. She stopped drawing, her chin dropped to her chest, and Challis sensed shame and bewilderment. One more question: 'Has your dad been home to see you?'

The girl said, 'He runded away.'

CHAPTER **TWENTY-NINE**

Tankard wasn't going to quit. Maybe if he made her a bit jealous? So he told her a story that was half true about a party he'd gone to back when he was in the police academy.

'I crack on to this chick, things hot up, I take her home, she goes, "Lose the threads," so I start getting my gear off, and then she goes—'

'Stop the car!'

Startled, he braked sharply. They were patrolling at the bottom end of High Street. The shops were sparser here. There was a bank, a pub, a real estate agency, an anonymous two-storey building with Lister Financial Services painted on the window. Even though it was Friday there was almost no one around.

'What?' Tankard said, glancing up and down, looking for the problem.

Nothing that he could see. 'What's got your bloomers in a twist? Or do you call them knickers? Scanties?'

'I need to see someone,' Pam said.

'Who?'

'Just someone,' she said irritably. 'I'll only be five minutes.'

And she got out, leaving him double-parked. He watched her dart across the road and into Lister Financial Services.

Tankard sank back into his seat. Tattered, sun-faded Christmas decorations still clung to a power pole. A gritty wind was gusting. The manhunt for Ian Munro was three days old but no one in Waterloo seemed bothered about it. An old man pedalled by on a bicycle hung with string bags crammed full of plastic shopping bags. Two teenagers were slumped, smoking, on a bench outside a struggling record shop, a sign saying 'This Business For Sale Inquire Within' pasted to the glass. A little red Golf drove carefully around the police van, an elderly woman at the wheel, disabled-parking sticker on her windscreen. He saw her brake in the street ahead of him and look with apparent longing at the disabled-parking bay outside the bank.

It was occupied.

'Stiff titty, love,' Tankard murmured, and he began to crack his knuckles for want of anything better to do.

Something niggled at him, somewhere in the back corner of his consciousness . . .

He turned toward the bank again. The vehicle parked in the disabled-parking bay was a chunky-looking Ford pickup. Nothing immediately remarkable about it except it didn't feel right, for some reason. Then he knew: your disabled person usually drove something a bit easier and tamer, like your little Jap job, or your Golf. For your average disabled person, driving an F100 would be like driving a truck.

Check out the disabled-parking spots, Kellock had said, and John Tankard, who had scoffed at the time, now thought there was something in the senior sergeant's theory of the self-selecting crim.

He backed up, waited for another parked car to leave, and swung the police van in next to the F100.

That had been a mistake, he realised later. A lot of grief might have been saved if he'd had the brains to pull in *behind* the F100 and block it in.

He got out, sauntered toward the rear of the big pickup, and noted the numberplate. Then he wandered around to the front, checked out the windscreen.

No disabled-parking sticker.

'Right, I'll have you, mate,' he muttered with satisfaction, returning to the van to call it in.

That's when he noticed a movement in the pickup. He paused, turned toward it for a closer look, and saw what he hadn't seen earlier, owing to the high sides of the vehicle's cab: a man stretched out along the seat, apparently reaching down for something in the passenger-side footwell. The window was partly open. Tankard came closer and tapped on the glass.

'Sir? Excuse me, sir?'

The man stiffened. What the hell was he doing? His back, his reaching arm, the bulky overhang of the dashboard, Tankard couldn't see clearly.

Maybe he *was* handicapped. Maybe his walking stick had fallen off the seat.

'Sir, my name is Constable Tankard and I'd like to talk to you about—'

That's when he saw a metallic gleam, some stray beam of autumn sunlight reflecting coldly off the twin barrels of a shotgun.

Tankard gasped, stepped back, trying to think. He couldn't think. He'd been trained to think in these sorts of situations, he'd learnt how to advance on an armed suspect, draw his weapon, fire two rounds, and reholster. He'd been taught to walk backwards, kneel, turn and fire without sighting, first with the right hand, then with the left.

He'd learnt how to aim at the largest body mass: trunk, shoulders, head. Your first shot could be your last, so make it count. Out at the shooting range, Tankard had regularly hit twenty-seven or twenty-eight targets out of thirty. Not very many officers could beat that kind of shooting.

He'd also been taught to at least take his revolver out of its holster . . .

God. Seconds were passing and his hands and mind weren't working. His mouth felt dry. He wondered if he should shout a warning. Finally his hand did find its way to the leather strap that held his revolver in its holster.

His fingers refused to find it, fumbling so that he had to look away to see what he was doing. By the time his nerveless hand was around the butt and he'd returned his gaze to the man in the F100, the open mouths of the shotgun were trained on his face and he was looking into the steady eyes of Ian Munro.

Hadn't even unsnapped his own gun.

'Take it out,' Munro said.

'What?' Tankard's voice was dry, a croak. He tried again. 'What?'

'Your gun. Take it out, two fingers, give it to me.'

Tankard swallowed. He complied, dropping his gun through the open window as if it were a dead mouse.

'Keys.'

'What?'

'Walk backwards to your van, reach in, take the keys out of the ignition or I'll blow your fucking head off.'

Tankard did as he was told. He had no choice but to obey the man's contemptuous, whipping voice. He felt sick to his stomach and knew that he was going to die now.

'Give them to me,' Munro said. He was actually snapping his fingers.

A kind of petulance came over Tankard. 'No,' he said, and he dropped the keys through a stormwater grate.

Munro laughed. 'I wasn't going to *steal* the van, you stupid prick.'

He laughed again and started the F100, slamming it into reverse. The tyres squealed briefly and he was gone.

Tankard supposed that the pickup was stolen but it took him some minutes to call it in and find out for sure, and meanwhile he had to run across to the men's room in the pub and sit there for a while, and when Pam Murphy reappeared he couldn't get the words out. It was she who went into the bank, expecting to find blood. There was none: Munro *had* had dealings with the manager there, but Tankard had apparently interrupted him before he could go in shooting. And it was Pam who asked Tankard where his service revolver was. That's when the shame really began to settle through him.

CHAPTER **THIRTY**

Special Operations police had questioned John Tankard first, meaning that by the time Challis had talked to him, the afternoon was almost gone. Challis drove home and, feeling unsettled in the dwindling light, began to rake leaves. His liquidambar wore a beautiful canopy of green in spring and summer, and was no less beautiful when hung with red and gold in autumn, but now the leaves were beginning to fall, forming a dull yellow mat on the grass, and he had a month of raking ahead of him.

First he circled the tree clockwise on his ride-on mower, letting the blades rake the leaves for him, pushing them in toward the trunk until he was at risk of jamming the blades, and then he resorted to raking the leaves into discrete piles. Finally he wheelbarrowed the leaves to the compost heap in the back yard, cursing when the top layers slithered off the barrow and marked his progress across the lawn and gravelled driveway.

Then an idea crept into his head: ask Kitty Casement to come to the opening of the footie season with him tomorrow, the Tigers versus the West Coast Eagles at the MCG. She'd once said that her husband rarely took her anywhere, he was always glued to his screen. Then, almost immediately, he abandoned the notion. She'd never say yes. She'd wonder why he'd asked, his intentions would look naked and obvious, the husband's first thought would be *what's going on?*

Ask Tessa instead. The way he was going, he would lose her.

And then he thought of the long drive and the traffic. And asked himself did he really want to go to the football? There'd been a time when your roots meant something. You barracked for the Tigers because you had direct links to Tigerland and so did the players. Not anymore. The players followed the money and you barracked for hybrid teams.

Plus, Challis knew that he was never good company at a football match. Partly it was his hatred of the herd instinct, but mainly his mind would drift and he'd lose himself in old or current murder cases. He'd even solved one or two in that dreamy state, but he was hardly a cheery companion.

Faintly he heard the telephone on his kitchen wall ring five times and cut out for the answering machine. He didn't follow it up but waited, and sure enough, a minute later his mobile vibrated in his pocket.

'Challis.'

'Hal? It's Marg.'

Marg Quinlan, his mother-in-law. 'Hello, Marg,' he said cautiously.

'It's about Angela.'

'I thought it might be.'

'She's not well.'

He said nothing, knowing he was making it difficult for his mother-in-law, who didn't deserve that, but unable to help himself.

'I think,' Marg said desperately, 'a visit from you would cheer her up.'

Challis said bleakly, 'All right,' as he always did.

'Oh, Hal, thank you, I know how hard it is but Bob and I do appreciate it.'

'It's all right, Marg.'

'We could meet you there.'

She was expecting him to say no, he'd go alone, but Challis disappointed her. 'Thanks, I'd appreciate that.'

'Oh. Well, would tomorrow suit you?'

'The afternoon.'

'The afternoon. Yes. Good. About two?'

And so at two o'clock the next day, about the time that the Tigers/West Coast Eagles game was starting, Challis met his parents-in-law in the waiting room of the women's prison on the outskirts of the city. The place depressed him. The few husbands or boyfriends there had the look of men stuck with children and responsibilities they would soon shed. As usual, there were also young women waiting outside—sisters, friends, partners of the inmates. One or two older people, grandparents perhaps. And several couples like Marg and Bob, aged in their fifties and sixties, who were parents of the inmates.

Not much cheer. A lot of hopelessness. And it seemed that everyone knew who he was, or smelt 'cop' on him.

Marg hugged and kissed him. She was a tall, large-boned woman with odd-looking hair. It had always looked to Challis like an untidy nest, as though Marg deliberately kept it that way and thought it fine. She wore slacks and a cardigan over a blouse, the collar faintly smudged with makeup beneath one ear. She looked unkempt but was rock-solid and full of love and kindness.

Bob matched her in size, shape and homeliness. He was losing his hair and his hearing, and tended to stand back, looking on pleasantly, whenever people conversed around him. Now and then he'd cup his ear and say, 'What was that?' In the early years of his daughter's incarceration he'd refused to visit her, but he'd softened over time. As he shook Challis's hand now, he turned it into an emotional gesture, trapping Challis's fingers for an eternity before letting go.

They loved him and they loved their daughter and were wracked with guilt.

Then children and young women were squealing hellos. The inmates were filing into the room.

To Challis's eye, his wife had declined since Good Friday. She had her parents' height and large bones, but the bones had become bowed and fleshless in the intervening time and so she looked smaller, hollower, sadder. She stood numbly as they kissed her one by one, but then as Challis pulled back from her she clasped him fiercely.

'Come on, Ange,' he said gently, 'let's sit down.'

Sometimes there was violence, and so the tables and chairs were plastic. Challis heard the chairs groan under the heavy frames of his parents-in-law. And the first thing his wife said was, 'I only wanted Hal,' her lip curling sulkily.

Marg and Bob jerked and twitched in the face of it. 'Well, dear . . .' they said.

Angela folded her arms. 'All right, I'm not saying anything then.'

She was as stubborn as a child, and perhaps her parents were reminded of the child she'd once been, for they sighed in unison and after some hemming and hawing, left the room.

'What do you want, Ange?'

'Don't be like that, all cold.'

'Look, I've come a long way to be here.'

In a ghastly show of demureness and coquettishness, Challis's wife wiggled forward in her chair and reached her hands under the table, finding his upper thigh. 'Hal, you don't know how much I miss it, locked up in here. God, just to touch you, I'm getting all wet.'

He said, 'Don't.'

She cocked her head and grinned and narrowed her eyes, testing him, and he saw how unhinged she was. He said, 'Don't,' a second time, his voice and face prohibitive this time, a chilling wind from a high plateau, and it was like a slap in the face for her.

She crumbled, put her hands over her face, and began to keen. Challis watched her for a time. The fear that he was five per cent responsible for her being here still sat in him like a stone and until he could rid himself of it he'd continue to be a decent man and listen to her, and help her cure herself, and serve out her punishment. But he didn't love her or want her back, and it was entirely possible that she would kill herself in here. He didn't want that to happen but if it did, would he experience guilt, or relief?

He came out feeling tense and jittery and the cure was not the long drive home. Instead, he drove into the city, to a multi-level carpark in Flinders Lane, a short walk from the top end of Collins Street.

'Timepiece' was a glass and gleaming brass shopfront between a bookshop and a clothing boutique. The ground shaking beneath him from a passing tram, Challis pushed open the heavy door and went in just as a grandfather clock struck four. All around him clocks were ticking, whirring, whispering.

'May I help you?'

A man with a cadaverous face watched disobligingly as Challis crossed the floor, reaching into an inside pocket for his CIB card. 'Detective Inspector Challis. Are you Mr Jelbart?'

'I am.'

'You'll remember that one of my detectives, DC Sutton, called you in regard to—'

'I remember. As I said at the time, I'd need something more than someone's word over the phone.'

'You've seen my ID now,' Challis said with irritation.

Sniff. 'That's hardly the same thing as a warrant.'

'Sir, forgive me, but there's been a murder. I'll not be looking at any of your other files or activities, I'm only interested in the Rolex found on the victim.'

Jelbart stared at him and Challis wanted to slap him about the face.

'Very well.'

'Thank you.'

Jelbart snapped his fingers impatiently. 'Details.'

Challis stared at the man. 'They were faxed to you.'

'I can't possibly keep track of everything that comes across my desk.'

Challis thought it likely that Jelbart did keep track of everything, but sighed and flipped through his notebook and recited the serial number found on the Rolex.

'Wait here.'

'Will this take long?'

'I have it on computer,' Jelbart said, as if Challis lived in the stone age.

Challis waited, hating the sounds of the clocks, and five minutes later Jelbart came back with a slip of paper.

'Found it.'

'Great,' Challis said, feeling relief. He looked at the name that Jelbart had scrawled for him. 'I was sure this was a wild goose chase.'

Jelbart glided back into the shadows between his clocks and Challis left the shop, wondering why, if Trevor Hubble of St Kilda was the Flinders Floater, his name had never shown up on the missing persons sheet.

CHAPTER **THIRTY-ONE**

Dwayne Venn had scarcely been released on bail when he struck again. At least, Ellen Destry believed it was Venn. The MO was slightly different: last night, Friday, a forty-year-old married architect had been having sex with his eighteen-year-old receptionist in the back seat of his car at a secluded turnoff beside the Devil Bend reservoir when they'd been interrupted by a man wearing a hooded zip-up jacket, baseball boots and nothing else. He'd forced them to have oral sex with each other while he watched and jerked off into a condom, and then he'd robbed them and thrown away the keys to the architect's car.

Now Ellen had them in separate interview rooms at the station. It's Saturday, they complained, you have no right . . . But Ellen prevailed and learnt that, yes, they'd heard a vehicle drive away shortly afterwards, but didn't know what kind or where it had been parked. No, they hadn't heard it pull up—but they were in the throes, so why would they? Ellen thought.

No, no distinguishing marks. Just an impression of an ordinary male groin. Legs? Spindly, said the architect. Strong-looking, said his receptionist. Penis? The architect had scowled, the woman had blushed, both had shrugged.

'Well, sometimes they're tattooed or wearing a ring in the foreskin,' Ellen said, wanting obscurely to embarrass the happy couple.

Face?

It was too dark, they told her. The hood was too concealing.

Did he ejaculate?

Apparently.

Did he remove the condom?

With a tissue. Shoved it all into his pocket.

How had he threatened them?

Mainly his manner. Very scary.

Did he have a knife?

No. A metal bar, like a tyre lever.

Did he take any souvenirs from you?

Eh?

Items of clothing, clippings of hair, that kind of thing?

Only our money.

So the details were sufficiently different to suggest someone other than Venn. Still, his alibi had to be checked. Ellen sent the architect and his receptionist home and questioned each of the Tully sisters.

Lisa first.

'He was with you the whole time? You're sure about that?'

Lisa nodded. They were in one of the interview rooms along the corridor behind the staff canteen, Ellen asking the questions, Scobie watching Lisa Tully stony-faced.

Donna Tully was waiting two doors down, drinking stewed black tea, watched over by another CIB officer. Both sisters were adamant: Dwayne Venn had been at home with them last night.

Is he sleeping with both of them? Ellen wondered.

'What's your relationship with Dwayne?'

'Whaddaya mean?'

'Is he a friend? Boyfriend? Fiancé? Boarder?'

'He's me sister's boyfriend. Whaddaya take me for?'

'You're close to your sister?'

'She's me sister.'

'Would you lie for her?'

'Whaddaya mean?'

'If she asked you to lie to the police to help or protect her,' Ellen enunciated heavily, 'would you do it?' And if you say *Whaddaya mean?* to me again I'll tip you out of your chair.

'What kinda question's that?' Lisa demanded. 'Lay off, why doncha. I'm the victim here.'

That had been Lisa Tully's refrain for the past ten or eleven months: *I'm the victim here.* Well, she *is* a victim, Ellen thought. Her two-year-old daughter was missing, presumed dead. But that had happened last year and had nothing to do with Dwayne Venn's nocturnal activities in the lovers' lanes of the Peninsula.

'Lisa, are you trying to protect your sister? Maybe she was ordered by Dwayne to provide him with an alibi for last night, and she in turn asked you to confirm the alibi. It's not really a lie. You've just got your sister's best interests at heart.'

Lisa Tully frowned suspiciously across the chipped laminex of the table as though Ellen had laid out a slippery plan requiring a level of concentration that might easily defeat her.

'Dunno what you mean.'

'So Dwayne was with you both the whole night. He didn't slip out for a packet of smokes or a six-pack of beer? Didn't meet his mates in the pub for an hour or so?'

'He stayed home, I'm tellin' ya.'

'What did you all do?'

Shrug. 'Had Maccas for tea, watched TV for a while.'

'Did you go to sleep in front of the TV at any stage?'

'Nup.'

'What was on?'

'The footie show.'

'Who do you go for?'

'Collingwood.'

'So do I,' said Ellen warmly. 'Who was on the footie show last night?'

Shrug. 'Dunno. I was in the kitchen.'

'The kitchen? Doing what?'

'Brad come round to see us.'

'Brad Pike?'

Belligerent. 'So? He's allowed'a.'

'You two are friends again?'

Shrug.

'You no longer think he was responsible for your daughter's disappearance?'

Shrug.

'You were in the kitchen with Bradley Pike. Where were Donna and Dwayne?'

'I told ya. Lounge room. Watching TV.'

'Didn't you and Brad want to watch TV?'

Shrug. 'Brad and Dwayne, you know . . .'

'They don't get on?'

'I dunno.'

'How long were you in the kitchen with Brad?'

'A while. Dunno.'

'What were you doing?'

Lisa shifted in her seat and the fluorescent light was harsh on the unhealthy face, limp bleached hair and pierced neck—the piercing new, inflamed, leaking. Ellen guessed that Brad Pike had brought around a couple of sweetheart joints for them to smoke.

'Just talking,' Lisa said finally.

'What about?'

'Stuff.'

Why not investigate the disappearance of Jasmine Tully last year as well as the alibi of Dwayne Venn last night? Ellen thought, and so she said, 'Do you like Brad?'

Shrug.

'Did he leave before or after Dwayne?'

'Before.'

'So Dwayne *did* leave?'

'No, I mean, Dwayne was there the whole time. Brad was there only a while.'

'What time did Dwayne leave?'

Lisa Tully hardened and said, 'You can't get me to say he went out last night so don't even try.'

'What time did Brad leave?'

'I dunno. Nine? Ten? No later.'

The architect and his receptionist had been attacked at eleven pm, so Brad Pike would not be able to say whether or not Venn had gone out. Ellen would question him, but she knew a dead end when she saw one.

She fared no better with Donna Tully. The older sister was sharper than Lisa, tapping long scarlet talons on the table as she snapped off her denials and waited out each of Ellen's questions.

So, the police had Venn on the Easter attack but not the earlier ones and not last night's. And a different MO last night, but Ellen knew in her bones it had been Venn. She wished she also knew who'd given them the tip-off that had given them Venn in the first place.

Ellen tracked Pam Murphy down in the canteen and said, 'Quick word, finish your coffee.'

Five minutes later, Pam Murphy was sitting in the hard chair across from Ellen's desk in the cubicle on the first floor. Murphy returned her gaze steadily.

'We encourage our officers to find informants,' Ellen began.

Pam nodded warily.

'But there are guidelines.'

'I know that, Sarge.'

'We like them to be registered.'

'Yes, Sarge.'

'You handle your own informant so long as a senior officer is there as a kind of cut-off or backup or consultant.'

'Yes, Sarge.'

'Except when it's a one-off tip from someone who's not likely to be in a position to offer information on a regular basis.'

Pam went very still. 'Sarge, is this about Dwayne Venn?'

'It is.'

And then, without prompting or pressure, Pam Murphy said simply, 'It was Brad Pike who told me about Venn.'

'Bugger,' Ellen muttered.

Meaning, although Bradley Pike had provided information good enough to trap Venn on Easter Saturday, he was not reliable and in general had too much at stake when it came to Venn and Venn's relationship with the Tully sisters.

'Bugger.'

'Yes, Sarge,' Pam said, as though she was disappointed too.

CHAPTER **THIRTY-TWO**

'I tried calling you at the station,' Carl Lister said on Monday morning. 'I was told it was your day off.'

'Not exactly,' Pam Murphy said. 'I worked on the weekend, so today I go on at four.'

She was strapping her surfboard to the roof rack of her new Subaru, mobile phone to one ear, listening to him with a lump of apprehension settling inside her.

Lister went on chattily: 'Though how they can let any of you have time off at the moment, I don't know. Have you caught Munro or those escapees yet?'

Lister had a battery of smiles: cheerful, blokish, winking, conniving. Pam could picture his smile now, probably sharkish and bearing no relation to what he was saying. 'I'm not at liberty to say.'

Lister laughed. It came at her harshly through the mobile phone. 'Now, Pam, a little matter that might have escaped your attention, what with manhunts and murders.'

Pam glanced guiltily at her new car. She knew what Lister wanted. She'd gone in to explain her side of things to him the day that Munro had bailed up Tankard in the street, only Lister had been with a client. She'd waited for almost ten minutes then left without seeing him. Still, she said, 'Yes?' in a puzzled voice.

'A little matter of your first weekly loan instalment. It was due last Thursday.'

'Oh.'

'Oh, indeed. Now I must insist on payment by the end of business today, understood?'

It was ten o'clock on a Monday morning, a lovely autumn day, the surf was up, and she was broke.

She began to stammer something when Lister interrupted her. 'If you can't manage payment then perhaps we can renegotiate the terms of your loan to make it easier for you. I'm not an unreasonable man, and you are a police officer, after all, and I have a lot of respect for the police, always have had.'

That was another line she got from time to time. If she wasn't called 'girlie' she was told she was respected because she was a copper. She got it from her landlord, she got it from shopkeepers, and now Lister was at it. For all they knew, she was corrupt, a rowdy tenant, a bad driver, chronically light-fingered.

She certainly couldn't manage her finances.

'When?' she said. She looked lovingly at the waxed surface of her board.

'No time like the present.'

And so she stacked the surfboard in the hallway behind her front door again and drove in to Waterloo, parking the Subaru where Lister wouldn't see her arrive or leave. She didn't know how reasonable he was. He might even commandeer the Subaru, though she doubted he could do that legally. Even so, he could make waves for her, like a quiet word to Senior Sergeant Kellock—for all she knew, they both belonged to Rotary—or an anonymous call to Ethical Standards.

At the street door to Lister's building she glanced across at the bank where Tank had encountered Munro. How would *she* have managed that situation? The way she was feeling now, butterflies in her stomach, she'd have wet her pants.

She pushed through the glass door stencilled with the words 'Lister Financial Services' and went up the stairs. The same receptionist was there, a blonde with big hair and hooked red nails the size of paperclips. God knows how she managed a keyboard or the telephone.

'Yes?' the receptionist said, staring at Pam as if she'd never seen her before.

'Mr Lister is expecting me.'

'And you are . . . ?'

'Father Christmas,' Pam said, stalking by her into Lister's office, expecting a protest, but the woman was silent.

Lister's office overlooked the street. Lister himself sat with his back to the window, the sunlight, banded by the slats of a venetian blind, falling across his head and shoulders and into her eyes, so that she couldn't see him clearly, and she immediately lost some of her resolve.

He didn't stand for her but gestured airily, 'Sit down, Pam.'

The only other chair was directly in front of his desk. Pam shaded her eyes with one hand and watched him, hoping he'd take the hint.

'Now, your interest payment,' he said.

'I've had a lot on,' Pam said. 'This Munro business, the mur—'

He halted her with his hand. 'I'm afraid that's irrelevant, sweetheart. You entered into an obligation and—'

'Surely I'm not the first one late with a payment?'

She'd heard things about Lister since she'd taken out the loan. How he targeted the battlers, giving loans to hopeless cases and subsequently repossessing their cars and houses; how he'd change pay cheques on the spot, but take a hefty percentage. Not quite a loan shark, no whispers of coming round with a baseball bat to get what was owed him, nothing the police could act on, but there was a strong impression of the predator about Lister nevertheless.

'No, Pam, you're not the first to miss a payment. And you won't be the last. But I—'

'I get paid this Thursday.'

'Do you now?' he said mildly. 'But you'll be a week behind by then and be obliged to make *two* payments, plus your penalty.'

'Penalty,' Pam said numbly.

'It was there in black and white in the contract. You did read the contract?'

Pam mumbled something. She hadn't read the contract, and he knew she hadn't. Tears came unbidden then. She could have been a child again, called into her father's study about something. Her brothers had never been called into his study. They were high achievers, university academics now, like their father. Pam had been good at sport, hopeless at all kinds of other things, and often found herself in her father's study, her father's voice quiet and full of reason, subtly putting her down.

'Pam, I'm a reasonable man,' Lister said. 'I don't like to see you get into a mess.'

She gulped and nodded, willing away the tears, hoping that with the sun banded across her face, he hadn't seen the wetness.

'We can come to some arrangement.'

'Thanks,' she said. 'What kind?'

'Would it help you to go onto a monthly schedule?'

'I don't know . . .'

And she didn't know. When she'd first negotiated the terms of the loan, the monthly instalment amount had seemed enormous, the weekly instalment much more palatable. But she couldn't even manage the weekly . . .

'Or you could pay less.'

She glanced at him. 'Over a longer period of time, you mean?'

She thought she could manage that, but to be beholden to Carl Lister for years and years was a terrible thought.

'Quid pro quo,' Lister said, lacing his fingers together over his chest.

'I don't understand.'

'I scratch your back, you scratch mine.'

She sat upright. 'I'm not going to sleep with you.'

He seemed genuinely astonished. 'God, no, sorry, didn't mean that at all.'

Now she felt bad for offending him. 'Oh. Sorry.'

'No, what I'm getting at is, I'm a businessman, right? I have fingers in lots of pies, I lend money to individuals at all rungs of society, I contribute to the community. Which all boils down to one thing: I'm vulnerable.'

She didn't understand.

He flashed her one of his grins, lopsided owing to his facial burns. 'Let's say I lend a young house painter ten thousand dollars to help him over a slump in business. Only he spends the ten thousand to . . . I don't know, buy stolen goods or finance a drug deal. What happens to my ten grand if he gets busted? Clearly I would have needed to know more about that young man before I lent him money.'

'A private detective could do more than I could.'

Lister shook his head. 'I'd need to know if the police were interested in my mythical young man.'

The world went still for a while. Pam Murphy, snitch, mole, spy, informant.

She coughed and said, 'I don't know if I can do that.'

Lister gestured, playing it down. 'Piece of cake, Pam. Nothing to it. I'm a discreet man. I won't use the information, I won't say where I got it from, I won't put anything in writing.'

In a small voice she said, 'What do I have to do?'

'Just keep me up to date. Who the police are interested in, whispers, advance notice of raids, that kind of thing.'

Her jaw dropped. 'Sounds like you want to know a lot.'

He shook his head. 'Just where it concerns drugs. That's my main fear, as a lender of money. I like to know what my money is being used for. So, keep me informed of who you're keeping your eye on. I'll make it worth your while.'

'How?'

'Let's say that for the first year your instalments are a measly fifty dollars a week. Think you can manage that?'

She nodded. Fifty? Piece of cake. Relief flooded through her.

'Okay then.'

CHAPTER **THIRTY-THREE**

A search of immigration and airline records on Monday morning showed that a Trevor Hubble, travelling on a British passport, had arrived in Australia a week before the body of the Floater was found. He'd not been reported missing in the UK and was not known to Interpol or Scotland Yard.

Nothing remarkable there. What *was* remarkable was that Trevor Hubble had a credit record in Australia and in fact had been making purchases by credit card for at least a year before he died—purchases in Australia, when apparently he'd been living in England.

But no spending since the Floater was found. Challis had just updated the file on Tuesday morning when the phone rang and Superintendent McQuarrie said, 'All eyes are upon you, Hal.'

Why did McQuarrie always bark down the phone? Challis held the receiver away from his ear. 'Yes, sir.'

'Munro shoots three people,' McQuarrie went on, 'and steals a policeman's gun—it's like he's running rings around us.'

'Sir,' Challis pointed out, 'I've nothing to do with the manhunt. My job is investigating the murders.'

'One and the same, Hal, one and the same.'

Well, no, they weren't, and it wasn't Challis's job to soothe his superintendent. 'Sir, I don't think the murders are related.'

'Have to be. Have to be. What's forensics tell you?'

'It's difficult with shotgun shootings, sir.'

Surely McQuarrie knew that? Ordinarily, the superintendent thought that forensic evidence was everything. In Challis's experience, forensic evidence was often imprecise and forensic experts were rarely expert enough, and in some instances had little or no training, or tried to do CIB's work for them. He didn't say any of this to McQuarrie, but went on to deflect the man, saying he'd seen him on television the night before.

'I thought you handled it well, sir. Impressive. Struck the right note.'

And in his mind's eye saw the man swell and beam on the other end of the telephone.

But he felt the pressure and called a briefing. The Special Operations commander reported first, brief and clipped as if he were a busy man and wanted to get this wrapped up so he could return to Melbourne where the air didn't smell of fishermen and orchardists.

'No sightings of Munro lately, but we did find those illegals,' he said with satisfaction. 'They were camping out at the tip.'

He said it as if he'd expected nothing less, and Challis was pleased to notice distaste in the faces of Ellen, Scobie and a couple of the others.

When the man was gone, Challis asked for updates from the CIB detectives investigating the shooting. 'Scobie?'

Sutton's lean, mournful face grew longer. 'I've been concentrating on Pearce's correspondence with the *Progress* and the shire. Both kept a file of his letters and I've been contacting those people he'd reported for littering, etcetera, etcetera. They were all puzzled, said, "How did you learn about that?" or "I'd forgotten about that". No one seemed pissed off enough to want to kill Pearce.'

'Did any of them say that Pearce contacted them direct, before he reported them?'

'No. That doesn't seem to have been his style, Hal.'

'True, but if he was impatient with officialdom dragging its heels, maybe he *did* take direct action. Also, check daily in case he sent letters that have been delayed in the post.'

'Done.'

'And his phone records.'

'Done.'

'And check the wife. Maybe *she* was the main target.'

Sutton nodded glumly. Challis turned to Ellen Destry. She looked tired. She'd hinted in the carpark earlier that there were problems at home. The daughter, the daughter's boy-friend, her husband, Challis thought. Or all of them. 'Ellen?' he said.

'I don't want to see another lawyer's caseload,' she said. 'Seigert dealt with wills, conveyancing and small business contracts. All deadly dull, all formulaic, nothing there to give rise to murderous passions. Except in someone like Ian Munro. There's a fat folder devoted to correspondence from Munro, Munro saying in effect that Seigert had sold him out and all lawyers are bastards and Seigert was going to get it in the neck one day when he least expected it.'

'A clear threat to kill?'

'More or less,' Ellen said.

'No witnesses? No sightings of Munro or his vehicle?'

'Nothing.'

Challis looked from Ellen to Scobie. 'What about cor-respondence received by Pearce? Anything at the house?'

Scobie shrugged. 'His mother wrote sometimes, there were some bills, receipts, junk mail, bank statements.'

'Any unusual payments in or out?'

'No.'

'That all?'

'Apart from his scrapbook,' Ellen said, glancing at Scobie, who muttered: 'You saw it, Hal, that day we found the bodies, all those Meddler notes and clippings from the local paper.'

Was Challis imagining it, or were Sutton and Destry stepping carefully where it came to Tessa Kane? They knew of his involvement with her. They probably wondered about its nature: mainly sexual? True love? Or was Challis using her to offer, and gather, information? Then his heart began to hammer: he hadn't told Tessa that Mostyn Pearce was the Meddler. He owed her that. Wanting to get Ellen and Scobie out of his office now, he said, 'Anything else in the house to interest us?'

'Only the damn ferret,' Ellen said. 'Which has escaped, by the way.'

'And the tapes,' Scobie said.

'What tapes?'

'Videos.'

Challis remembered. TV programs, films, documentaries, football grand finals . . . Nothing there to stir the heart.

'Any personal stuff on tape?'

'Their wedding.'

'My weary bones,' Challis said, his way of saying that it was time to go back to work and it would be thankless.

When they were gone, he dialled Tessa's mobile number. 'It's me.'

There was a pause, then a bright, 'Hello, me.'

He didn't want to banter just then. 'I thought you should know—Mostyn Pearce was the Meddler.'

This time the pause spoke volumes and her voice when it came was strained. 'You're only just *now* telling me this? It's been days. Are you sure? No, forget I said that, of course you're sure—but didn't you think I was important enough, *central* enough, to be informed?'

The phone went dead in his ear before he could add that the escaped asylum seekers had been found; and he thought absurdly that he didn't want to lose her.

CHAPTER **THIRTY-FOUR**

When Carl Lister had said he wanted to be kept informed, he hadn't said it would be *every bloody day*. Here he was, Tuesday morning, on her doorstep.

Pam yawned. 'I was on till midnight. I'm on again this evening. I'll be hopeless if I don't get my sleep.'

He pushed past her and she seemed to blink and find herself making him instant coffee in her kitchen. The autumn sun was streaming in and ordinarily she'd have loved to sit there at the table over a steaming coffee, half awake in the warm splash of sunlight.

'I haven't got anything for you,' she said.

'You must have something. Dealers, pushers, runners, importers, addicts, the local Mr Big. Who's supplying the local school kids, the clubs? Who's pushing in the mall? Who's growing it, who's manufacturing it? These are the type of people who might come to me for money. I need to know beforehand if they're known to the police.'

So she told him about Ian Munro's marijuana crop.

He dismissed Munro with a wave of his hand. 'Everyone knows that. What else have you got?'

The Waterloo police station was full of names and drug-related activities: possession, possession with intent, all small-time stuff. She gave Lister a few names. 'Dwayne Venn,' she said. 'Brad Pike.'

'Pike? Piece of shit,' Lister snarled. He looked at her closely. 'Do you think he's responsible?'

Pam looked at him in bewilderment. Surely Bradley Pike wasn't a major league player in the local drug scene?

'For killing his girlfriend's kid,' Lister explained irritably.

'Oh. Yes. Guilty as sin.'

'I agree. Any other names?'

'No.'

Lister got up to leave, his coffee untouched. 'I'll need more, girlie. Otherwise I start calling in your loan the old-fashioned way.'

What did that mean? Court action? Bailiffs? A knee-capping?

John Tankard was on duty but felt so miserable half the time that he wanted to cry. Plus he was knackered, but unable to sleep. And his judgement was shot to pieces.

So he went herbing off to Penzance Beach in the divisional van and sounded the siren outside Pam Murphy's place for a bit of a giggle. Maybe she'd ask him in or he could talk her into going to the Fiddler's Creek pub later for a glass of suds.

Fat chance. She really spewed when she saw him, said she'd been on duty and was catching up on sleep, so why didn't he just bugger off and leave her alone.

'My second visitor this morning,' she snarled. 'What the hell do you want?'

So who'd been the first visitor? 'Don't be like that,' Tankard said.

'Like what? You come here in broad daylight, siren blasting when I'm trying to sleep, and you expect me to like it? God knows what the neighbours think.' She laughed without humour. 'Probably take one look, see who's making the racket, and think to themselves: typical, it's the stormtrooper.'

Last year someone had gone around placing anonymous leaflets on windscreens complaining about John Tankard's Nazi stormtrooper tactics. He flushed. 'Can I come in?'

'No. Why?'

'Pammy, please, I'm falling apart here.'

And she must have seen something in his face and manner that convinced her, for she gave him a subtle look of understanding and stood back as he stepped past her into the house. She was wearing pyjamas. Half of him was thinking, God I want a piece of that, and the other half wanted to grab hold of her for dear life and cry his heart out.

'Five minutes tops, okay?' she demanded.

'Okay,' he mumbled, and he watched her disappear into her bedroom and come back wearing a dressing gown guaranteed to kill all desire.

So he talked to her mate-to-mate about his bewilderment, his shame, his loss of nerve, and how it was all down to Ian Munro.

And she listened, mate-to-mate.

This time Dwayne Venn was there when Brad Pike called round to see Lisa Tully.

'If it isn't little Bradley.'

'Gedday.'

'Come in, son, come in.'

Two o'clock on Tuesday afternoon and the house was doped up, curtains drawn, air dense, Lisa and Donna sprawled on the floor, high as kites.

He had a lot of catching up to do, hadn't had a hit of anything since yesterday, and eyed the bowl on the coffee table. You had your speed there, your ecstasy, your hand-rolled joints, even—if he wasn't mistaken—a baggie of coke and heroin in a twist of aluminium foil.

Plus your bottles of Southern Comfort.

It all felt right, somehow. All of a piece with the Native American posters and the Confederate flag and Dwayne's Harley Davidson parked in the hallway.

'Got something to chill me out?' Pike asked.

'Have we ever,' Venn said, and slowly, over the next hour or so, Brad Pike began to unwind and talk and enter into the spirit of things. The last time he'd had the undivided attention of anyone in this town was when the cops had grilled him about Lisa's kid.

After lunch on Tuesday Ellen rang her husband and said, 'Alan, I'm sorry, I shouldn't have said what I did.'

He didn't respond and she pictured him there in the kitchen, heavy jaw set hard against her, swotting for the sergeants' exam. It was not that she owed him an apology. It just made sense to apologise. She figured that if she could keep things sweet at home until after the exam, then he'd manage the exam better and life would be easier on everyone.

Then he coughed and said, 'Okay.' Not 'Thank you' or 'It was all my fault,' just 'Okay,' so she put some brightness into her voice and asked, 'Did Skip call?'

'No.'

Overnight, it seemed, Skip had dumped Larrayne. He'd not called her, taken her out over the weekend, or responded to the messages that Larrayne had recorded on the Listers' answering machine. Larrayne was distraught. 'What did I do wrong?' she'd wailed. 'Has he met someone else?' The dialogue out of a bad romance novel, but heartfelt and anguished even so.

'Okay, just checking in, hope it goes well today,' Ellen babbled, still playing the guilty one, and she hung up, almost banging the phone down.

And now it was the afternoon and she wanted a word with Aileen Munro.

She got to the farm in time to see Carl Lister trying to shake off a handful of journalists. He was in his car and looked ropeable enough to ram them but recognised her and called her name. 'Ellen, can't you do something?'

She got out of her car and approached them. 'Come on, guys, let the man leave.'

'But what is he doing here?' they wanted to know. 'Is he a friend of the family? Does he know where Ian Munro is?'

All good questions, Ellen thought. She cleared a path for Carl and was about to ask him how Skip was, had he gone on a trip, Larrayne would appreciate a call, but he sped away before she could get the words out. She gave a wry shrug to the waiting journalists, who mobbed her good-naturedly.

'Sergeant Destry, any news on Munro?'

'Any chance of an interview, Sergeant?'

'Is there a reason why you're calling on Mrs Munro at this time?'

And so on.

She grinned and turned away from them. As she did so she came face to face with Tessa Kane, the editor of the *Progress*. Ellen nodded. 'Tessa.'

'Ellen.'

There was a pause; then, to let Tessa know that she sympathised with her position on the asylum seekers, Ellen said, 'Did you hear? They found those poor Iraqi men camping at the tip.'

Tessa flashed a bleak smile of thanks. 'They'll go into solitary confinement and eventually be deported.'

Ellen didn't know why, but she said, 'I don't know where Hal is today. Following up something, somewhere.'

Tessa shrugged. She didn't seem to care. Instead, she said, 'Who was that man in the car just then?'

Ellen considered the question. There seemed to be no harm in saying, 'Carl Lister. He's more or less a neighbour. Why?'

'Oh, no reason,' Tessa Kane said, and Ellen knew at once that there was a very good reason for the question.

CHAPTER **THIRTY-FIVE**

Challis worked until four on Tuesday afternoon and then drove to the aerodrome, intending to work on the Dragon's cockpit for a couple of hours before he went home. Home these days meant early- or late-evening darkness, his answering machine full of his wife's hysteria, a comfortless instant meal—for he was often too tired to care about cooking—and a barely refreshing sleep before he got up to a chilly morning, the sun weak through the leafless trees in his back yard.

Home could also mean Tessa's place. The opening was there, but he still felt vaguely disconnected from her. And in today's *Progress* she'd been scathing about the community's selective hysteria, its focus on the asylum seekers and blindness to the things that really affected the local community, like the increased dealing and pushing of drugs. She was on the warpath and when she was like that, seeing the world in black-and-white terms, he felt that his lack of fire would show, and she'd be disappointed in him.

Oddly enough, she'd published the Meddler column—probably hadn't had time to pull it before going to press, he thought.

At the aerodrome he could forget himself for a while. Draw comfort from working with his hands. Maybe Kitty would be there.

What did he think he'd do—save her from a loveless marriage? Who said it was loveless? He *wanted* it to be loveless. A big difference. Or they could have an affair. That would suit a man who has good reasons to shy away from commitment.

But it's all in my head, Challis thought, when he walked into the hangar and saw Kitty Casement and got a pre-occupied smile and wave from her and nothing more. 'Catching up on paperwork,' she called, waving an invoice at him, her voice losing itself in the hollow reaches of the high steel walls and oil-stained concrete floor.

'Have fun,' Challis called back, climbing into his overalls and hauling himself onto the Dragon's bottom wing.

And slowly he felt better. He managed to forget himself for a while, one part of his mind absorbed in mapping out the stages of a physical task, the other dreaming of a time in history, 1942, when this very aeroplane had helped ferry Dutch refugees, who were fleeing the Japanese invasion of Java, from Broome to Perth. Or earlier, 1934, when a Vacuum Oil Company geologist had flown it over tricky magnetic country in the remote desert region of central and northern Australia.

That's where the history stopped. Challis had no idea how the Dragon had subsequently come to be a wreck in a barn near Toowoomba in Queensland.

They called it synchronicity, didn't they? Or something like that. For just at that moment Kitty rapped her knuckles on the fuselage and when he'd uncoiled himself from beneath the instrument panel and poked his head out, he saw her waving a book at him. 'This came in the post,' she said.

Challis straightened the kinks in his back and climbed out to join her. The book was evidently self-published, everything about it looking amateurish, rough and ready, including the photograph on the front cover.

'A few weeks ago I got Rex off the computer long enough to search the Internet,' Kitty said with a laugh. 'I couldn't believe it when I found sites devoted to the Kittyhawk. Apparently the man who flew my plane died a few years ago, but one of his friends sent me this.'

The cover photograph showed a Kittyhawk fighter on an airstrip in the hot sun, a young man in shorts, boots and dogtags grinning at the camera. Challis guessed that he was the author as a young man, Lt Andy H. Ludecki, from New Jersey.

'Darwin?' Challis guessed, pointing at the photograph.

'Yes.'

Kitty couldn't control her pleasure. Her face was wreathed in smiles. 'He even mentions my plane and the man who flew her.'

But Challis felt only an unwarranted chill. 'I don't under-stand the title,' he said.

'*Kittyhawk Down*? Oh, that's just a quote from a radio transmission the day Darwin was bombed.'

'Shot down?'

'Yes.'

'Kitty,' Challis said, 'be careful, won't you?'

She looked at him oddly for a moment, touched his sleeve with a brief grin, and turned away, saying she'd better get back to work.

Shortly after that Challis's mobile phone rang. It was Tessa Kane, sounding less strained now, saying she had some information for him. Challis, feeling an obscure loneliness and pain, suggested a drink and bar snacks at the Heritage in Balnarring.

· · ·

Six o'clock. A dewy evening was settling and the moon hung in the skeletal trees. Challis could smell chimney smoke as he got out of his car; good, they'd lit the open fire in the side room. Tessa Kane's car was already there, parked in a corner under a tree. No other cars yet. They'd have the place to themselves for a while. A glass of red and a plate of nachos by the open fire. Get a glow on and forget about Kitty Casement.

Challis found Tessa on the massive leather couch. She got lightly to her feet and kissed him affectionately. 'Sorry I got mad at you last time,' she said. 'I know you're under pressure and can't always divulge things when you want to.'

Challis felt a rush of affection and gratitude tinged with guilt: she didn't warrant his neglect. His heart lifted: the firelight, the beautiful woman, the promise.

'I ordered a bottle of Elan,' she said.

'Good.'

'Nachos, and guacamole and chilli dip.'

'Great.'

She turned a wicked, full-voltage grin on to him. 'Chilli dip prepared by someone else, you'll be glad to know.'

Challis snorted, blushed, shifted about, suddenly embarrassed. A few days before Easter he'd prepared a curry meal for them, and was slicing hot fresh chillies on his chopping board when she arrived. They kissed, and found themselves stripping, then making love, and afterwards, prone on the sitting-room rug, had felt a burning sensation in their genitals.

Tessa laughed. 'Sit, Hal.'

She swung her slim knees toward him when they were seated, and immediately began to speak. 'Remember I told you about the Easter walk and the men in the four-wheel-drive looking for something on the beach?'

Challis stiffened, then relaxed. This wasn't an attack. She was generous and forgiving by nature, and this was plainly business. 'Yes.'

'I saw one of them again.'

'Where?'

'The Munro place.'

Challis watched her carefully. 'Do you know who he is?'

'Lister. Carl Lister.'

'Are you sure?'

'Fairly sure. He was the passenger, not the driver, that day on the beach. At the time, I didn't think I'd seen him clearly, but I must have, subconsciously. I remember the scarring on his neck.'

'How do you know his name?'

'I was hoping to get an interview with Aileen Munro— you know, local paper, sympathetic hearing, not some hotshot from the *Age* or the *Herald Sun*—when this Lister character drives out. Almost ran over a couple of reporters. Anyway, I recognised him as the man in the passenger seat of the Toyota.'

Challis frowned. Toyota. Ian Munro owned a Toyota. 'But how do you know his name?'

She touched his wrist. 'Hold your horses. Drink your wine. Eat your nachos.'

He breathed out, grinned, swallowed his wine.

'That's better. The reason I know his name is that Ellen Destry arrived at that moment, and she helped Lister avoid the scrum, and told me his name.'

'Carl Lister,' Challis said to himself. Then: 'But the driver, that day on the beach. Could he have been—'

'Ian Munro? Yes, possibly, though he wore a beanie and shades and his face was distorted with all the shouting he was doing.'

Challis stared into the flames, losing himself in them. Lister and drugs, Munro and a drug crop . . .

'Hal?'

He turned to Tessa.

'What are you thinking?'

She wasn't asking it as a lover—or only partly—but as a journalist. She had that intent, narrowed gaze. But he found that she was holding his hand, so he told her that he was thinking not about the past but the here and now.

CHAPTER **THIRTY-SIX**

Larrayne was subdued, teary, on Wednesday morning. She didn't want to get up, and for the past two days had taken to wandering around with her mobile phone in her hand.

'Why won't he ring?'

'Perhaps he's away, sweetie. Studying for exams. Staying with friends.'

'Well, why didn't he tell me? I'm sick of leaving messages.'

Larrayne recognised the anguish well enough from her youth. There's nothing worse than waiting for calls that never come, the calls of the beloved.

'I love him, Mum.' Said frankly and devoutly, as though Ellen doubted it or no one before Larrayne had ever loved.

'I know you do. It will sort itself out, you'll see.'

'He's avoiding me, I can feel it.'

In the end, Ellen told Larrayne to get dressed, go to school, take her mind off Skip.

Fat chance, but it was worth a try.

She dropped Larrayne at the school gates and drove to the police station, and Challis nabbed her as soon as she walked in to CIB. 'Carl Lister was seen visiting Aileen Munro.'

And at once Ellen connected the dots: Lister, his son, Munro, marijuana, and saw good reasons why Skip had suddenly stopped seeing Larrayne.

Three-thirty that afternoon, just before the four o'clock shift went on, found Pam sitting with John Tankard and Sergeant van Alphen around a table in the canteen. They were full of coffee and someone's leftover birthday cake and disinclined to start work.

'Get this,' Tank said from behind yesterday's *Progress*. 'Says here: "With labels like 'illegals' and 'queue jumpers' we demonise the asylum seekers". I'll give her labels.'

He poked his head around to see that Pam was paying attention. 'Challis's girlfriend,' he explained unnecessarily.

Pam said sweetly, 'And what labels would those be, Tank?'

Caught on the back foot, he looked flummoxed, then mustered himself: 'Poser, do-gooder, un-Australian, wanker. That do you? Want me to go on?'

Pam thought that John Tankard would know all about labels, he who'd been called a stormtrooper. 'What do you think, Sarge?'

Van Alphen said, 'So long as it doesn't affect his job.'

She had no idea what he was talking about. Tankard's job? 'Sarge?'

'Challis,' van Alphen said. 'So long as his work isn't compromised by what his girlfriend thinks.'

'Hadn't thought of it that way, Sarge,' Pam said, thinking that Challis's relationship with Tessa Kane wasn't the issue here. The issue was the asylum seekers and their reception and treatment. People were funny. Funny and limited.

As Wednesday evening settled, the sun flattening red over the mangroves and smokestacks of Westernport, Brad Pike's skin crawled with need and loss, and he left his flat beside the strip of used-car yards and drove through the side streets to the cop shop at the roundabout. Plenty of parking outside so he zipped in, braked, turned off the ignition, waited a few seconds while the motor ran on and coughed and died with a rattle, then went in and said that he was being stalked.

The cop on desk duty—looked like a probationer—called Sergeant van Alphen. Shit, shit, shit.

Van Alphen came in, lean, dark, a repressive cast to his face. 'Well, if it isn't young Bradley. How's things, Brad?'

'Not bad. Yourself?' Pike said automatically, then kicked himself for being polite to a cop.

'So, what weird shit have you been up to now, Bradley?'

'No need to be like that.'

'Like what?'

'I come in here on legitimate business,' Pike said, the word 'legitimate' tangling his tongue a little.

'Your only business with us is telling us where you buried Lisa Tully's kid.'

Pike felt his face grow hot. 'The charges were dropped.'

'But that's not the same as being found innocent, though, is it, Brad?'

Twice lately he'd been told that. Van Alphen was a hard nut, dark and hard, like old leather. They reckon he'd gone off the rails a bit last year, but if that was true then he'd long recovered. He'd been on Pike's case from the start. In some ways he was as fucking bad as John Tankard.

'I come in here to make a complaint.'

'Don't tell me, you're being stalked. You said that on Monday, you said it last week . . .'

'So how come no one's listening?'

'Because you're full of shit. You're a slime bag and don't deserve to live.'

The probationary constable was looking on with his eyes and pimply mouth wide open.

'It's true, someone's following me.'

'Constable Tankard,' laughed van Alphen.

How did van Alphen know that? Had he put Tankard up to it?

'I dunno who it is,' Pike said. 'I get, like, these phone calls in the middle of the night, these letters. I can feel someone's behind me all the time. I think it's Lisa's sister, maybe Dwayne Venn. When I'm out walking and stuff.'

'Out walking? You never walked a millimetre in your worthless life.' Van Alphen leaned forward over the front desk, disturbing a pile of brochures. 'You know what I think? It's in your mind, a delusion. The world hates you for what you did to Lisa Tully's kid—hell, *you* are probably stalking *Lisa*— so you're twisting it around, pursuing the joys of victimhood.'

A deep, slow flush spread through Pike. But van Alphen wasn't finished.

'You're a lonely, isolated, pitiful specimen of humanity. You know it, the world knows it, and you're desperate for sympathy. You're intent on blaming others for your own shitty life. You can't accept any responsibility for that shitty life.'

Then van Alphen stood back and folded his arms dismissively. 'So forgive me if I'm sceptical, Brad.'

Pike opened and closed his mouth a few times and turned to leave, just as the station boss, Kellock, burst in, calling, 'We need a couple of cars out at the aerodrome. There's been another shooting.'

'Munro?'

'Don't know. Security guard called it in.'

Then Kellock grew aware of Pike and shut down, growing cold and still, but Pike was thinking, I'm out of here, and he pushed through the glass doors to the footpath outside.

To his car, where Scobie Sutton was standing with his hands in his pockets. 'Brad,' he said mildly, 'perhaps you're not aware of it, but you're in a no-standing zone, police vehicles only. And I see your registration is long overdue.'

'So sue me,' Pike said with a sob, and he got in and turned the motor over for a long few seconds before it fired.

CHAPTER **THIRTY-SEVEN**

'She often worked late,' the security guard said.

Challis nodded. He knew that she did. He felt awful and was grinding his jaw in an effort not to weep.

'I could see a light on in the hangar. If there's no light I just check the doors are locked and continue on my way. If there's a light on I go in and natter for a few minutes, you know, the weather and that.'

I bet that thrilled her, Challis thought, and immediately regretted it. Maybe she liked having the guy come in and wish her good evening.

'You didn't see or hear anything?'

'Not a thing.'

'Anyone around? Pilots, mechanics . . .'

The security guard shook his head. 'You don't find anyone here after six, usually. Except Mrs Casement.'

'And what time did you find her?'

The man glanced at his watch. His breathing was habitually laboured and it was some time before he replied. 'Forty-five minutes ago. About seven-thirty.'

'Was this the start or finish of your rounds?'

'The start.'

'What did you do after calling it in?'

The guard looked embarrassed. 'I'm on a strict timetable. I thought if it took the police a while to get here I might as well finish checking the other buildings.'

'And did you?'

'Yes,' he said defiantly. 'Plus I thought I might spot who done it.'

Challis said, 'Look, that's fine. Better to do something than stand around letting a dead body get under your skin.'

The guard shuddered. 'Bad choice of words, mate.'

It was. Challis had seen the body. Massive shotgun wounds to the torso and head, indicating that the killer had fired twice. If it was Munro, and he had the double-barrelled shottie with him, then he'd fired both barrels. Or he'd had the single with him and reloaded it after the first shot.

Or he had an automatic shotgun.

Either way, Kitty Casement was dead.

Challis continued to work it out, trying to think like a policeman when all he wanted to do was chuck the job in. Kitty was a woman he'd only ever brushed against accidentally and certainly never kissed, but she'd lodged in his head and had died terribly. He swallowed. The image came back, unbidden: a corner of the hangar; harsh shadows cast by the unremitting fluorescent lights bolted to the steel rafters overhead; a tumble of empty fuel drums and greasy rags; the cold, chipped, oil-stained concrete black and sticky where her blood had pooled; her body splayed like something tossed aside.

The *smell*. Aviation fuel and grease and blood thickly spilt over the ground.

The security guard was talking to him. 'Sorry, what?'

'Can I go now?' the guard repeated. 'I've got me rounds to finish. Schools, the antique place, coupla supermarkets . . .'

Challis rubbed his face tiredly. 'Come down to the station tomorrow and give a statement, okay?'

'Sure, no drama.'

Challis watched the guard wheel out of the aerodrome in a little white van, then turned reluctantly back to the hangar. The crime scene technicians were working the corner where the body lay. Ellen Destry watched from the sidelines, looking up as she sensed his approach. She crossed toward him as though to head him off.

'Nasty one, Hal.' She paused, cocking her head in concern. 'You okay?'

Challis nodded. 'I want a doorknock of the houses out on the main road. They're a bit far away, and used to people coming and going here, but someone might have seen or heard something.'

'Seen Ian Munro, you mean. This *has* to be him, doesn't it?'

Challis turned on her irritably and said, 'Nothing has to be anything, Ellen,' and immediately wondered what he'd meant.

She backed away, hands up placatingly. 'All right, stay cool, I'll get onto it.'

'Then I want you to come with me to speak to the husband.'

'You don't think it was him, surely?'

The irritation came back into his voice before he could stop himself. 'He has to be *told*, doesn't he?'

As their tyres growled softly along the loose gravel of the Casements' driveway, Ellen said, 'He'd have to be wondering where she is by now.'

Challis was slumped against the passenger door. He'd not said a word since getting into the car. Now he roused himself, rubbed his hands raspingly over his face. 'Not necessarily. She often worked late. And he's apparently on the Net day and night.'

They parked, knocked on the front door, and then in unison turned on the doorstep and looked out at the distant bay. The water lay dense and black but lit here and there by the moon, while beyond the dark mass lay Phillip Island, full of twinkling lights.

They'd not heard footsteps but a spotlight illuminating the driveway and doorstep went on and a latch was turned. Rex Casement swung open the door, blinked as the light hit him, and stared past them into the gloom. He seemed dazed— exactly, Challis thought, like a man dragged away from an obsession.

'Who . . . I was . . . are you . . . ?' Casement said.

Ellen moved toward him and said gently, 'May we come in, Mr Casement?'

Casement recovered and said, 'Is anything wrong? I was on the Net,' he added, glancing at them in turn. 'I don't think Kitty's home yet, actually.'

He wore tracksuit pants, slippers and what looked like a pyjama top under a fleecy striped football jumper. His hair was badly tufted and even as Challis watched he tugged at a clump of it. Maybe he'd made a bad on-line investment, Challis thought.

'Actually it's you we've come to see, Mr Casement,' Ellen said.

Frowning doubtfully, Casement took them to the kitchen. 'This is the cheeriest room at night, hope you don't mind. Tea? Coffee? Something stronger?'

He was washing his hands as though to stave off the inevitable, and when Challis told him the reason for the visit, he stopped fussing at the sink and collapsed into a chair. 'Oh no, oh no.' He looked up. 'Shot?'

'Yes.'

'This Munro character did it?'

'Mr Casement,' Ellen said, 'I realise this is a distressing time, but I have to ask you what your movements were this evening.'

Casement turned to her, jaw open, making a massive effort to comprehend her. 'Me?'

'Yes.'

'I was here, working.'

'On the Internet?'

'Yes. Why?'

'You didn't go out at all?'

'No.'

'Do you have a separate phone line for the Net?'

'Yes.'

'Did anyone ring you this evening?'

'Not that I recall. There's an answering machine.' He crossed to what appeared to be an all-purpose corner of the kitchen bench: notices fluttering from a little pinboard, Rolodex, scrap paper and pens, phone and answering machine. He pressed a button and the machine beeped and they heard Kitty Casement say that she'd be working late.

Casement sobbed and swung away, returning to his chair at the table.

'Did you go out this evening?'

Challis saw a change pass across Casement's face, dazed grief giving way to incredulity. 'You're checking *me* out? That's a bit harsh.'

'No it's not,' said Challis evenly. 'It's statistically likely, and we're obliged to ask.'

'If you bastards had arrested Munro this wouldn't—'

Challis cut in. 'Can you think of anyone else who might have wanted to harm your wife?'

'Apart from Munro? No. He's the obvious one, so why are you questioning me? Leave me alone. Go on, piss off and catch—'

Ellen touched his arm. 'Is there anyone we can contact for you, Mr Casement? Friend, neighbour, relative?'

'I'd rather be by myself,' Casement said, diminished by the night and the solitude that was coming for him.

CHAPTER **THIRTY-EIGHT**

It was fully dark and Pike was in a real state when he got to Lisa's. They let him in, Venn was there, and they were high as kites as usual.

'Well, if it isn't young Bradley,' Venn said, when Lisa ushered him into the sitting room. Donna scowled at him. Lisa herself could have been a bit warmer. They were all looking at him like he was a bad smell.

And he wished Dwayne wouldn't keep saying the same thing each time he visited. 'Change the record, Dwayne,' Pike said, keeping his voice light and cheery, rubbing his hands together dryly. The place smelt of dope and dirty clothing, like they hadn't been out for days. Probably hadn't. When was he last here? Yesterday? Day before? They were really coked up, so he said, 'Looks like I've got some catching up to do.'

And that's what he did for the next hour. Smoked dope, drank Jim Beam, and when he was well blissed out, ticking over nicely, too sluggish to move, he caught Venn exchanging glances with the Tully sisters. 'What?' he slurred.

'We got some new stuff for you to try,' Lisa said.

She went out and came back with a syringe. 'This is good stuff.'

'What is it?'

She tapped the side of her nose and grinned like she was really pumped about something. 'Wait and see, lover boy.'

He liked the way she said that. Then she sat on the sofa, patted the cushions. 'Come on, your turn, we've had stacks.'

Gratified, Pike collapsed onto the sofa next to her and flexed his arm, tied it off with a length of rubber tubing supplied by Donna, tapped a vein.

Lisa got closer. Her thigh was warm against him. 'Now,' she breathed, 'want me to do it for you?'

That was an ultimate act of love and he nodded and watched her slide the needle in and depress the plunger. He tore his eyes away and, waiting for the rush, said to her, 'Lisa, I'm sorry I jacked up about that intervention order you took out on me.'

'That's all right.'

'Shouldn't of forced you to go through all that stuff in court again. I could see you was really cut.'

'No drama.'

Then she walked away from him and joined the others, all three of them now standing in a line, watching him as if from a great distance.

'What?' he said.

'It's not working,' Lisa said.

'Give it time,' Venn said.

They continued to watch. Pike tried to move but was too sleepy, too relaxed. The stuff in his veins wasn't doing anything, however. There was a kind of discomfort, that's all, maybe a faint burning sensation, very faint.

From far away he heard Donna hiss, 'It's not working.'

'It has to work,' Venn said. 'It's battery acid.'

They watched, and Pike thought, acid? Haven't had a good acid trip in a while.

He felt drowsy, but jumpy too, and tried to focus on their faces. 'Talk to me.'

'You're a pest and a nuisance, Brad,' Lisa said.

'Don't say that.'

'You been following us around,' Donna said. 'Stalking us.'

Hurt, Pike said, 'Haven't.'

Venn was all sharpness and hard angles. 'You're a maggot, a dog. You dobbed me in to the cops.'

'No way.'

'You're going to die, Brad, and good riddance,' Donna said. 'There was real acid in that needle.'

'What a blast,' Pike said.

'No, I mean *real* acid, like we did experiments with in the lab at school. From that car place Dwayne works at,' Donna said nastily. 'It's going to eat your insides out.'

The truth got through to Pike eventually and he stirred, rising from the sofa. 'I need to go to the hospital.'

Venn pushed him down. 'No way known.'

'Not till you tell me what you done to Jasmine,' Lisa said.

Pike glanced at them one by one. 'Is it true?'

'Is what true?'

'You put fucking battery acid in me?'

'Yep.'

'Take me to the doctor. Please.'

'Not till you tell us what you did to my niece,' Donna said, the words 'my niece' giving her a little prideful lift.

'And not till you tell me you dobbed me in to the cops,' Venn said.

Pike thrashed around on the sofa, in fear and pain now, and said, 'It was an accident, all right? We were mucking around and something happened.'

Lisa's eyes narrowed. 'What kind of mucking around?'

'On the carpet, you know, playing horsey and that, tickling and wrestling and that.'

'*You had sex with her,*' screeched Lisa. '*You had sex with my baby.*'

'I never.'

'*You did.*'

'Yeah, you did, Brad,' Donna said.

'She went all floppy on me. I think her neck got broke,' Pike said. 'Anyway, you shouldn't of left her with me. She wasn't my kid. What do I know about little kids? It's all your fault, fucking slag.'

Lisa groaned. 'Where is she?'

'Don't worry, I give her a decent burial. Over by the boardwalk.' Which crossed mangrove swamps and was an area of crabs, gluey mud, sucking tides and scraps of plastic and paper.

Lisa began to sob, her hands over her face.

'Take me to the hospital. At least call an ambulance,' Pike said.

Venn looked at the women. 'The acid's not working.'

'I *told* you that,' Donna said.

Venn went out and came back with a baseball bat and swung it at Pike's head. It struck him obliquely and curved downwards at a tangent to splinter against the edge of the coffee table. Pike grunted, swayed, fell to his knees. There was blood. He felt bad, inside and out, and looked up blindly through the blood. 'Don't hit me. I told ya, I'm sorry, okay? Get me to the doctor.'

'Now the fucking bat's broke,' Venn muttered. His voice was far away. 'Still don't know if he dobbed me in to the cops or not. Did you?' he screamed, poking Pike with the jagged end of the bat handle.

'I know,' Donna said eagerly, and Pike heard her rummage in a drawer. Then she was next to him on the floor, slipping a plastic bag over his head. He heard her say, 'This'll work,' before the plastic sucked wetly to his nostrils and lips and sealed him off against the world.

CHAPTER **THIRTY-NINE**

On Thursday morning, Aileen Munro said, 'You again.'

'I don't have time for this,' Challis said. 'Last time I was here you told me that you never have visitors.'

'We don't.'

Ellen leaned forward. 'Aileen, on Tuesday Carl Lister came to see you.'

'Well, yes.'

'So you do have visitors from time to time.'

'But he's a neighbour. He lives up the road in one of them big houses on the ridge.'

'Has he been a regular visitor?'

'You don't call them visitors when they're your neighbour,' she muttered at the floor, then looked up and said, 'He pops in now and then.'

'Sits down and has a cup of tea with you?' Challis asked.

'Not really. They weren't that kind of visit.'

'What kind were they then?'

'He always come to ask Ian a favour,' Aileen said. 'Like, could Ian take his tractor up there and slash his grass for him, or he was bogged and could Ian come and pull him out, that kind of thing.' She folded her arms aggrievedly. 'He wasn't visiting. It was work, kind of thing.'

'Work,' Challis said, his lean face prohibitive in the dim light. Since Kitty's murder he'd felt close to heartsick and was barely hiding it.

'Yeah, work.'

'Did Lister help your husband to grow the marijuana?'

'I told you, I never knew about that. Why don't you believe me?'

'Were they partners?'

'I'm not answering any more of your stupid questions if you don't believe what I say.'

'Or did Lister pay your husband to grow the marijuana?'

Aileen Munro assumed the behaviour of a stubborn child, humming loudly to block out their voices, tapping her foot and gazing about the room. It irritated Challis even as he understood the reason for it.

'Mrs Munro, did Ian go off somewhere with Lister on Easter Saturday?'

She frowned. 'Might of done. Can't remember.'

'Did they say anything about going to one of the beaches?'

'One of the beaches?' Aileen was dumbfounded. 'What, like fishing?'

'Or for a walk, something like that.'

Aileen shook her head in wonder. 'I've never seen Ian within cooee of a beach.'

'Did Ian ever make deliveries for Lister, or fetch things for him?'

She screwed her face up in doubt that merged into disbelief. 'Nah.'

'You never saw him with packages?'

'Nup.'

'Did Ian take drugs?'

Aileen drew herself up, as though the question reflected badly on her or the choices she'd made in life. 'Never.'

Ellen said, 'Aileen, where is Ian now?'

'Haven't the foggiest.'

'Is he with Mr Lister? Is Mr Lister hiding him?'

'You'll have to ask him.'

Challis said, 'What did Lister want with you yesterday?'

'Dropped in to see how I was getting on.'

They gazed at her, wanting, expecting more, and were rewarded when she said into the silence: 'Asked me about you lot.'

Challis sat back and watched her levelly with a half-smile. 'Asked just out of passing interest, or was it more than that?'

She thought about it. 'He seemed a bit bothered.'

'About what, exactly?'

'He asked the kind of questions you've been asking. Did I know about the marijuana. Did I know what Ian had been up to. Had I told the police anything. I thought he was just being nosy.'

Then she muttered something and went pink.

Challis snapped forward. 'I didn't catch that, Aileen.'

She glared at him defiantly. 'He give me some money.'

'How much?'

'Hundred dollars.'

Challis guessed a few hundred. 'Did he say why?'

'In case I need anything. Ian did all the banking and stuff.'

'Did he place conditions on the loan?'

'Wasn't a loan!'

'Was it hush money, is what the inspector is asking,' Ellen said. 'In other words, did he ask you not to tell the police certain things?'

'He said the police don't have to know all my dirty washing,' Aileen Munro said sulkily. Then: 'Will I have to give it back?'

Challis shook his head. 'Keep it.'

'Good, because it'd be useful. For the bills and that.'

In the car afterwards, Ellen said, 'They were growing marijuana together, or Munro was growing it on Lister's behalf. Then the aerial photograph turns up and they destroy the crop in a hurry, or at least remove the plants and put them somewhere to dry, assuming the plants were ready for drying and processing.'

'But now they can't risk growing another crop,' Challis said, taking up the narrative, 'in case it's spotted from the air again.'

'So they switch to something else: ecstasy, cocaine, amphetamines, heroin, dropped off at sea.'

'But there's rough weather and one of their shipments is washed away or destroyed.'

They fell silent. Scobie was driving, and now he said, 'But how long have they been doing it? Was this the first time? For that matter, was the stuff washed away, or were the goods maybe snatched by someone else?'

Challis pictured Tessa Kane on her Easter walk, trudging along a lonely beach, a strong wind kicking sand into her eyes. A Toyota pickup appears, Munro and Lister inside, clearly angry and suspecting that their drugs shipment had been stolen.

Had the marijuana crop been stolen from them too?

Had Kitty Casement recognised the crop and harvested the plants under the cover of darkness? Had she then monitored Munro's and Lister's movements and got to the seaborne drugs first?

Challis was not surprised to hear Ellen ask, 'Have we got a turf war on our hands?'

Or to hear Sutton ask, 'Do we know anything about Kitty Casement's husband?'

'The smell,' Ellen said suddenly.

'What smell?' Challis said, even as his skin tingled and the hairs stood up on his neck, responding to her.

'There's a distinct chemical smell in the air around Lister's place.'

Challis continued to register the stirring of his skin. 'You're right, I noticed it too.'

'A lab?' Scobie said. 'He's cooking speed in a hidden lab?'

'Cooking something,' Ellen said.

They had reached High Street and the roundabout. 'But where's his lab? I didn't see any sheds there the other day,' Challis said.

'If you walk further along the fenceline you can glimpse part of the grounds at the rear of the house,' Ellen said. 'It's been landscaped, sort of terraced, with cement structures set in the ground. I'd assumed they were retaining walls or underground rainwater tanks, but they could be a laboratory.'

Scobie Sutton mused on it as he parked the car. 'These guys like to steal sinus tablets and process them in labs.'

Challis nodded. They crossed the asphalt surface to the back door of the station.

Sutton went on: 'So was Lister leaving the finished product to be collected, or was he taking delivery of sinus tablets?'

'Don't really know, Scobe,' Ellen said. She grew tired of Sutton sometimes.

Challis stopped suddenly. The others collided with him. 'Hal?' Ellen said, steadying herself, one hand on his upper arm.

'The beach.'

'What about it?'

'Miles of coastline,' Challis said, 'and none of it's been searched. We've been looking for Munro in the wrong place.'

CHAPTER **FORTY**

'A bit nipple out,' Tankard said, shoulders hunched against the chilly wind. Four-thirty in the afternoon, a warmish autumn, how come it was so cold here on the beach?

He trudged on with Pam Murphy, glancing at her chest for a glimpse of hardened nipple—too much clothing—then looking at her face to see how she'd taken the nipple comment. Didn't even crack a smile. She was restlessly scanning the ti-trees for signs of Ian Munro. Like, was he going to pitch a tent in the bushes? Tankard had hoped, after his tearful visit to her place the other day, that she'd chill out a bit with him today. He could still feel her comforting arm around his shoulders, smell the talc in her dressing gown before she'd changed into jeans and a windcheater.

Now here she was in a uniform as stiff and impractical and out-of-place as his own, ploughing along getting sand in her shoes, cursing occasionally, ignoring him. The thought came into his head from nowhere: what would it take to get you to love me?

Love? Going a bit far there, mate.

So Tankard hunched his shoulders a little more, plunged his hands into his pockets, tried to avoid the kelp and the dog shit.

He'd never been a beach person, never been to this stretch of sand before. Penzance Beach seemed to merge with Myers Point, yet on the map they were separate places. A handful of costly holiday houses ranged up and down the cliffs, but mostly he was looking at the flat areas in between, where tiny fibro shacks, nestled in ti-tree clumps, sat right on the edge of the sand.

Their job was to doorknock and look for signs of life or break-and-enter in the apparently empty houses, search any caves they might see in the sides of the cliffs, check out the yacht club, see if anyone was camping, talk to people. Other uniformed police were scouring the empty stretches toward Point Leo in one direction and the navy base in the other. According to Sergeant van Alphen at the briefing, CIB had urged Special Ops to search the beachfront but these requests had been shrugged off, so this was purely a Waterloo operation. There was backup in the form of two patrol cars in radio contact.

Autumn, a chilly wind blowing in off the bay, the place was practically deserted. Every single holiday house was shut up, there was a geezer sewing a torn sail at the yacht club, the ti-trees were impenetrable, one or two retirees walked their dogs, but that was it.

'Everyone else has more sense than to be walking on the beach today,' Tankard said. 'A bloody long shot, if you ask me.'

Pam ignored him. She was treating the exercise as if it was a dead certainty that they'd find Ian Munro and return to the station as heroes.

Come to think of it, she'd hardly said boo since they came on shift. Charging along as though obsessed, face set in an unyielding expression, not interested in talking.

'Cat got your tongue?'

A seagull slipped down the channels in the sky above him and shat at his feet.

'Did you see that? Christ, we need danger money.'

She forged on as if he'd not spoken. He had to hurry to keep pace with her, and his vast inner thighs chafed, his breathing was laboured, he felt sweaty despite the cold wind. 'Oi, slow down, will ya?'

She ignored him.

'What's got your knickers in a twist?'

He hoped *he* hadn't got her knickers in a twist. Hoped she didn't regret taking him in and comforting him. His eyes pricked with tears to remember the pain he felt that day, and still felt sometimes, and which she'd kindly soothed away.

'How's the new car?' he called, knowing that was a safe topic.

If anything, she increased her pace, her back stiffened, her swinging arms positively punched the air around her.

Christ, what had he said wrong now?

Maybe she'd pranged it already. Maybe it was a lemon and kept breaking down. Piece of Japanese shit, give him a V8 Holden any day.

Suddenly she stopped. 'What?' he demanded.

They were at the base of a sheer cliff. On either side of it there was scrub, but the cliff-face itself was yellowish stone and clay. Behind them the sea frothed over rocks that would sandpaper your skin off, the Penzance Beach shop lay to the east, Myers Point around a headland to the west. Tankard and Murphy were alone now, and for the first time he felt spooked.

'What?' he said again.

She pointed at a narrow bit of farmland separating the two townships. 'There's a house up there. Abandoned. Overgrown with creepers and stuff.'

He didn't know of any house on the cliff-top. 'You sure?'

'There's a path here somewhere,' she said, and she veered away from the stony face of the cliff and into the dense ti-tree and bracken thickets at the base. He followed her, and soon they were swallowed up in cool, mysterious hollows and cut off from the sounds of the wind and the sea. The path zigzagged, slowly traversing a gentler slope of the cliffs. The only sound was their breathing, and the sunlight, heavily filtered by the dense canopy of leaves, lay like coins at their feet. Tankard was taken back to the dim recesses of bedtime stories, and shivered.

At the top they broke out into a blackberry thicket and there was the house, of grey, weathered, mouldy fibro and rusted corrugated iron, choked by ferns and bracken. Torn flyscreens on the windows, a torn flyscreen door, bricks missing from the chimney. Tankard glanced again at the chimney. Munro wouldn't be stupid enough to light a fire. The smoke would be a dead giveaway that someone was staying in the house.

But Munro was there. Tankard could feel it in his bones and whispered, 'You stay here, I'll circle around the back.'

'And?'

He hadn't thought that far ahead. He was prepared for events to find their own course, but glanced at his watch and said, 'Allow two minutes, then we both knock and shout, "Police, open up."'

She shrugged. 'It's a plan. But we were told not to approach but to call it in.'

'No time,' Tankard said. He held up his finger, whispered, 'Two minutes,' and began to circle to his right, where the undergrowth was less dense.

And came upon Ian Munro outside the back door of the house, standing waiting for him on a patch of hard-packed, grassless dirt, apparently amused as Tankard blundered around the corner. 'Blundered' was how Tankard replayed the scene in his head later, but right now Munro had a shotgun pointed fair and square at his chest and was full of lean, muscular contempt.

'Hello, copper.'

Tankard froze.

'Don't learn real quick, do you, sunshine?'

Tankard found that his hands were in the air.

'How many of you?'

Tankard swallowed and managed to say, 'A whole heap.'

Munro considered this. 'I don't think so. One other, maybe. Take your gun out—I see they gave you another one.'

That was when Pam rapped her fist on the door at the other end of the house and called, '*Police*,' but it all sounded impossibly far away to John Tankard. Had it really been two minutes? He seemed to inhabit a dream. He saw Munro, momentarily startled, swing the shotgun toward the house, and he seemed to watch his own hands stop clawing at the sky and drop to his holster to unstrap his service revolver. It was smooth, by-the-book, but impossibly slow, and the shotgun swung round on him again to fix on his defenceless chest.

Tankard got his gun out and fired, then dropped it because it kicked so much and numbed his fingers. The shotgun roared, the shot spraying with a whump above his head, and then Munro was collapsing.

When Pam Murphy found him, Tankard was standing over Munro, streaked with tears, asking her over and over again: 'What have I done?'

CHAPTER **FORTY-ONE**

Pam Murphy called it in and detectives and senior uniformed police took control of the scene—and thank God for that, because John Tankard had fallen in a heap. She gave a brief verbal report, then asked if she could take him back to the station.

'You'd be better off taking him to see a doctor,' Sergeant van Alphen said, glancing critically at Tank, who sat weeping on the back porch of the shack. 'Get him tranquillised. Later on he'll have to see a psychologist.'

He looked at Pam then, kindness there somewhere under his wintry features. Not for the first time, Pam was struck by his external resemblance to Inspector Challis: the same stillness and sense of economy, the same dark, intense, considering scrutiny. Except Challis seemed stable where van Alphen had shown last year that he could go off the rails a little. So he should know it when he saw it. Pam watched him look again at Tank and shake his head minutely.

'Sarge?' she said. 'He'll be okay, won't he? I mean, there'll be an inquiry, but there was nothing dirty about the shooting.'

Van Alphen grinned like a shark at her. 'Hell, this is Munro here, dead. They'll give John a medal.'

'Thanks, Sarge.'

'Take him home. No, take him to the station first, familiar surroundings, maybe he'll be up to giving a statement. When the investigators turn up tomorrow, I'll keep them sidetracked for a day or so, give him time to recover.'

'Thanks, Sarge.'

Pam very briefly and discreetly hugged van Alphen, who after a moment's hesitation squeezed her shoulders awkwardly and stared at the ground.

Then she got John Tankard to his feet and begged a lift back to their car from Scobie Sutton, who said, 'Good result, guys.'

He prattled on, praising, talking about the importance of counselling now. Pam knew there was another side to Scobie Sutton, but right now he was a long streak of sweetness and light, as if he should have been a clergyman. 'Thanks,' she said, glad to get herself and Tank out of the CIB car and into their divisional van.

Then back at the station there was more backslapping. She took Tank through to the lockers, telling him to get changed. He was looking stunned, watery eyed, practically had to be led by the hand. Forget giving a statement: she was taking him home.

Except Senior Sergeant Kellock came in then, said, 'Good result, you two,' and took Tank away to make a statement.

So Pam sat there for a while, and thought about Lister, and realised how she could make the loan go away: simply sell the car.

But back out in the corridor she ran into Sergeant Destry, who gave her a cracking smile full of warmth and said, 'Good result today,' and Pam, badly in need of a confessor, found herself saying, 'Sarge, could I have a quick word?'

Ellen Destry was always reminded of her younger self whenever she saw Pam Murphy. Murphy was keen, sharp, ambitious, obliged to put up with lechers and Neanderthals, apt to be secretive and not above stuffing things up.

What she didn't expect to hear was this thing about money: the constant anxiety about it, the lack of it, the hopelessness with managing it. Ellen shook her head, thinking unaccountably of her daughter at that moment, thinking: we keep failing to teach our kids how to live their lives.

Then bad memories came flooding in. Money's going to get *me* into trouble one day too, she thought, and flushed to think of that time last year when she'd pocketed five hundred dollars that she'd found at an arson scene. It was something she did every once in a long while, usually small amounts belonging to crims and never missed. But it was wrong and she liked to think she'd got on top of her problem. Last year she'd given the five hundred dollars to charity: it had been too hard to take it back to the arson scene. It was a kind of light-fingeredness that lingered from childhood, when she'd lifted lollies and comics from the corner shop after school.

She shook off the memories. 'But I thought Lister was an accountant,' she said now, looking intently at Pam Murphy in the hard chair on the other side of her desk.

'He is,' Pam said, apparently surprised not to get bawled out, her head bitten off. 'But he loans money too.'

'And he loaned you thirty thousand.'

'Yes, Sarge.'

'A lot of money.'

'Yes, Sarge.'

'If you'd borrowed something more manageable, like ten thousand—you can get a decent car for under ten thousand—you wouldn't be in this bind.'

Ellen saw Pam bow her head. 'Yes, Sarge.'

'But you don't want a lecture from me. How are you going to repay the loan?'

Pam looked up and with a crooked grin said, 'I'm going to sell the car.'

'You'll lose money on the deal.'

Pam shook her head. 'Not necessarily. It was newish second-hand, so it had already depreciated in value when I bought it. There's a big demand for Subarus, and with any luck I'll get my money back or make a small profit. If there's any shortfall, I'll borrow it from my mother. Once the debt is cleared, Lister can't touch me.'

You're naïve, Ellen thought, giving the younger woman a pitying look. She turned harsh. 'As soon as we arrest him or even question him about anything he'll say he's had his hooks into you. He'll say you gave him sensitive information in exchange for money and you'll face disciplinary action and possibly lose your job.'

Her mind drifted as she spoke, so that she was unmoved by Pam's crestfallen face and hot spurt of tears. She was thinking that Ian Munro borrowed money from Lister because no one else would lend to him, got behind in his repayments, and found himself agreeing to grow marijuana for the man.

But was Skip involved? Had Skip been a spy for his father, urged to visit the Destry household and learn all he could of local police intelligence? The thought was too terrible to contemplate. It would absolutely devastate Larrayne.

'Oh, Christ,' she muttered, and came back to reality only when Pam Murphy said, 'Sarge?'

'So, what are we going to do with you?'

'Don't know, Sarge.'

'How much information did you give to Lister?'

'Nothing that wasn't already public knowledge,' Pam said, clearly trying to make light of it.

'The thing is, Constable, you gave him information for gain. That's how it's going to be seen. Doesn't matter how sensitive or worthless that information was.'

Pam Murphy hung her head. 'Sarge.'

'Did Lister say why he wanted that information?'

'He said he didn't want to lend money to people the police were interested in. He was afraid they'd get arrested and he'd never get his money back.'

'Convenient story.'

'Yes, Sarge. The thing is, he only wanted to know about who was involved with drugs, who the police had their eye on locally, the dealers and pushers.'

Ellen nodded. If Lister was setting up or moving in or manufacturing and selling, or even fighting a turf war, he'd want the kind of information that only the police had.

She didn't say any of this to Pam Murphy. Instead: 'The thing is, Lister's name has cropped up in relation to another matter. Your experience with him helps round out the picture for us. Let's keep this under wraps for now. If asked, I will say that you came to me immediately Lister tried to recruit you, and that we decided to go with it and feed him innocuous information until we could see what he intended to do with it.'

This was a reprieve, and the cares dropped away from Pam Murphy's bowed shoulders and drawn face. 'Thanks heaps, Sarge.'

But Ellen held up a warning hand. 'That doesn't mean that at a later date the truth won't come out if the whole thing goes pear-shaped. You did do the wrong thing.'

'Yes, Sarge.'

'Still, better late than never.'

'Thanks, Sarge.'

As Pam went out the door, Ellen said, 'Did you hear about Brad Pike?'

'Sarge?'

'Dead as a dodo.'

Meanwhile, that Thursday afternoon Scobie Sutton was questioning Dwayne Venn. When the tape was rolling and

Venn had been cautioned and had again waived his right to have a lawyer present, Scobie began, Challis to one side, distracted, looking deeply, darkly fatigued, the way he leaned one shoulder against the grimy wall. If there was a tide mark on the wall at floor-mop height, there was also another at shoulder height, where weary or frankly disbelieving detectives liked to rest their head and shoulders.

'Dwayne, take us through it again.'

'I already told you what happened.'

'This time for the tape.'

Venn looked sleepy yet wired, as if he'd been taking a drug cocktail for the past few days. He needed a shave and smelt badly unwashed under the white paper suit he'd been obliged to wear after his jeans, T-shirt and trainers had been taken away for testing.

'Well, Brad come round last night and—'

'He came to the house? Lisa Tully's house?'

'Actually the lease is in Donna's name.'

'Who lives there?'

'Lisa and Donna.'

'Anyone else?'

'No, mate.'

'You were there too?'

'Just visiting.'

'Do you live there, Mr Venn?' Challis said suddenly.

'It's not, like, my place, but I like to pop in now and then, yeah.'

'Are you sleeping with Lisa? Donna? Both of them?' Challis demanded.

'Buggered if I'm telling you about my sex life. Look, me and Lisa and Donna come here in good faith, told you we solved the case you fuckers couldn't solve, and what happens? You want to know about my fucking sex life. No wonder you couldn't find Lisa's kid. She—'

'It's only background we're after, Dwayne.' Bloody Challis, Sutton thought. He put his hands up placatingly. 'So, tell us what happened next. You were at the Tully sisters' house when Brad Pike showed up, correct?'

'Yeah.'

'Then what happened?'

'We got talking and—'

'Were you drinking?' Challis said harshly.

'So what if we were?'

'Drugs? Dope, speed?'

'No way.'

'Dwayne,' Sutton said gently, 'the house was reeking with it.'

Venn folded his arms stubbornly. 'Brad brung some stuff with him. We didn't want any. It was him stunk the place up.'

'We're only trying to get the truth of what happened, Dwayne. If your judgement was impaired because of drugs, that could be seen as mitigating circumstances in court.'

A light seemed to come on in Venn's eyes and he narrowed them. 'Hang on, Pike come at me, tried to kill me. I had to defend myself.'

Challis snapped forward across the rocky table, hard and implacable. 'The evidence suggests otherwise. He was beaten about the head with a cricket bat or something similar and—'

'Cricket bat?'

Scobie, watching Venn at that moment, thought, this is a man who surrounds himself with Jim Beam whisky, a Harley Davidson motorbike, posters and artifacts of the American Indians—what does he know about cricket, a game for Englishmen? 'Or baseball bat,' he said. 'We found a broken one in the alley behind the house.'

'Never underestimate the stupidity of your local crim,' Challis snarled.

What's got into Challis? Sutton thought. Like a bear with a sore tooth. 'Okay, Dwayne, Pike attacked you. Then what?'

'I defended myself.'

'How?'

'Me fists. I got in a lucky one and he went down and hit his head on something. Maybe a bottle, that would explain the type of mark on his head.'

'Very full of himself. A man with all the answers,' Challis said.

'Fuck you. I come here in good faith and—'

'The pathologist said that Pike was asphyxiated,' Sutton said. 'From the way the blood is smeared against Pike's face she thinks a plastic bag was used. We haven't found the bag yet, but we will, just as we'll find traces of the bag on Pike.' Giving Challis a sharp, sidelong glance as he said it, as if to say, I can come on strong too, just back off for a while, okay?

Venn said stubbornly, 'I'm not saying no more.'

At least he hasn't asked for a lawyer yet, Scobie thought. 'Then what happened?'

Venn looked at him sulkily. After a few seconds of that, he deigned to answer. 'Before Brad passed out he told us what he done with Lisa's kid.'

'You believed him?'

'Well, yeah. It was a deathbed confession,' Venn said, enunciating 'deathbed confession' carefully, apparently pleased with the expression.

What a dickhead, Scobie thought, and he began the recitation: 'Dwayne Venn, I'm arresting you on suspicion in the murder of Bradley Pike on the fifteenth of—'

Venn's jaw dropped. 'You can't do that. We come here in good faith and—'

John Tankard said, 'I can't get it out of my head.'

'I know,' Pam said.

She was driving, taking him home, a comforting presence beside him. Every now and then she said, 'I know,' smiling kindly. How could he resist the power of her kindness, her weary compassion? She wasn't judging him, coming on hard and sharp like Kellock back at the station a few minutes ago, Kellock half pleased that Munro was dead but mostly worried about what the press would say, police involved in another fatal shooting.

'I just shot. It was instinct. Pure instinct, Pam. Pow, just like that.'

Funny how his feelings seesawed. One minute he wanted to hide or die or cry all day, then a surge of elation.

'I mean, God . . .'

'You probably saved both our lives,' Pam said.

Now his feelings were going the other way again. Everyone patting him on the back like he was this quick-shooting, quick-thinking hero, when really he'd more or less panicked again, got in a lucky shot. The gun hadn't felt good in his hand. It was a lucky, panicky shot.

And he'd killed a man.

'Oh God,' he said, and put his hands over his face.

Thank Christ they'd been obliged to take his gun into evidence. He didn't want to see another gun as long as he lived.

They reached his flat and as she parked against the kerb he said, 'Look, I need to be alone, no offence, I just—'

'If you're sure, Tank,' Pam said, giving him a brief hug and thanking him again for saving their lives.

So his feelings soared again.

Then she was driving away quickly, too quickly, and he wondered how genuine she really was. Bitch.

CHAPTER **FORTY-TWO**

It was early evening and the phone rang and his wife said, 'Hal, I'm so miserable.'

Challis said nothing. He listened to time tick away. He didn't want to encourage her.

'If it wasn't for you I don't know what I'd do. I've always needed you.'

This time he reacted. 'No you haven't, Ange. There was a time when you didn't want or need me at all.'

'Don't be like that.'

'Like what?'

'All mean.'

He said nothing. He was a fool to have said anything.

'I just lost my head for a while back then, that's all. Besides, you were always working, never home. But I soon got my head together. It was you I've always really wanted.'

'Ange, it's too late.'

He hadn't said that to her before. Or not so directly, for fear of her fragile state. But now he didn't care about that.

She wailed, 'No it's not.'

'We divorce, we go our separate ways.'

'No.' Then she unravelled further. 'No, you can't do this to me.'

He said gently, 'I have to.'

'I'll kill myself if I can't have you.'

She'd said that before, she'd go on saying it. He said goodbye, replaced the receiver on the wall mount, and five minutes later Tessa Kane rang. His nerves were on edge when he answered.

'I'm trying to get an angle on the Janet Casement thing.'

'It's not a thing. She's not a thing. There is no angle. Someone hated her enough to kill her, and it's tragic, okay?'

'Who got out on the wrong side of the bed this morning? And there *is* an angle, Hal. You said it yourself, someone hated her enough to shoot her, which raises two questions: one, are you saying Munro *didn't* do it? Two, whether he did or didn't, *why* was she shot? Come on, Hal, I need a good story here.'

'Tess, you've had wall-to-wall good stories for the past fortnight.'

'Fine, I'll go elsewhere.'

'You do that.'

'I'll speak to you when you're feeling more civil.'

'Fine.'

She didn't say anything but broke the connection and then McQuarrie called. 'Good result, Hal.'

'Yes, sir.'

'One more mongrel off the streets.'

As if to say that Munro had been roaming the streets shooting innocent people. 'Yes.'

'Good for our clean-up rate: four murders, one culprit.'

'Sir, I have grave doubts about that.'

'Don't be silly, Hal. Do us all a favour. Look at the common denominators: a shotgun was used, and one disaffected man, who owns a number of shotguns, had a reason to kill all four victims.' The superintendent paused. 'All right, indulge me. How do you see it?'

'I think Janet Casement's killing was opportunistic. I think the fact that a shotgun was used in the other killings is coincidental.'

'You're not saying three killers, one for each scene?'

'No. I think there were two.'

'Can you prove it?'

'I don't know. I'm working on it.'

'Image is important, Hal. Image matters. So does morale. If your leads don't pan out, it's not going to be the end of the world if Munro is saddled with all four deaths.'

Challis had been dealing with politicians like McQuarrie for all of his life. Something happened when you got too senior, within reach of Force Command. You stopped policing and started politicking.

Seven forty-five, mid-evening. The three calls soured Challis, spoilt the air for him. He could be in St Kilda within an hour, and have more chance of learning something about Trevor Hubble than if he called during the day, when people might not be at home.

He locked the house and drove out of his gate, heading for the highway. It was good to be on the move but, inexorably, Kitty Casement was there in his head again. The preliminary post-mortem results had come in that afternoon and were as expected: she hadn't been poisoned or bludgeoned before she was shot. She had no fatal illnesses or diseases. Her stomach contents revealed that she'd eaten a sandwich some hours earlier and nothing since then. So, cause of death was a shotgun wound to the occipital region, most likely a contact wound, given the massive but localised damage to bone and tissue.

Fortunately they knew who she was, for the damage to her facial bones, tissue and teeth would have made it next to impossible to reconstruct her face or to match dental records.

Blood type O, about half of the population.

Challis sighed, shook Kitty out of his head, determined to get something positive from the evening.

By twenty to nine he was on Beaconsfield Parade, buoyed by the lights on the water, the streaming cars and the hint of cheerful seediness in the guesthouses and flats that faced the bay. He found Duke Street, found a young woman at home at Hubble's old address.

Her name was Sienna. Just Sienna. She was an artist.

'Oh, he moved back to England,' she said, showing Challis into a sitting room. He glanced around: glossy hardwood floors, thick woollen rugs, black leather sofa and armchairs, floor-to-ceiling bookshelves. A hint of linseed oil in the air, and he guessed that she had a studio in one of the other rooms.

'Do you know where in England?'

'He's a Londoner, I think. He was homesick. Went back there with his girlfriend a couple of years ago.'

'You bought this house from him?'

Sienna folded her thin arms and shook her head emphatically. 'I already owned it—with my husband. Trevor Hubble rented it from us.'

'You moved in when he left?'

'Not quite. His friend took over his lease.'

'His friend. Do you have a name?'

'Something Billings.'

'Could I see a copy of the lease?'

Sienna looked embarrassed. 'It was all pretty casual. We didn't draw up a new lease for this Billings—I mean, he was Trevor's friend and very personable and everything. He always paid the rent on time, in cash, didn't trash the place, seemed like a nice guy. Silly of me, I suppose, but I trusted him.'

'Where is Billings now?'

'I don't know. He left kind of suddenly and I don't have a forwarding address.'

'When did you move in?'

Sienna kicked one foot and played with an earring as she watched Challis. 'Late October last year.'

Around the time that Trevor Hubble had returned to Australia and the Floater was found, he thought. 'You weren't interested in finding someone else to rent the house?'

'My husband and I had just separated, so when Billings said he was moving out, I moved in.'

'What about his mail?'

'There's never been any for him. I get some for Trevor from time to time, but I don't have an address for him either.'

'You never saw Trevor Hubble again?'

'Far as I know, he's still in England.'

Challis shook his head. 'In fact, he came back just before you moved in here.'

Sienna didn't know what to make of that, and looked at him as though he'd subtly accused her of something. 'Oh, well . . .'

'Yet there's evidence,' Challis said, 'that he was living here during the period he was supposedly in London.'

She looked bewildered. 'How do you know?'

'We've tracked down credit card statements, phone and electricity bills . . .'

'Perhaps Billings paid the bills in Trevor's name,' she mused, 'but surely he wouldn't use Trevor's credit card?'

Challis merely watched her.

'Look, all I know is, Trev said goodbye and moved back to England in 1999. Billings moved in, and I didn't hear anything about Trevor returning to Australia. His girlfriend did, but Trevor didn't. She only lasted in England a few months.'

'Did you see her again?'

'We got kind of friendly when she lived here with Trev. It was always she who brought me the rent. We'd natter, you know. Then when she came back from England she asked me if it would be all right if she took a room here. It was all right with me, but Billings didn't like the idea. He'd been friendly with her when Trevor was on the scene, but now he was quite cold with her.'

'Do you stay in touch with her?'

'She moved to Queensland.'

'But do you stay in touch?'

'I've got her number somewhere.'

She crossed to a small cabinet and took out an address book, scribbled a number on a scrap of notepaper, and handed it to Challis. 'Look, can you tell me what this is all about? I should have asked you at the start, but I didn't want to seem as if I was poking my nose in, but now my curiosity has got the better of me,' she said, half embarrassed, half imploring, running out of breath as though she knew that something bad had happened to people she'd known and trusted.

'We think we've found Trevor Hubble's body,' Challis said. 'He'd been murdered.'

Her jaw dropped. 'Where? Here in Australia?'

'Yes.'

'When?'

'About the time that Billings moved out of this house.'

He could see her thinking about that. 'Was Billings pretending to be him?'

Challis's gesture said that he didn't know but she'd probably made a good guess.

CHAPTER **FORTY-THREE**

He'd tried the number for Hubble's girlfriend last night, in the car, driving back to the Peninsula in a settling fog, and got a sleepy, surly voice saying she'd left Queensland and moved to Melbourne. Challis scrawled her new phone number into his notebook but didn't call. It was late by then, too late to call.

So he thought he'd try from work on Friday morning, but just as he'd brewed the coffee and was reaching for the phone, Ellen Destry appeared in his doorway and said, 'Got a minute?'

Challis closed his notebook and gestured to the chair on the other side of his desk. 'My time is yours.'

'You've never thought Munro shot the Meddler and his wife, right?'

'Right.'

'Do you think he shot Janet Casement?'

'Everyone else seems to think so.' Challis folded his arms and leaned back in his chair. 'The super practically told me so. "Good result, Hal," he said, in that glorious way of his.'

Ellen gave him a grin, her face losing its seriousness, becoming briefly ironical, likeable, disrespectful. Then it faded and she said, 'I think we can put Carl Lister in the frame.'

Challis nodded slowly. 'Go on.'

'He's a loan shark on the side.'

'Uh-huh.'

'This next bit's in confidence. It involves one of the uniforms and I don't want to get this officer into unnecessary trouble.'

Challis stared hard at her, then shrugged. 'It's your call, Ells.'

'Pam Murphy.'

'She's a good officer,' Challis said.

'You keep saying that. The thing is, well, she seems to have stuffed things up a little.'

'Go on.'

'She borrowed money from Lister to buy a new car. Couldn't meet the repayments, so Lister kindly came to an arrangement with her.'

Challis frowned. 'Sex? What's that got to do with the shootings?'

Challis saw Ellen shudder. 'I can't imagine Murphy agreeing to have sex with that creep. No, in exchange for information, Lister went easy on the interest payments. Basically, he wanted police intelligence on the local drug scene.'

Challis swung in his chair and stared moodily out of the window, toying with his coffee mug. 'You think Munro owed him money too?'

'Bet on it.'

'Couldn't meet the repayments so Lister told him to put in a marijuana crop.'

'Yes.'

Challis swung back. He felt the interest stirring in him again. 'The Meddler somehow got wind of it, blackmailed them maybe, or was seen poking around, so Lister shot him and his wife.'

'It was more of a Lister kind of shooting than a Munro kind of shooting, if you get me,' Ellen said. 'Carefully staged, etcetera, etcetera.'

'You don't like him, do you?'

'Never did. Not from the very start. I think he's got his son involved in selling and distributing drugs up at the university and probably the local rave scene, kids' parties, that kind of thing. I think he wanted to know what *we* know so he could stay a step ahead or undermine the opposition. He always struck me as calculating. Munro was more hot-headed. Munro was always going to run off the rails.'

'Did Pam Murphy give Lister anything useful?'

'She says not—or nothing crucial. Says she named a couple of local junkies, that's all. But says that Lister was starting to get nasty, starting to put pressure on her.'

'Is that when she came to see you?'

Ellen nodded.

'And you think Lister killed Kitty too?'

'It makes sense, doesn't it?'

'It does if she was killed because of that photograph.'

'Hal, what if it wasn't just the photograph?'

'Look, Ellen, Kitty is dead now, I feel bad about it but it's not as if there was ever anything between us, despite what you think. So if you think she was bent, please just say so.'

'I never thought you were romantically involved. I never thought that. But I could tell you liked her.'

'Okay, I liked her. But I didn't know much about her, so I don't know why she was murdered. So for Christ's sake, lay out your theories.'

Ellen made a brief face at him, then said, 'Well, we've more or less been over it all before. She was innocently involved. She sold Munro the photograph without knowing what it depicted. Munro told Lister, and it's the kind of thing that festers, and eventually he decides to get rid of her.'

'Strange way to go about it, though, first trying to ram her plane.'

'In some ways, maybe, but it had the same throw-the-police-off-the-scent elements about it as the murder-suicide of the Meddler and his wife. Perhaps he hoped we'd think it was drunken kids joyriding in a stolen car, and waste a lot of time investigating in that direction.'

Challis nodded. 'I see your point. But then she was simply shot. Nothing complicated or ambiguous about that.'

'Opportunistic,' Ellen said.

Challis felt a slow burn inside. He leaned his forearms on the desk. A cloud passed over the face of the sun, darkening his window then flooding it with autumn light again. 'This is how Lister figures it. Munro has gone off the rails. He's out there roaming around with a shotgun, which he's already used on people he hates. So why not pin another death on Munro? He's bound to be shot dead by the police, and if he isn't, who's going to believe that he didn't shoot Kitty?'

Ellen nodded.

'But why?' Challis said. 'That's what it comes down to.'

'The photo.'

'I need more than that. Kitty showed that photo to Munro months ago. Why would Lister fear it now?'

'We've already covered that. Kitty knew what it depicted and blackmailed Munro, who told Lister, or she ripped them off, or she bought into their little racket.'

Not the Kitty I knew, Challis wanted to say. They were silent. Then Ellen said, 'Have we got enough for a warrant to search Lister's place?'

'Not even close.'

'Can we go and talk to him at least?'

Challis reached for his jacket. 'Don't see why not.'

On the way there in the Triumph, Challis said, 'What does the son study?'

'Chemical engineering.'

'Chemical?' Challis said heavily.

He sensed a stillness in Ellen, and went on: 'The father has burns to his face and arms.'

Ellen began to nod her head. 'Lab explosion,' she said. 'But I ran his name past the Drug Squad, and they don't know him.'

'That doesn't mean anything. He was careful, that's all. Just not careful enough with the old Bunsen burners.'

'Bunsen burners,' Ellen said with feeling. 'God, that takes me back.' She sank into her seat and glanced at Challis. 'Ever visited a high school, you know, to give a talk?'

Challis nodded. 'They all smell the same,' he said. 'Sweaty socks, chem lab, hormones.'

'Chalk, whiteboard markers, tampons, cleaning fluids.'

They came to Carl Lister's gate. Challis pressed the intercom, announced who he was, and some time later both Listers appeared, Skip from around the side of the house, Carl through the front door.

'Interesting,' Challis murmured.

'Think Skip was in the lab? Carl warned him to come out?'

'Possibly. Let's see if Carl will allow us to take a bit of a stroll in the grounds.'

Lister reached the gate ahead of his son and said, 'What can I do for you?' He peered. 'Ellen, hi.'

Then Skip was there. He wouldn't meet their gaze but muttered, 'Hello, Mrs Destry.'

'Hello, Skip.' Challis saw her staring hard at the boy, then heard her say, 'Larrayne would appreciate it if you could give her a call.'

Skip shuffled under the scrutiny, shaping the gravel with the toe of his shoe.

'What can we do for you?' Carl said again.

'Perhaps we could come in and have a quick word?'

'What about? It's just that I've been sweeping leaves—they're all over the back lawn—and then I have to meet a client and I don't really have much time for—'

'It won't take a moment. Better than all of us yelling through the gate at each other,' Ellen said.

Lister exchanged a glance with Skip. 'Put the rake away, son.'

Skip frowned, then his brow cleared and he strolled away with his hands in his pockets toward the rear of the house. But he was too tightly sprung, hurrying a little too much, to pass it off as a casual stroll. Challis watched him go down the side of the house and disappear.

Only then did Lister open the gate for the Triumph. He left it open, as though he didn't expect them to stay long. Challis drove past him and along the driveway, parking outside the front door. He got out, Ellen got out, just as Lister reached them. The chemical smell was stronger here and Lister, apparently conscious of it, said, 'Come in out of the cold. Days are getting chilly, have you noticed?'

'Perhaps we should take a brisk walk,' Ellen said, 'get the circulation going.'

Lister forced a laugh. 'What? And disturb my leaves, all nicely raked into neat piles? No, no, come inside.'

They stepped onto the verandah. The sound when it came was muffled, but clearly an explosion. The ground shook, reaching them as a diminishing shock wave, and Challis ran to the rear of the house in time to see acrid smoke boiling out of a rupture in the dirt. Then there was another explosion and part of a concrete slab tore free from the grass and more smoke poured out.

Lister screamed, '*Skip*,' and began to run. Afterwards Ellen told Challis that there was more heartbreak in the voice than she'd have thought possible.

CHAPTER **FORTY-FOUR**

'So there's no doubt?' said Scobie on Saturday morning, in the passenger seat this time.

'None,' Challis said. 'Lister confessed, for a start. And the evidence is there, despite the explosion. A pill-pressing machine, buckets full of powder, dye, sinus tablets, you name it.'

'And the kid?'

'Badly burnt, but he'll live, just.'

Sutton shook his head. 'Burns. It's what I fear most, Roslyn pulling a saucepan down on herself, or playing with matches and her clothes catch fire.'

Challis tuned out. Lister, distraught to the point of collapse, and then wracked with guilt, had told them everything yesterday. Yes, he'd been manufacturing amphetamines in an underground laboratory behind the house. Skip had been helping him. He was not proud of that fact. He was not a good father. He'd *made* the kid help him; had brought the kid up in a culture of sly dealing.

Ellen had burst out: 'My daughter loved him.'

Lister had hung his head. 'I know. And I think he was keen on her. But he felt guilty. He—'

Challis broke in. 'Tell us about your burns.'

A lab explosion a few years ago, Lister explained. He'd been living in Sydney then. This time he'd thought he was safer: more know-how, better equipment, Skip's university training.

Then he'd collapsed and they'd had to postpone the questioning.

Later, with a mild sedative under his belt, he'd continued to spill . . .

Yes, he was a loan shark. If anyone couldn't make the repayments he'd work something out with them, *quid pro quo*.

'Ian Munro?'

'He put the marijuana crop in for me. Actually, he leapt at the idea. Unstable bugger. I should never—'

'You harvested the crop? Sold it?'

Lister had shaken his head. 'Burnt it to the ground as soon as that aerial photograph showed up.'

'Is that why Janet Casement had to die? She was a loose end? Why wait so long?'

'I was going to ignore it but it kept niggling at me. Plus Munro was getting more and more unstable and I thought if he got himself arrested for punching someone from the shire or whatever, then the cops might start sniffing around.'

'You would have been better off killing Munro than Janet Casement.'

'You can say that again.'

'So why try to ram her plane? Why not just shoot her to begin with?'

'I wanted it to look like an accident. I mean, like maybe a drunk or someone stoned was responsible. Less suspicious that way.'

'It turned out to be *very* suspicious,' Challis told him. 'From my point of view, anyway. Who drove? You? Munro?'

'Munro didn't know anything about it. No, it was me.'

'Taking a risk,' said Ellen flatly.

Lister shrugged. 'I was going to hire a junkie, but that would've been a greater risk.'

'When that failed,' Challis said, 'you told Munro to shoot her. Or was that you?'

Lister had shaken his head, looking puzzled. 'Wasn't me, I'm telling you that now. Must've been Munro, mustn't it? I mean, he shot his lawyer, even told me he was going to do it, and I tried to talk him out of it. He might have shot that other couple as well, and the Casement woman, but I don't really know. He never mentioned them, and I never put him up to any shooting.'

'Oh, that's convenient,' Ellen said. 'You cough up to the lesser charge, an attempt on someone's life, but not to being a party to an actual killing. Having second thoughts, are you? Starting to regret spilling your guts the moment your son is almost killed, trying to claw back some lost ground now, is that right? You disgust me, Carl.'

And Carl Lister had turned a damp, distressed face to her and said, 'I know I do. You should throw away the key. But I don't know anything about the shootings, none of them.'

'And that's where we stand,' Challis said now, Scobie beside him in the passenger seat.

'I wonder how Ellen's kid is taking it,' Scobie said. He sat with one finger inside a street directory and was ducking his long, narrow head to peer up at passing street signs.

'Not good, apparently,' Challis said. 'That's why Ellen's taken the day off.'

'Think of the misery that guy's caused.'

'Lister, or the son?'

'Lister, mainly.'

'Where were you on Easter Saturday?' Challis had asked him.

Lister cocked his head. 'You're talking about the beach, right? When I saw that reporter at Munro's place the other day, I thought I recognised her. We went to the beach to collect a shipment of sinus tablets—brought down from Queensland by boat, it's safer that way than by road. Didn't count on the storm.'

Then Ellen asked him about Pam Murphy. Lister had waved it away. 'She didn't tell me anything I didn't already know.'

'She came to me and reported the blackmail.'

'So?'

'So I don't want you using it in any way. It won't help in your defence, it'll only make things worse for you if we call it attempting to blackmail a police officer.'

Lister had shrugged. 'I've got nothing against her. Water under the bridge.' He went on without a change of pace: 'I feel shithouse about Skip, can't you see that? I want to get things off my chest.'

Ellen had stared at him in disbelief. 'Constable Murphy is going to sell her car and pay back the loan.'

Lister rubbed his face violently, clearly fatigued now. 'I suppose it will come in handy. Legal fees. Hospital expenses.'

'You disgust me,' Ellen had said.

Challis didn't say any of this to Scobie Sutton now. Sutton wouldn't blab or use it in any way, but the Pam Murphy business should stay buried.

'Here we are,' Sutton said, 'next street on your right.'

They'd taken the Peninsula Freeway to Frankston, then cut across to the Nepean Highway, which hugged the bay one street back from the water, glimpsed now and then down the side streets. It was a cheerless, red-tile stretch of the city, despite the water: flat, sun-baked, a sameness to the houses relieved only by ugly Italianate villas, their terracotta tiles and white plaster columns glaring in the autumn sunlight.

Challis turned right, across traffic and into a narrow street that dropped away in a curve of 1950s triple-fronted brick veneers. Number 40 was in cream brick, the lawn parched, a Mazda bubble car in the carport at the side.

'Someone's home,' Sutton murmured.

Challis gave a faint headshake of irritation. He wouldn't have come all this way without checking that fact first.

Louise Cook was about forty, with shapeless carroty hair and the dry, lined face of a chain smoker. She had a smoker's cough and took them into her sitting room as if desperate for the relief of her armchair and nearby coffee table and ashtray.

But then she struggled to her feet again, saying breathlessly, 'Tea? Coffee?'

'Nothing thanks,' Challis said firmly. He didn't want to stay here for long, and saw her sit back relievedly and give him an expectant look.

'You want to know about Trevor?'

'You went to England with him in 1999.'

'That's right.'

'But you came back and he stayed on.'

'Yes. He was from London originally, but I'm from here, and I got homesick. Plus it was so cold and expensive in London.'

'Did you stay in touch?'

'Off and on. It was a fairly amicable split. No grand passion or anything.'

'What can you tell me about Billings, the man who took over Trevor's rental agreement for the St Kilda house?'

'He was a nasty piece of work. All I wanted when I got back to Australia was a room for a while, till I was on my feet again, kind of thing. Bastard shut the door in my face.'

'Before then. When you and Trevor Hubble first met him, before you went to London.'

'Trev and I had this carpet cleaning business. That's how we met Billings. We got talking, got friendly, he and Trev both came from the same part of London so they had stuff in common, and in the end he invested in our business so we could afford to go to England. He retained financial control, kind of thing.'

'What happened to the business?'

Cook gestured. 'You tell me. We wrote to him from England but he never replied. Then when I came back and tried to see him, he slammed the door in my face.'

'But he was friendly at the start and gave you money?'

'More or less, yeah. It was all legal.'

'I'm not interested in the financial aspects, or not as such,' Challis said. 'Tell me more about Billings.'

'Well, like I said, he was friendly, generous, offered to look after the business for us. I know Trev left a lot of paperwork with him.'

'What kind?'

'Banking matters and stuff like that. Documents. For safe-keeping, kind of thing.' She gestured at Scobie Sutton. 'What's his story? Doesn't he speak? Is he your boss or something?'

Sutton, who'd found out about the active accounts and bills in Hubble's name, gave her a tired smile and said, 'When did you last see Mr Hubble?'

'I told you, when I said goodbye in London.'

'But you stayed in touch after that?'

'Couple of letters,' she muttered. 'Couple of phone calls. He didn't seem very happy.'

'With your leaving him?'

'No, well, maybe, but mainly he was unhappy living in London again. Too expensive, couldn't get a decent job, couldn't start up in business, had no family left, no friends to speak of.'

Now Challis knew why no one reported him missing in either country. 'So he came back to Australia?'

She shrugged, which seemed to aggravate her cough. They waited until she'd finished, half concerned that she might die in the meantime, for the coughing fit left her washed out.

'All I know is, he said he thought he'd come back here and take up where he'd left off.'

'Cleaning carpets?'

'I suppose.'

'Did he tell Billings to expect him?'

She shrugged. 'I suppose so.'

'What about you? Didn't you want to be part of the business again?'

'It wasn't like I'd put money into it. Plus Trevor and I were finished, and the chemicals used to give me a rash, and I'd met someone else.' She seemed to incline her head toward the hallway that led to the bedrooms. 'We live together. He's at work now. He's never met Trevor or Billings, in case you want to question him.'

Challis shook his head. He leaned forward. 'So it's probable that Trevor told Billings he was returning to Australia.'

She barely shrugged.

'Have you got a photo of Trevor Hubble?'

'Somewhere.'

'And anything he might have handled, like a photo album, a book . . .'

She frowned. 'I'll have a look, but what's this about? What's he done?'

'Nothing that we know of.'

'But it sounds like you need his fingerprints. That plus a photo . . .'

'Identification purposes,' Scobie said.

She stared at him and finally said, 'You found a body.'

Challis said gently, 'Yes. In the bay.'

She got excited now, jerking in her chair, coughing, which left her red-faced and gasping. 'Billings had a boat.'

'Did he now?'

'Go and arrest the bastard.'

'Do you know where he is?'

'No.'

'Can you tell us anything about him? Movements, habits . . . any photographs?'

She was thinking glumly, holding her chest and wheezing a little. She glanced up. 'I've got a mobile phone number somewhere.'

In the end it was Sutton who got up and went into the kitchen for her, coming back with a buttery address book. He looked up 'Billings' and wrote the number in his notebook.

'Try it,' Challis said.

'He's probably changed the number by now, people do that, they chop and change companies.'

'These days you can keep your number even if you change companies,' Louise Cook said, watching them with brightening eyes. She's enjoying this, Challis thought.

'Let me try it,' he said, fishing for his mobile phone.

Scobie read him the number, he dialled, and a calm English voice crackled in his ear immediately: 'Rex Casement.'

CHAPTER **FORTY-FIVE**

Back in the Displan room in Waterloo, Challis called Ellen at home, saying he needed her for an urgent briefing, and when they were all gathered he took them through the Casement story as he saw it. 'So,' he concluded, 'we got him because he kept his old mobile phone number.'

They shook their heads. They'd seen it time and time again. This was a variation on Kellock's illegal parking theory. Ellen said, 'He simply announced his name?'

'Yes.'

'How does he keep track of who he's supposed to be?'

'This guy is focused. He has to be.'

'Except he kept his old phone number.'

'Except for that.'

'What did he say?'

'Very cagey. Wanted to know how I'd got his number. I'd thought of hanging up, saying wrong number, but I thought that would look more suspicious.'

And so Challis had improvised, telling Casement that he was simply doing his job, that he was sitting in a call centre full of similar operators, going down a list of mobile phone numbers on behalf of a charity. Who gave you the list of numbers? Casement had demanded. Challis had said he didn't know, he was just doing his job, but maybe the phone company itself had sold the list. 'Bastards,' Casement had said.

'So I apologised and got off the phone quickly.'

'He didn't recognise your voice?'

'Don't think so. Not in that context.'

'So who is he?'

'I've contacted Scotland Yard, asked them to look into the names Casement and Billings. Given that he used original documents to pass himself off as both names, it's possible they're actual people—who might or might not be dead now.'

'So we're looking at him for killing his wife?'

'And Trevor Hubble,' Challis said, perching on the table next to the whiteboard. 'Let's deal with Hubble first. Suppose Casement is on the run. He comes to Australia using the name Billings, meets Hubble, and takes on Hubble's identity when Hubble gets homesick and returns to England. But then Hubble gets restless again and returns to Australia, so Casement/Billings feels threatened. He takes Hubble out on his boat, kills him, leaves the St Kilda house and moves down to the Peninsula. He meets Kitty and they get married. Being married was good cover and gave him some badly needed legitimacy.'

He paused. 'We need hard evidence. His boat, for starters. We know from Louise Cook that he had one. Does he still have it? Where is it moored? Can we get a warrant to search it? Hubble's fingerprints would be nice.'

'Global positioning system,' Scobie said suddenly.

'What's that when it's at home?' asked van Alphen, who was there on loan from Kellock.

'Something to do with navigation. It can tell us where the yacht has been, and when.'

Challis pointed to van Alphen. 'Van, I want you to find the yacht and get a warrant to search it and examine its global positioning gizmo. There's also the matter of the anchor used to weigh down Hubble's body. Has it turned up yet?'

They shook their heads, unsurprised by the world. Cops stole or misplaced or borrowed evidence all the time. Who would miss an anchor? Why would it ever be needed again?

'Next, Janet, his wife,' Challis went on. 'It's possible that she got too nosy, or twigged to who he was, or maybe she'd been in on the deal from the start and had become a liability. Either way, it was an opportunistic killing because it could be blamed on Munro.'

'Maybe she was bringing unwanted police attention home with her,' Ellen said. 'First when Lister rammed her plane, then when we found the photograph.'

Van Alphen scoffed. 'So why kill her and *guarantee* police attention?'

'Sympathy, not suspicion,' Challis said. 'And it could be that he stands to gain in other ways. Scobie, I want you to look into their finances. Does Casement have money of his own? Did Kitty? Does Casement inherit? How much? Did he take out any insurance policies on her life lately? And so on.'

Scobie and the others made to close their folders and go, but Challis held up his hand. 'Not yet. There's the matter of the Meddler and his wife.'

He could see sceptical faces watching him. 'Bear with me. Lister told us that he didn't shoot them or order them shot, and I believe him. He also said that Munro talked of killing the lawyer, but not of killing the Meddler and his wife. Why be coy about them? He also said nothing to Lister about shooting Janet Casement. I think Rex Casement goes to the top of the list for the Meddler shootings as well.'

'Motive?'

'This is the Meddler we're talking about. He got up people's noses. He dobbed them in or threatened to. What if he found out who Casement really was?'

'If he did, why didn't he report him to the police?'

'Frustration?' Challis said. 'Greed? Perhaps he thought he could profit from it in some way, try a bit of blackmail. He's not going to try blackmailing someone who dumps rubbish or doesn't feed his sheep, but Casement was a different kettle of fish. If he's living under assumed names then it's probably for something big, like fraud—something worth black-mailing for.'

'So we need to hear back from Scotland Yard?'

'And we need to go back and search the Pearce house again,' Challis said. 'Ellen, you come with me. The rest of you, you know what to do.'

They were crossing the carpark when his mobile phone rang.

'Inspector Challis? You gave me your number just in case.'

'Who's talking?'

'Louise Cook.'

'Yes, Louise.'

'Um, I think I did something stupid. But I was that mad.'

Challis clenched inside, knowing what to expect. 'What did you do?'

'I rang that mobile phone number I gave you. Billings answered and it definitely *was* him, even though he gave a different name.'

'And?'

'And I got mad at him. Told him I knew he killed Trevor.'

'Christ.'

'Look, I'm really sorry. It's just I felt—'

'When?'

'What?'

'When the bloody hell did you call him?'

'There's no need to be like that. I did the right thing, I called you straightaway, soon as I realised it was him.'

'But you warned him, and now he'll run and now your own life is in danger. Christ.'

CHAPTER **FORTY-SIX**

'How's John Tankard?'

'Not too bad,' Pam Murphy said. She was driving, Challis beside her, van Alphen and Ellen in the back seat.

'Is he getting couselling?'

Challis sensed resistance in her. She's protecting her own, he thought. She doesn't like this line of questioning. She drove expertly, at speed, along the coast road toward Penzance Beach and the turnoff for Upper Penzance, and deflected him: 'Will Casement run, sir?'

'He has before. He'll have a contingency plan, new ID to slip into.'

'Do you think he'll be there?'

'I hope so, but drive like the clappers even so.'

'Will he be armed if he is?'

'There's a good chance.'

And so they were armed. And armed backup would follow behind them as soon as Senior Sergeant Kellock could muster some more uniforms. Unfortunately there were officers down with the flu and others attending at a four-car pile-up at the corner of Myers and Coolart roads. The Meddler had been right about that intersection: why the hell had they installed give-way rather than stop signs?

Challis watched Pam Murphy brake and corner with a flick of the wheel onto Five Furlong Road. There was something a little staged about the manoeuvre, something a little self-conscious. She'd driven pursuit cars in her last posting; she was still young enough to want to show off. She wanted to join CIB but the uniform allowed her to do the fun stuff, like drive at speed, siren on, telling the world to step out of her way.

'Damn, there he is,' Challis said.

This part of Five Furlong Road was narrow, rutted, pot-holed, with treacherous gravel verges. Two cars passing from opposite directions were obliged to slow to a crawl and pull over to the side, outside wheels in the ditch if that were shallow enough. If not, you risked bottoming out and scraping away your sump and exhaust system. But Casement, in the familiar Mercedes station wagon that his wife had driven, was not slowing, pulling over, stopping. Pam swung into the bracken between two peppermint gums, bouncing the chassis over clumps of hardened mud cast up by a shire grader, while Challis craned his head around to peer through the rear window at Casement, who had flashed past, churning up a dense blanket of gritty dust. They heard small stones ping against the rear of the police car.

'Quick,' Challis said, immediately regretting the obviousness of it.

'I *am*, sir,' Pam said, showing irritation and anxiety in the face of his scrutiny.

She spurted forward, looking for a farm gate, nosed in, reversed, then a horn brapped sharply. Before she could complete the turn and demand right of way, a Telstra linesman passed, his van top-heavy with ladders. Challis read alarm in his face and then he was past them and they were crawling behind him. He seemed panicked to have the police on his tail, to be hindering them, and slowed to a walking pace; but the edges were soft gravel, and overhanging branches threatened to tear off his ladders. Challis's own road resembled Five Furlong Road. At least once a year he called the shire's emergency number to fetch the tree-removal crew. Why none of the neighbours ever called it in, he didn't know.

'Sound your siren,' van Alphen said from the back seat.

'It's all right,' Challis said. 'He knows we're here, he'll pull over when he can.'

Beside him Pam Murphy flashed him a look of thanks.

Then they were past the van and picking up speed. Dust lingered. They reached the intersection with the coast road and Pam said, 'Sir? Left? Right?'

The answer came to Challis. There was something neat and ironical about it. 'The aerodrome. We know he can fly.'

Pam laughed. 'I've got visions of chasing him up and down the landing strip.'

It should be possible to box him in, Challis thought. The Waterloo airfield was laid out in a simple T-shape, aligned north–south and east–west. Plenty of grass between the strips and the perimeter fence, like a large open paddock, hangars to one side, a couple of gates, cyclone fence.

'And if he's not there?' Pam said.

'Better call it in,' van Alphen said, taking out his mobile phone and murmuring, then shouting to be heard, finally shutting down the phone and pocketing it.

'I can never get a decent signal around here,' he said. 'The Peninsula's full of dead spots.'

They ignored him. Pam hammered the police car along the coast road back to Waterloo. Challis guessed they'd lost about two minutes back there on Five Furlong Road. Casement would have put on speed when he saw them. He would have guessed they were after him. Was two minutes enough time to fire up a plane?

Which plane?

The Cessna? It was being repaired in a separate hangar. Challis didn't know if it was ready or not.

The Kittyhawk? The Kittyhawk would give him speed, but also stand out everywhere, and you didn't just step into an old war-era cockpit and trundle out onto the strip to take off.

They were there in nine minutes. If Pam Murphy had been driving at the safe—let alone the *legal*—limit it would have taken them at least fifteen minutes to reach the aerodrome. She braked at the dirt road outside the perimeter fence, fishtailed at the gate, swung through.

It was late afternoon by now, the place had almost shut down for the day, and it was apparent that Casement wasn't there.

'Shit. Sorry, sir.'

'Don't stop,' Challis told her. 'He'll have driven into a hangar.'

Pam accelerated, spurting between the hangars to the landing strip itself, and now they could see an open hangar door and the dusty Mercedes deep in the shadows. She braked and they piled out, Challis directing them.

'We can't be sure when our backup's going to arrive, so Van and Ellen, you check the planes,' he said, pointing to a dozen light aircraft parked on an asphalt clearing beyond the hangars. 'Pam, you come with me. All of you be ready to draw your firearms, but warn him first, the usual drill.'

They spread out and began the search. Five minutes passed, then ten, and as the evening light spread from horizon to horizon, filling the aeroplanes and hangars and their hidden niches with tricky shadows, Challis began to wonder whether they were too late, if Casement was already in the air, maybe having hijacked the pilot of a plane that had been about to take off.

Stupid. He should have checked with the ground staff.

And now it was the end of the work day for the ground staff. He could see them driving toward the gate one by one in a motley collection of family station wagons, four-wheel-drives and small Japanese sedans, craning their necks to see what the drama was.

'Blast!' Challis said.

He ran back to the police car, remembered the keys too late, was about to look for Pam Murphy, double-checked the ignition, saw she'd left the keys there.

He got in, fired up the motor, chased after the departing ground staff. They'd left the airfield itself and were driving in single file on the dirt road that led to the main road. Challis gunned the motor and swung out onto the grass to pass them, sideswiping a tree along the avenue of gumtrees before veering across the nose of the first car and braking, effectively cutting them all off.

Piling out with his service revolver held in two hands up next to his head where it could be seen, Challis then motioned for the cars to stop, the drivers to get out. A woman slipped out of the first car, very jittery and, following Challis's gestures, ran for the shelter of the gums. Then a man got out of the second car and scurried away in a half-crouch, and two men got out of a little Daihatsu, but the driver of a Land Rover just sat there staring at Challis, hands fixed tightly to the wheel.

When the other drivers and passengers were free of their cars, Challis advanced on the Land Rover, down the left flank so that the abandoned cars gave him some cover.

He approached until he was behind a Holden a few metres away from the Land Rover and saw that the driver was the head mechanic and that he was trembling. Challis paused, called out: 'Is Casement there with you?'

The man nodded.

'In the back seat?'

Another nod.

'Armed?'

A final nod, the mechanic clenched tight with fear, and it was then that Challis saw the shotgun emerge between the gaps in the seats and press upwards into the hinge of the mechanic's jaw.

'Casement? Can you hear me?'

The window went down, the twin barrels swung away from the driver, and Challis's answer was a blast from the shotgun. He ducked and heard the pellets humming over his head and slamming into the flank of the Holden.

There was no second shot until he raised his head. This time the blast was better aimed, the shot flying low, peppering a rear tyre and zipping about his feet, branding his right shin bone and calf.

Challis ran before the pain could set in, ran before the blood slopped in the bottom of his shoe, ran before Casement could reload or prove to him that he had a magazine full of shells.

CHAPTER **FORTY-SEVEN**

In the middle of the questioning, the paperwork, his patching-up visits to the hospital over the next three days, Challis's wife killed herself, and his first thought was: I'm tired of all the dying.

Succeeded in killing herself, to be precise, sleeping pills this time, stolen and accumulated when she was recuperating in the prison hospital, the pills succeeding where sharpened plastic and half-hearted cutting motions had failed to work.

She left a note blaming him but he didn't feel any responsibility and went to the funeral and stared at the coffin, feeling nothing but pity for Bob and Marg, who clung to his arms and said how sorry they were.

Sorry for their daughter, sorry he'd been shot, holding his arms as much in need of support as to offer support and sympathy to him, with his bandaged leg and hospital crutch.

But that was on the third day. Hours of fruitless questioning had come before that, Challis with a temporary hospital patch-up on the first evening, so that he wouldn't lose the momentum with Casement, then a session in surgery while they removed the pellets, then back for another swipe at Casement.

Who'd had a lawyer right from the start, an overweight, heavily suited, idly contemptuous-looking man who slumped precariously in the plastic interview room chair. 'My client freely admits to attempted abduction and various weapons charges, but he denies killing anyone.'

'Ian Munro shot my wife,' Casement said, looking relaxed. 'For all I know, he also shot the Pearces. As for Trevor Hubble, I don't know anything about that.'

'You admit to knowing him, though.'

'Years ago.'

'Two years, in fact. You were business partners, you took over the business when he returned to England, but then he came back last October and you killed him because you'd taken over his identity and he was a threat to that.'

'It was easier for my client to leave the paperwork in Mr Hubble's name, that's all,' the lawyer said. 'He paid his taxes, he doesn't owe anybody anything.'

But the next day Challis was able to tell the lawyer: 'We sent your client's prints to Interpol and Scotland Yard. His real name is Michael Trigg and he's wanted for theft, fraud and money laundering. We intend to send him back to England as soon as he's served his sentence here.'

'My client will challenge any charge the English police try to pin on him. Meanwhile I doubt he'll serve much time for attempted abduction and firearms charges in this country.'

'You're forgetting murder,' Challis said. 'Four counts.'

'On what evidence?'

They didn't have any. Challis stuck with what he knew. 'According to Scotland Yard your client defrauded a circle of business acquaintances of three or four million pounds. He laundered that money through dozens of bank accounts. He disappeared before his trial and has remained at large by adopting a series of false identities.'

It was easier to say 'your client' than 'Casement', 'Billings' or 'Trigg', yet, in Challis's head, Trigg was Casement.

'As I said, my client is confident that—'

'Does your client have anything to say for himself?' Challis demanded. He was in pain, uncomfortable, irritable.

'I can only repeat what my lawyer has so ably said,' Casement replied levelly. He seemed to be enjoying himself and Challis guessed that he was entirely unmoved by the things that normally move us.

Challis went on: 'We know that you took the identity of at least two of your victims: Billings and Casement. Stripped a million quid from each of them, apparently.'

Casement shrugged.

'Did you use Hubble's carpet-cleaning business to launder the money you stole?'

No reply.

'Now it's safer and easier to sink your stolen money into Internet share trading, is that it?'

No reply.

'We found oil paintings, gold bars, cash and a selection of identity documents hidden in your house.'

This time Casement shrugged.

Challis went on: 'What did you do with your yacht?'

'What yacht?'

'According to Louise Cook, Hubble's girlfriend, when you were known as Billings you owned a yacht.'

'Do I look like a yachtsman to you?'

Casement could have owned the yacht under an alias the police were yet to trace, Challis thought. 'Where is the yacht moored now?'

'My client didn't own a yacht. Please don't harp on it, Inspector.'

'We'll find it,' Challis said. 'We'll match the anchor to it, we'll take a reading from the global positioning unit, we'll probably find your client's prints on it along with Trevor Hubble's.'

There was a flicker in Casement, a tiny shift, but the lawyer stepped in saying, 'I understand you don't have the anchor, Inspector. That it's gone missing.'

'These things always turn up,' Challis said.

And it did, in a second-hand chandlery store along the beachfront at Rosebud. No, the owner couldn't remember where he'd got the anchor.

And then the yacht was found. Casement had tucked it away down a drainage channel near Tooradin, some distance away, where it might never have come to anyone's attention if it hadn't dragged its anchor chain and damaged someone's dinghy. Crime scene technicians found Casement's prints, Hubble's prints.

'So I owned a yacht? So what?'

'So you lied to us.'

'My client is understandably nervous about these murder charges, Inspector Challis. As a result he's forgetful but also inclined to be self-protective. You can understand that.'

'Oh, I quite understand,' Challis said. 'He's trying desperately to save his neck. But that doesn't change the fact that we have your client's prints and his victim's prints on a boat he denies owning.'

'The correct term is yacht, not boat,' said Casement automatically.

'Terribly sorry. But as I said—'

'And there's an innocent explanation,' Casement said. 'I expect Trev's prints have been there for ages, from back when we went sailing on weekends, before he flew to London.'

'So who killed him and why a death at sea?'

'Why not ask Louise Cook about that? She wanted him dead, I heard her say so often enough when she came back to Australia without him. "I hate his guts," she'd say. "I'd happily shoot him." That's where you should be looking.'

Challis made a mental note to do just that, and said, 'The global positioning system puts you off Flinders at the time of the murder.'

'But that's not proof that my client was on the boat at the time or that he killed Trevor Hubble or that Hubble was on the yacht at the time. Other people may have taken the boat out.'

'Yacht,' Casement said.

'Why did you kill the Pearces? What did Pearce have on you?'

'My client has already denied—'

'Did Pearce discover your true identity? Did he see you kill Hubble? Was he sniffing around, asking uncomfortable questions?'

'Didn't know the chappie, sorry,' Casement said languidly.

'Why did you kill your wife?' Challis went on. 'Was she onto you? Did Pearce approach her separately, telling her who you were? Or did she already know and you had a falling out? Or was she bringing unwanted police attention to herself, so you felt threatened? Was it money? I understand there is some cash and property and an insurance policy for half a million dollars.'

'My client has already denied—'

Stalemate.

Casement was called a flight risk and placed on remand on the abduction and weapons charges, so he wasn't going anywhere, which gave Challis the space to breathe and think.

What he thought about was constancy, and counting his blessings. His wife had not been constant in love but constant as a thorn in his side. Now he was free of her. Kitty Casement had been constant until she was murdered, constant but remote, and not free to love him.

Love. That was a dream because he'd been unhappy at the time.

Tessa Kane had shown herself willing to be a constant in his life, and he was free to love her now—unless he'd driven her away. He found himself wondering how he should tell her that his wife was dead. Would she say 'Too late'? Would she say 'Too convenient'? Would she wonder what other impediments he might bring to their relationship?

But he should count her as a blessing. Whether she counted him as one was another matter.

And so it was that the day after the funeral his unconscious mind prompted him and he said to Scobie Sutton: 'We were going to search the Meddler's house again, if you remember.'

It wasn't a sharpening of Challis's faculties, for he rode drowsily in the car and dreamed while Sutton talked.

'Aileen Munro took her kids out of the school.'

'Uh-huh.'

'Poor little beggars.'

'Yes.'

'How do you tell kids that young what happened? It's been hard enough explaining to *my* kid. Given rise to some heavy questions. "Dad, where do you go when you die?" kind of thing.'

Challis let Sutton talk, and trailed behind him into the Pearces' house. In the days since the murder something other than blood had thickened the air. Strangely, it was the smell that woke Challis. He tracked it down to a small bin under the sink, a lidless bin crammed with packaging, as though one of the Pearces' last acts had been to put away the shopping. The bad smell came from skin and fat trimmed from a chicken, he realised, as he carried the bin out into the back yard and tipped the contents into a wheelie bin.

That's when he saw the cellophane wrapping and an empty sheet of stick-on videocassette labels at the bottom of the bin, together with a cash register receipt dated two days before the murder, and these everyday things took him back into the house and the VCR and the video labelled 'International Most Wanted' still there in the machine, waiting to spell out the link between Casement and the Meddler.

No proof yet that Casement had shot Kitty, but first things first.